MOTORB

MOTORBIKES
and
CAMELS

Nejoud Al-Yagout

LUMINARE PRESS
WWW.LUMINAREPRESS.COM

Luminare Press
438 Charnelton St., Suite 101
Eugene, OR 97401
www.luminarepress.com

LCCN: 2018953912
ISBN: 978-1-944733-99-5

"To the ostracized, the voiceless, the subjugated, the forgotten, the mistreated, the violated; to the eyes of mothers, seeing gazelles in monkeys. And to the gems and lanterns for flickering together in the dark."

—Gus O. Y. Al Qatami

1

SALMA

*"And if you release them internally,
they have no power externally."*
—Basimah Ramala

Salma wasn't used to being around members of the opposite sex. She had been educated at all-girl facilities prior to college. And in high school, only bad girls spoke to boys. They would climb over the wall during school hours and get into their boyfriends' cars. Once, when she was in the bathroom with a classmate, Salma watched her swallow a pink pill.

"You want one?" she had asked Salma.

"What is it?"

"Oh, it'll make you real high. Try it. I take it before meeting Jassim. It gives me courage, you know?"

"Who's Jassim?"

"My boyfriend."

Salma didn't take the pill, nor did she speak to the girl again. She witnessed all kinds of behavior. There was the girl who poured whiskey into a mug of hot chocolate at the cafeteria, the girls who smoked behind the gym, and the ones who pretended to be ill so they could sleep in the nurse's office. But she didn't report her fellow pupils to the principal because they would get in big trouble with their families. She developed a reputation on campus as a prude, but a trustworthy one. She once walked into the locker room and a few of her classmates were huddled in a corner. One of the girls hushed the others when they noticed it was Salma, but they continued speaking about how to steal a cheat sheet. Many of her fellow students had told her all their juicy secrets, and one by one, Salma stopped speaking to each of them. She was alone.

The wild girls were nice enough but unrefined. She had to stay away from them. You are a diamond, pure and lustrous, her mother warned her once. Don't play in coal.

BADER WAS THE FIRST YOUNG MAN TO APPROACH SALMA at university. Salma had never seen eyelashes so long on a man. He had curly jet-black hair and green eyes, a rare combination for a local.

"Did you study?" Those were the first words he asked her as they waited in line outside the classroom door for the bell to ring.

"Excuse me?" She was facing this handsome man and was flustered.

"Do I need to repeat myself?" He smirked.

There was the same stirring below her stomach that she

had experienced when she watched uncensored romance movies hidden in her parents' closet while in high school. They were not dirty movies, but her mother didn't approve of her watching anything unless it was on television. For a couple of years, she got away with it, but her mother caught her rummaging through her closet one night.

"I moved them away, Salma. I noticed the DVDs weren't in alphabetical order. Poor Rita, I thought she was secretly watching them. I almost fired her for lying. But it's you who was doing this? Why would you want to watch such movies?"

Salma didn't tell her it was her father who had shown her where the movies were when she had complained to him that the local cinemas censored love stories but not violence. She was sad her mother had threatened to fire Rita. Her parents treated Rita well. She was the granddaughter of Alice, the nanny who had raised her mother. Rita had been with them for seven years.

Her mother had accused Rita without any proof—Rita, who had told Salma more than once how lucky she was to live with them. Rita, who had defended her mother when Salma said she couldn't understand why the staff had only one day off a week. She insisted to Salma the employees in the house were happy and treated well, so Salma shouldn't worry about them. Good treatment was more important than freedom, according to Rita.

But Salma said they were adults and had the right to go out when their work was completed. Good treatment and freedom were equally valuable, she wanted to add. But who was she to kill Rita's joy when her mother was good to her?

"You have to apologize to Rita," her mother demanded.

"I didn't say anything to her. You're the one who should apologize for accusing her without evidence."

"Salma, behave yourself."

"Uff, Mama. I'm just saying you should apologize, not me."

"Is that what these movies teach you, to talk back to your parents? What does the Koran teach us? We should not say uff to our parents."

"They're love movies. They have nothing to do with talking back to parents. And why do you quote the Koran when you're losing an argument? You know how much I love and respect you, but I can't say sorry to Rita if I did nothing wrong to her."

Her mother slapped her. It was the first time she had ever hit her. Salma kept her hand on her cheek for a while, for dramatic effect. Her mother gently removed Salma's hand and kissed the spot where she had slapped her. Then she held her in her arms.

"I'm sorry, my love. Oh my God. Please forgive me. I don't know what came over me. I'll apologize to Rita. Let's go downstairs. We can sit in the garden and have tea and biscuits."

"I have to study."

"Please, Salma. It's not good for you to spend all that time holed up in your room."

"But you make such a fuss when I don't do well at school. You should be happy I'm studying. I don't get you."

"I want you to get good grades, but you need to take breaks. Now come down and have tea with me. We don't spend enough time with each other."

Salma didn't want to change the subject. Movies were on her mind. "Mom whenever we do, you nag. And now you're going to bring up the movies again."

"I promise I won't say a word about them. But you have to promise not to watch them again."

"You watch them too, Mama. And Aunty Zayna watches love series all the time. I think that's where she learns how to be romantic with Uncle Mohammed."

"She's married. And she's not romantic with Mohammed. Forget about love now. Focus on your studies. Be careful. These movies will put bad ideas into your head. It's not part of our culture. When you're married, you can watch these kinds of movies with your husband."

Salma switched to watching movies on her laptop. Her mother was wrong. These movies were good for unmarried women. At least they could teach them how to make their future husbands fall in love with them. The women were immaculately dressed. And men were constantly chasing them. Most of the directors were men, so she learned what men desired. Though she was shy to dress the way women did in movies, she could buy these clothes privately to wear for her husband one day.

She learned men had double standards with women. In one movie about a high school reunion, a man was reminiscing about a girl he had slept with in high school. It turned out two other men had slept with her as well. They all called her the school slut. But one man in the movie was called a stud for bedding two women on the same night. She watched as the men high-fived him.

In the same movie, the main character ended up falling in love with the girl next door. There were exceptions, but the male directors loved to make romantic comedies about men marrying good girls. There were plenty of bad girls in the movies, but they didn't get the heroes. In time, Salma realized that most of these movies had predictable scenarios and endings, so she turned her interest to documentaries.

But Salma's obsession with movies was resurrected when she met Bader. She changed the way she walked and started taking care of her appearance. It was best to avoid Bader, so he would have an urge to run after her. But much to her dismay, a week after their first encounter, as she was entering the main gate of the campus, he was standing close to another girl. She was the one from Salma's history class. What was her name? Maha. How could Salma be jealous? She didn't even know Bader well enough. Maybe Maha was a friend? Or his sister?

She would have to ask for advice from Aisha, her new friend, a soft-spoken hijabi with a skeletal frame, olive skin covered in acne, and crooked yellow teeth. Aisha was not conventionally pretty, but she was alluring. Salma couldn't put her finger on it, but her devout, chaste friend was, dare she think it, sexy.

Salma had known Aisha for six months at the time. They had met at a public lecture for women's rights where Aisha was the moderator. Salma was impressed a veiled woman was on the panel, and when she went to talk to her afterward, she was even more impressed by Aisha's intelligence.

Salma learned that when Aisha had graduated from high school, her dream was to be a young mother. After several years of waiting for a potential suitor, her moment had arrived when she impressed Hussam's mother with her belly-dancing moves at a wedding. Hussam's mother asked who she was and cornered Aisha's mother at the buffet to schedule a meeting for their son and daughter to meet.

Hussam's mother was confident Aisha's family would not refuse him. The first time they went over to Aisha's family home, Hussam's mother was already suggesting a few destinations for the honeymoon. And she told Aisha they would be living in the Jemali district after the wedding.

Aisha was delighted they would not be living with the in-laws or in an apartment. Her future husband's parents had built a house for him in preparation for his life as a married man. Hussam's mother would call Aisha to arrange more meetings, and after one month, his mother set the wedding date.

Aisha was an engaging storyteller. She recounted to Salma that Hussam's mother told her mother they should not wait since they were obviously suited to one another.

"Unbelievable. What did you say? What did your mother say?"

"She was too busy grinning to say a word. And Hussam and I stared at the ground."

Aisha and Salma laughed.

"So you're engaged without actually approving?"

"Who would say no to Hussam? Would you?"

"I guess not."

"You guess not?"

"OK, you win. You love him?"

"I feel comfortable with him. He's more mature than other men. And at least he's financially stable."

"I wouldn't call a billionaire's son financially stable. And sorry, Aisha, but you're hardly one to compare him to other men. You know nothing about them."

"Yes, well, I read a lot."

"Reading about men is not the same as being with them. Anyway, how does he feel about you not having a university degree?"

"He's marrying me, so he obviously doesn't care."

"I think you'd be stellar at university. I mean you're already a force to reckon with, so imagine what a degree would do."

"I want to be a mother, and I consider myself educated. What does a degree have to do with that? I'm invited to give lectures or moderate them because I'm qualified. I sit on panels with experts who have post-graduate degrees. Nobody asked me for a certificate."

"You know what? You're right. I parrot things, like I'm a mouthpiece for society or academia. I mean, who cares? You're smart and I'm excited you're getting married."

"We're keeping the engagement short. Don't tell anyone, but we're getting married in two months."

Salma had developed a deep respect for her friend. And though Aisha had no experience with men, Salma trusted her opinion.

AISHA GLARED AT SALMA AS THOUGH SHE HAD PUNCHED her in the gut. "Why would you do this to yourself? Don't speak to a man before marriage unless both your parents know. Don't. One thing will lead to another."

"Do what?"

"Stay away from him, Salma. Boys at this age want one thing. If he wants to marry you, he knows how to find you. He knows your name and your last name. Why let him enter through the window when he can knock at the front door?"

It was odd that Aisha the feminist would use such an archaic saying. She had only ever heard her grandmother say that before.

"I just want to talk to him. Maybe he's the one for me."

"The one? How cliché. Are you mad? Where do you get such ideas from? Men want two things: sex or marriage. And I can bet you this Bader guy is looking for the former."

"Sex?" Salma asked, startling Aisha by shouting the word. "Now you are out of your mind. I'm not going to sleep with him. Why is everything dirty when it comes to women and men? Who said anything about sex?"

Her fantasies about Bader did involve making love and exchanging tender kisses, but Salma had no intention of acting on them. It embarrassed her Aisha had read her mind. She changed the subject.

Two days later, Salma was sitting on the grass studying when Bader entered Luna, the campus coffee shop. She got up slowly and trailed behind him. It was crowded inside, and Salma had to wait in line for thirty minutes. The air conditioning was on full blast, and she was shivering. She'd have to bring a cardigan to school to wear indoors and leave it in her locker.

Bader was sitting with Maha. When it was Salma's turn at the counter, she ordered a cappuccino with skimmed milk. The cashier asked her if she would like anything else. No thanks. One day she would say: If I wanted anything else, I would ask for it.

Salma sat down at a table facing Bader and placed her mug on the checkered pink and yellow tablecloth. Artwork covered the brown brick wall beside her. She was drawn to a painting of a veiled woman riding a motorcycle. Walking behind her was a man in jeans and a shirt holding a camel on a leash. She scanned the artist's name: Hashim A. Hantab. Although she didn't know much about art, she had come across his name on social media. He was famous. Beneath the frame, Salma read verse inscribed by Zead Banash, a renowned local poet, who wrote: *In this and that, lies the mystery of life. Portals of peace, portals of strife.* She had no idea what the words meant.

Salma stared at Maha. When Salma turned her gaze toward Bader, he was smiling at her. She had to turn away. Now. Instead, she smiled back. She took a sip of her drink. It was still hot. She pretended to be distracted by her phone. She turned toward the painting again. Suddenly, she couldn't breathe. She left her cappuccino on the table and rushed out, trying, but failing, to catch her breath. Bader came rushing out behind her.

"Are you OK?"

"I can't breathe. I need to go to the hospital."

"Relax. It must be a panic attack."

He held her shoulder, and she recoiled, pretending to be repulsed by his electrifying touch. If he had kissed her then and there, like men did in the movies, she would have let him even while the whole world watched. Nothing was more natural to her than the attraction she had for Bader. If men could kiss girls, then women could kiss them back, right?

"Salma, did you hear what I said?"

"A-a-a what?" A few students were watching them. Blood rushed to her face as she tried to avoid their stares. He grabbed hold of her arm, leading her gently to a corridor inside.

"Breathe." He inhaled deeply. "Just breathe."

Salma heeded him, confused and hypnotized, while synchronizing the gasps coming out of her mouth. Could she recover that fast? "It's gone."

"Yup, it's a panic attack. I wasn't too sure, but…" He tilted his head, his eyes focused on her mouth. At this angle, he reminded her of the moment right before a man leaned in to kiss his object of affection in movies. She repeated the phrase God forgive me in her mind again and again. She uttered it aloud by mistake the seventh time.

He smirked, which made her more flustered, more self-conscious. How could he understand her struggle? His confidence angered her. Why didn't he blush? Why was he calm around her? Men were different. Just like in the movies.

"Do you even know what a panic attack is?"

"Of course I do." She had no idea what one was. It must be a condition not severe enough to warrant a visit to the hospital. Otherwise, Bader would have taken her to a doctor. Was it going to happen again? Why wasn't he worried about her? Would she have to take medicine? A cousin of hers took pills for anxiety. Was this anxiety? Did she need to visit a doctor? All these questions raced through her head.

"Well, you're OK now."

"Thank you," she said, trying to prolong the conversation, though she had nothing else to say.

"Oh shit. Maha. I have to run. I left her at Luna."

He left her with the sound of his shoes hitting the pavement. She closed her eyes. The tune of Beethoven's Fifth Symphony reverberated in her mind. This must be love.

Salma couldn't sleep. She scrolled through her Facebook feed and came across a friend request. And there he was: Bader Essam. She had sensed the connection was mutual. Why else did he come rushing out of the coffee shop behind her so swiftly? But what was his story with Maha? Was he dating her? She was not his sister. Who runs that fast for a sister?

She ignored his friend request. She wouldn't start a relationship with Bader until she was sure he wasn't dating Maha.

Bader had been parking outside Gate 1A lately, so she chose a new spot on the grass beside this entrance the next day. He was usually at university an hour before his first class and had breakfast at Luna. When he entered through the gate, she tried to get up but couldn't move. But he didn't walk toward the coffee shop. Instead, he came straight to where she was sitting.

"Did you study?" he asked.

"You're asking me again?" She raised her eyebrow.

"You didn't answer the first time around. I learned when you want to know something, you have to persist."

"I studied. OK? What else do you want to know? And who is Maha to you?"

"Relax, Salma."

She wished she had not blurted out Maha's name, but Bader's face was beaming. "I like a girl who's upfront. It's not going to work with Maha right now. I like someone else."

Salma blushed. It was becoming a habit around him, but she enjoyed it because blushing would validate her innocence to Bader.

"I have to go to class," Salma said.

"Can I walk with you?"

"No. I don't want people talking about us."

"Nobody here cares. Within these four walls, we live a different life than out there. Man, is it just me or is it hot today?" He rolled up his sleeves. There was a tattoo on his left forearm with the initials O.L. He caught her staring at it.

He must have been used to people asking what it meant, because he told her it stood for one love.

"Are you with someone you love?"

Nejoud Al-Yagout

"No, it means one love," Bader said.

"I don't get it. Have you found her or not?"

"Oh, no. One love isn't about a woman. It's about all this." He spread his arms out and sighed deeply. "The sacred space around us. The beloved." The last word was enunciated. Who was this beloved?

"I don't understand." She looked around to see what he was referring to.

"When you go beyond rituals and tradition, you will." He joined his hands in prayer pose and bowed his head.

"Rituals and tradition are my life."

"And the beloved is my life. I found the one through my own guidance."

Salma got up and walked away.

"Don't be scared." He grabbed her wrist but she yanked it away.

"I don't wear a hijab, Bader. But it doesn't mean I'm not religious. I pray five times a day. I fast in Ramadan. I can't stay here while you tell me rituals and traditions are a waste of time."

"I didn't say that. You aren't listening. I was talking about going beyond. It has nothing to do with giving up prayer. You can find bliss while performing rituals. They'll feel different though, more enhanced." Bader was twirling around like a Sufi. She looked around, self-consciously.

"There's no need to impose your beliefs on mine."

"You wanted to know what I meant by one love and the beloved. I respect your beliefs. Can you respect mine? They're the same, though they appear different."

"Aren't you a believer?"

"Aren't you listening to a word I'm saying? Yes, I'm a believer. Are you happy now? But I don't need to tell you whether or not I am. It's not important."

"It's important to *me*. Anyway, I don't want to talk about this anymore." How could she be in a relationship with him? He spoke in a way she couldn't understand.

"Have you read Ramana Maharshi's *Who Am I?*" he asked. "Just read it, and let me know what you think."

"OK," she said, with no intention of reading the book.

When Salma went back home, she replayed her conversation with Bader. She had pretended to be offended to conceal her ignorance. This epiphany made her more intrigued by him. What did he know that she didn't?

During the night prayer, she prayed with more intensity. She asked Allah to guide Bader to the straight path, the *sirat al mustaqeem*. While supplicating, she called God the Beloved. She repeated this, one of his ninety-nine names, over and over. That's the beloved he was referring to. How stupid of her.

After praying, she opened her laptop and accepted Bader's Facebook friend request. She would take time to get back to him if he messaged her. She couldn't reveal how eager she was to talk to him. A male character in a movie she had watched emphasized men liked independent women. She had to become like those women.

She no longer feared being in public with him. There were many couples on campus. She went out on dates with Bader, and after three months of dating, he invited her over to his house.

Salma fantasized about him all day. Although it would be a mistake to go to his place, she had a strong desire to be alone with him. And she would do everything but *that*. She took a shower, waxed her legs and armpits, and spritzed *oud* scent all over her body. When she was younger, she watched her mother spray the same traditional perfume before her father came home. What was going to happen tonight? Though they had stolen kisses at his friends' houses and parties, though he had even managed to touch her breasts one time, from outside her shirt, of course, this was the first time they wouldn't be interrupted.

Two hours later, she walked into his house and he greeted her with a firm kiss on her lips. They walked to his bedroom. He closed the shutters and there was a flickering dim light from the bathroom. He was breathing loudly, and he kissed her lips softly. After taking off her clothes, and then his, he penetrated her gently. But, unlike the movies, he didn't cuddle her afterward. He got up and went to the bathroom. She heard water running. She checked the bed for bloodstains. Nothing. She put on her clothes and sat on the edge of the bed.

Ten minutes later, he came out with wet hair. He was wearing shorts and a wife-beater. He walked toward her and handed her a towel.

"No thank you," she said. "I'll take a shower when I'm home. Want to go out for dinner? I know a new pizza place near here."

"You go ahead. I have to study."

THE NEXT DAY ON CAMPUS HE WAS WITH MAHA. SHE wasn't worried. She trusted him. They were just friends. She was sure.

She sent him a message to meet her at her spot on the grass. He did not reply. Later, she searched for him at Luna, but he was sitting with Maha again. Salma had an exam but didn't turn her phone off. She kept it on silent in her backpack outside the classroom. When the bell rang, she rushed out to check her phone. Nothing.

A few hours later, he called her back.

"Hi, Salma. You called?"

"Yes. I miss you. Do you want to hang out again tonight?" She had lost her virginity, so they could have sex all the time. There was no need to play hard to get. He got what he wanted. Didn't she get what she wanted too? No. She wanted more. Did he?

"I can't. It's a hectic time for me. I have to go now, but see you around."

See you around? How could he be so insensitive? Her chest tightened, her throat constricted. She couldn't breathe. She had read about panic attacks after her first one. They were recurrent but safe. She learned how to relax. Breathe. Breathe. Even through the dizziness, she remained calm by inhaling and visualizing an ocean. She tried to imagine sand beneath her feet, but Bader was on the beach beside her. She had read the best thing to do during an attack was not to resist any thoughts, so she let Bader fill her mind, encompass her being. She lay down on her bed and started crying. She was battling death yet again in her mind, and her breathing had become shallow. I am healthy, she repeated while inhaling and exhaling slowly. What had he done to her? Would she ever get over these attacks?

One website encouraged sufferers to take medical tests to rule out anything serious. She had every possible test done. Nothing was physically wrong with her, according to the doctor. She would have to learn how to deal with her state of mind on her own or visit a therapist. Salma chose the former.

Salma had to confront Bader to alleviate her anxiety. The next morning, she waited for him outside his fourth-period class.

"Hey, Salma."

He liked upfront girls, as he had once mentioned, so she told him they needed to talk.

"Sure, let's go to Luna."

"No, somewhere private."

"I have class in a bit."

"Do you have to go now?"

"OK, let's walk across the street to Mario's. But I can't stay long."

When they sat down at the table, Salma started crying. Maybe Bader would have compassion for her.

She had to tell him she was a virgin before their night at his place. Her mother had said the first thing men looked for were bloodstains. Her mother meant husbands, of course. When she used the bathroom at home, there were drops of pink blood on the toilet paper. But Bader must have checked his bed after she left and thought she had been with others. Is that why he was ignoring her? She asked him if he was thinking of marrying her.

"Whoa, Salma. Marriage? I don't want to get married. I'm way too young. It's not even on my mind. Are you kidding me?" He was scratching the corner of the wooden table.

"Why didn't you say anything before you slept with me?"

"I didn't sleep with you. We slept with each other. It was a natural flow. Our bodies were attracted to each other. Why make such a fuss about it?"

"So all this time it was just an attraction? Oh no. Nobody will marry me now."

"We've only been together a few months. And we're freshmen. What the hell were you expecting? And you want to marry me because nobody else will?" He scrunched his forehead.

"I'm not saying we should get married now. But I want to know we will." Salma was fidgeting with the sugar bowl and spilled sugar over the table. A waiter came running to clear it up for her.

"Salma, I don't want to get married. And not just because of my age. I thought we could be together until this thing we had ended. And it ran its course." For the first time since they had met, he blushed. But from the tone of his voice, it was anger, not shyness. He was biting off the skin around his index finger.

"How convenient. Right after our night together? You're a cheat. You tricked me. I don't ever want to see you again." Salma spoke softly. A waitress was staring at them.

"Why are you taking this so seriously?" Bader asked.

The waitress came to the table and asked if they would like a menu. Salma said they would call her when they were ready to order.

They sat in silence and the waitress left them alone.

"Oh it's not serious at all for you? Do you think I wasn't a virgin? Is that why you don't want to marry me? I swear by Allah you're the first man who ever touched me. I never even kissed anyone before. How can you do this to me?"

"Why are you putting this all on me? Why didn't you tell me you wanted to get married before we had sex?" Bader bent his elbows and joined his hands together. He rested his mouth on his knuckles and stared at her, his eyebrows raised.

"Would it have changed anything?"

"Well, I wouldn't have slept with you, for starters. None of this makes sense to me. I don't care about all this virginity stuff. It takes two to tango. I might as well shun myself if I shun a woman for doing the same thing I did."

"Stop philosophizing. I think you do that to avoid having a real conversation."

"Go ahead and analyze me. I don't mind. Hey, I'm sorry it had to end this way, but if you want to get married, let the guy know beforehand. Make your intentions crystal-clear so there's no room for misinterpretation. Look, it's not a big deal. There's no reason to get all emotional about sex."

Why did he have to be rude? No reason to get emotional about sex? Where the hell did he think he was living?

She got up without saying a word and walked out of the restaurant. Bader could easily reach her. He would come back. She had to wait patiently.

BADER IGNORED HER. IN CLASS, NEITHER OF THEM SPOKE to each other. This continued for a while, and he was regularly with Maha on campus. He had moved on and she had to as well.

Aisha had been right all along about Bader. But Salma had hidden her relationship with him from her, and now she hid her grief. Instead, she prayed more than the required amount and fasted on Mondays and Thursdays, asking God for forgiveness. Maybe the panic attacks were a punishment. They started when she developed a crush on Bader.

And still, whenever Salma walked past Bader, she would have trouble breathing. On days when the anxiety was potent, she sat on a bench or on the grass so she wouldn't faint. The months dragged by slowly until it was summer. She had survived her freshman year.

WHEN SHE CAME BACK TO UNIVERSITY AFTER A LONG holiday in London, she met Khaled. He shared the same religious beliefs as her, but how she wished she were a virgin like Aisha had been before her wedding.

Salma met up with Khaled often. And a couple of months into the relationship, she confessed she was not a virgin, but she would not sleep with him until they got married. Salma could have lied to him because she hadn't bled in Bader's bed, but, to her, Khaled deserved the truth. He told her he was not a virgin either and there was no difference between *al zani wa al zania*, the adulterer and the adulteress, as mentioned in the Koran.

Her parents embraced Khaled, but a few weeks into the engagement, her father's stance toward him changed.

"Baba, why do you suddenly hate him?"

"I don't feel comfortable around this man. Trust me *habibti*. It's my intuition as a father. What do you know about his past?"

"I don't care about his past, and neither should you. As long as he treats me well when we're married, nothing else matters."

"A man's past shapes his future. One's reputation is built on what he has done, not what he'll do. If he has hurt others, he'll hurt you."

"Baba, please. You're not making any sense. He hasn't hurt anyone, as far as I know. And I want to get married. Don't stand in my way, unless you heard something."

It was part of the tradition during the engagement period for family members to ask about a suitor's reputation. But her father told her nobody had said anything.

A year later, they got married. Both Khaled and Salma continued with their studies. Juggling marriage and university wasn't hard for Salma, because Khaled was out most of the time. She had plenty of time to study without distractions.

Khaled hadn't given her any indication he drank alcohol until their honeymoon, although they had been to several parties together while dating. They both agreed when they got married, they would stop going to parties and devote their lives to settling down and raising a family.

Khaled was perverted and violent in bed. He persuaded her to do things she was not comfortable with, but before her wedding night her mother had said: Husbands want whores in the bedroom. After the honeymoon, when they settled into a rental villa, he was drunk at least three nights a week. He wouldn't touch her when he was sober.

Khaled had constant headaches or stomachaches or backaches. Salma even called an ambulance to take him to the hospital one morning because his chest hurt, but the doctor said it was stress. Most nights, he couldn't get an erection. She didn't admit it to him, but she was relieved. Sex had become a chore she dreaded. But she was worried about his health. He was too young for all these medical issues, but Khaled, who was obsessed with psychology, told her they were just phantom symptoms.

───────────

Though they weren't using protection, Salma couldn't get pregnant, even after more than three years of marriage. Her mother-in-law insisted she visit a gynecologist. Salma and Khaled got tested. She went to pick up the results alone the following week. He was too hung-over to join her.

On the way home, she called her husband and asked if he was home, without telling him she had visited the doctor. She told him to meet her in the garden.

She took off her heels and walked toward him. He was sitting under a green and white striped bistro umbrella beside the pool. The grass was lush and the garden was scattered with palm trees. The house was rented and Salma had asked Khaled to buy the property, but he told her they should wait a couple of years, in case a better place emerged. There was a jug of iced-tea and two plastic glasses.

"I told Abby not to serve plastic," Salma said.

"Why not?"

"For the environment. There's a new campaign and people are pledging to curb the use of plastic, so I thought we'd start with cutlery and glasses."

He rang the bell and Abby came running out of the house.

"Yes sir. You called?"

"Throw away these plastic cups." Khaled handed her the glasses.

"Listen, Abby, you know that garbage bag I showed you the other day filled with the plastic water bottles? Put these glasses in there. OK?" Salma looked at Abby, waiting for an answer.

Abby looked at Khaled. "What should I do sir?"

"Do exactly what Salma told you to do."

"Yes sir." Abby picked up the glasses and walked indoors without looking at Salma.

"Wow, she has a soft spot for me, huh?" Salma asked.

"Don't start. Why are you dumping the plastic? Isn't that more waste?"

"There's a company that picks up used plastic so I'm filling up a special garbage bag."

"Mmm … OK. Now what did you want me out here for?"

"I got the results from the doctor. Here…" She opened her bag and handed him the results. "See your sperm count is low," she said, pointing at the diagnosis.

He skimmed through it, crumpled the paper, then threw it on the table.

"I shouldn't have married you. What's the point of being together if we can't have children? This feels like a life sentence to me."

"I'm the one who's suffering," Salma said. "You think I enjoy being with an alcoholic?"

"I started drinking after we got married. Not such a good sign, huh?"

"Yeah right. You're saying you started drinking out of the blue. You never had alcohol before you married me?"

"I tried it in high school but I hated it. But you got me to marry you and I needed an escape."

"You're blaming me for drinking? You married me. You chose me. And you started on our honeymoon. I didn't do anything to deserve this treatment. And I didn't want to marry a drinker."

"Oh you're judging me for drinking. That's funny coming from a woman who wasn't even a virgin."

"The adulterer and the adulteress, remember? You weren't a virgin either."

"I'm a man, no matter what, Salma. You're an insult to our society. I'm glad you can't be the mother of my children. If we had girls, what kind of an example would you be?"

"I'm sick of your cruelty toward me. I hate you."

SHE WAS STUCK IN A MARRIAGE, SUFFERING. AND AISHA was suffering, so she waited to tell her about Khaled. Married with a daughter, Aisha's husband had turned out to be gay. They had not had sex since the discovery. Her friend had saved her virginity for a man who was gay. How tragic. She cared about Aisha, but was relieved she was not the only one in a failed marriage. Salma learned all the details. It had all begun when Aisha found a pornographic magazine featuring naked men beneath the bathroom sink.

How could Aisha stay with him after that? The more she got to know Aisha, the further Aisha demonstrated behavior of a feminist. She was angry at her friend for staying with Hussam. All this for society?

A part of her suspected it was because of Hussam's family wealth. Aisha's father was a renowned local businessman, but the Salama family was among the richest in the world. Then again, maybe Aisha was staying for her daughter, Dania.

Why was she staying with Khaled? He was a heavy drinker. They had no children. She didn't need his money, and her father harbored an inexplicable hatred of Khaled, which would serve her well if she left, because she would be welcome back home.

Khaled behaved well in front of her parents, and they were clueless about her marital struggles, so Salma couldn't figure out why her Baba despised Khaled. Aisha once told her it was because many fathers are obsessed with their daughters, not sexually, but in a distorted, protective way.

"Sort of like a reversed Oedipus complex?" Salma asked.

"Huh? No. A reverse of the Oedipus complex is known as the Electra complex. It's when a daughter competes with her mother for her father's affection. But nice try."

A WHILE AFTER SALMA DISCOVERED KHALED COULDN'T give her children, she discovered a couple of messages from a girl named Saadia to Khaled. He had left his phone in the bedroom and she read them on his screen. Saadia told him they could be friends and she wasn't in love with him anymore. Who was this girl? And what had Khaled said to her? Did they just break up? She took his phone and walked out of the room. He was taking a nap in the living room.

"Who is she?"

Khaled opened his eyes and sat upright. He was wearing boxers and a *gahfiya*. How could anyone sleep in a skullcap?

"Who is she?" She gave him his phone and sat on the floor, facing him.

"A girl I used to know. It's not what you think." He unlocked his phone and was staring at his screen.

"Let me see the other messages if it's nothing." Salma snatched his phone from him and ran to the bathroom. She locked the door. She scrolled through their conversation while Khaled pounded on the door. He kicked the door and threatened to break it open, but she was entranced reading their messages.

"Open the door, you bitch!" Khaled shouted.

When she finally opened the door, around fifteen minutes later, Khaled was on the ground. His legs were crossed and he was bent over, head in his hands. She towered above him and threw his phone across the hall.

"You make me sick."

"I-I-I'm so sorry." He stood up and ran to pick up his phone. It was cracked. He looked at her, shaking his head, then walked toward her, and led her by the hand to the bedroom.

"What are you doing? Let go of me!"

Once inside, he let go of her and sat on the bed, patting a spot beside him. "Come, I'll explain everything. It's not what you think."

"It's more than what I think. You wrote her a message saying you regret leaving her and you would marry her in an instant if she approved. I read it all."

"Nothing happened. I swear by Allah."

She sat beside him. "I know nothing happened. I saw her responses. She said she wouldn't cheat on her husband and wasn't in love with you anymore. She even told you to focus on me. But it would've been a full-blown affair if she were indecent like you. Why did you marry me when you were, and still are, in love with another woman?" Salma was not jealous. She was angry, humiliated that she had wasted time on a man who cheated on her. A man she hated.

"Salma, please. My father was against it. She comes from a low-class family, the Lathis, who are from the Akashi tribe. I had to think of my sister. Who would marry her after I married an Akashiya? Imagine."

"You're willing to marry her now. What changed? And I'm sorry, but your parents should be more concerned with Jawa's health than any future husband. Haven't you guys noticed she has lost weight again? She needs serious help."

"Why the hell are you bringing my sister's issues into this?"

"I care about her. I should've known by the way you treat her that you have no concern for anyone but yourself."

"The way I treat her? I don't bother her. I leave her alone."

"Yeah well maybe that's the problem. If you can't be there for your own family, how can I expect anything from you?"

"Go to hell Salma. I can't handle seeing Jawa like that. It doesn't mean I don't care about her. You think it doesn't kill me to see her wasting away? And I sacrificed my own happiness for her and my family. I let go of the one person who mattered to me to please them. I'm not having this conversation. If you want to leave me, go ahead. But I'm not going to argue with you."

Khaled walked to the cupboard. Though he usually wore jeans and a shirt, he took out a *dishdasha*, the traditional white robe he wore for formal occasions, and *ghutra*, headgear, and threw the hangers on the floor. He dressed facing a mirror. Then, he put on transparent white pants underneath and opened a drawer and placed the black-ringed *egal*, which keeps the headgear in place, on the top of his head.

"Where are you going?"

"Well you know I'm not meeting her, so what are you worrying about?"

"Is there a fling on the side?"

"Didn't you check my other messages?"

"You could've deleted them."

"I have to meet my dad. You can call him and check."

"I want to discuss Saadia. This is serious."

He looked at his watch. "We have ten minutes."

She followed him to the living room and they sat down next to each other.

"What do you want to know?" Khaled asked, staring at the ground.

"What's your story? Why didn't you guys get married?"

"I told you. I couldn't do that to my family. Her mother had raised her alone without a father. She used to leave us alone. Her own mother. They had mixed parties at home. I couldn't have married her. You know that type of woman."

"No, I don't. But you want to marry that type of woman now."

"You won't understand. You live a sheltered life. Her family is too open for our society. Her brother isn't a man. He let his sister take me into her bedroom. And Saadia's mother is not originally from here." He removed his *egal* and *ghutra* and placed them on the glass table in front of them. He scratched his head.

"So you suddenly think all of that is OK? What the hell changed?" Why was she berating a man she didn't love? A divorce was inevitable. Maybe she could go back to Bader now. He must have matured now. He must miss her. The moment she got in touch with him, he'd come running back.

"Come on Salma. Stop pretending. Don't you feel stuck too? I know you don't want to be with me either."

"What're we going to do?"

"I don't want a divorce." He held her hand and kissed it.

She sensed he was lying. He was waiting for her to initiate it.

"Then why did you keep proposing to her, telling her to leave her husband so you could be together? Were you planning on making her a second wife?"

"I can't even handle one wife, let alone two."

What was the name of the television series where she had heard that line? Or was it a movie?

"Khaled, I want you to swear by Allah you never cheated on me. Swear on your father's head. Have you cheated on me? I want to know." Her dignity had prodded her to ask him.

"I didn't see Saadia while we were married. You have physical proof of that."

"You know I mean in general."

Al sukoot alamat al ridha was one of her mother's favorite sayings: Silence is a sign of agreement. Salma didn't need any further comment from him.

Khaled got up and walked out of the room. He had left his *ghutra* and *egal* on the table. She jolted from the couch, picked them up, and then sat back down on the couch again. She put his *egal* back on the table, and cried into his *ghutra*. It smelled of incense and musk. The marriage was over.

Saadia wasn't the only reason she left. But as her mother would say: It was the straw that broke the camel's back. And now her past and present were colliding. She had lost her virginity to Bader, struggled through university, graduated, been in an unhappy and childless marriage, had gotten a divorce, and was now questioning everything she believed. It was difficult for her to pray.

She had started praying regularly at the age of ten, mostly to impress her father and her Uncle Mohammed. She liked spreading her mat toward the *qibla* facing Mecca, in the living room right in front of them, and hearing her uncle Mohammed whisper to her father: *Mashallah*. It filled her with a sense of pride.

When she completed the voluntary prayer, the *sunnah,* her uncle would tell her he was proud she was a devout girl. Her father never said a word. One day, when she was older, she asked him why he didn't praise her while she prayed and he said: Prayer isn't about impressing other people. It's about a relationship with God. But whatever Salma's intentions were at the time, since her childhood, she'd been obsessed with God.

And here she was, an adult, losing her grip on the religion of her birth. She downloaded Maharshi's *Who Am I?* Maharshi emphasized self-inquiry for liberation. The language was simple, and she finished the book in a day. Was this where Bader had learned about one love? The name of the book was still crystal-clear in her mind after all these years. She ached for him.

She downloaded other books about enlightenment and bought Nisargadatta Maharaj's *I Am That* online. She could not complete it, but read a few passages here and there. His ideas were blasphemous to her but brought her peace.

Salma had become a prolific reader like Aisha. At first, she couldn't understand how Aisha was interested in books. You haven't discovered your genre yet, Aisha had told her. It could be poetry, fiction or nonfiction, her friend added.

"I suppose."

"Or subgenres: women's fiction, thrillers, critiques, autobiographies…" Aisha was grinning widely.

Salma had a genre—or was it a subgenre?—now: spirituality. She couldn't wait to tell Aisha. She spent most of her time meditating and practicing *Atma Vichara*, self-inquiry. Who am I? She repeated this phrase silently throughout the day, even when she was in the shower or driving. Who am I? Who. Am. I?

One night she had a dream of Maharshi. He was standing next to Nisargadatta Maharaj. They beckoned her toward them and spoke to her of universal oneness and love. She was enveloped in light. When she woke up, there were no signs of enlightenment or all-encompassing love, but she had discovered her spiritual path. And it was through meditation.

The question that most annoyed Salma was 'Did you pray?' This was followed by 'Are you sure?' Salma's mother sensed her spiritual crisis and was committed to saving her. Every day after her mother woke up from her nap, she would come into Salma's room, without knocking, at the time of the *Asr* prayer and check on her. She didn't ask her whether she prayed during the other four scheduled times, but Salma didn't bring it up in case she started checking on her throughout the rest of the day, too.

At the time for the afternoon prayer, Salma would sit on her mat, her prayer *thoub* covering her head and body, and wait for her mother to come in and find her praying or she would act as if she were performing *dua*, supplications, which gave her a chance to turn around and catch her Mama smiling at her. *Taqabul Allah taatich,* may God accept your efforts, she would say to Salma each time. These were the words to dutifully express to fellow believers who finished their obligatory prayers.

When her mother left, she would remove the *thoub* and meditate or read.

She discovered the verse of Rabia al-Adawiyya:

"O God, if I worship You for fear of Hell, burn me in Hell,

And if I worship You in the hope of Paradise, Exclude me from Paradise.

But if I worship You for Your Own sake, Grudge me not Your everlasting Beauty."

In the midst of reading it, Salma's phone flashed. It was her mother. She ignored her. If she needed her, she could come to her room. Her mother had a habit of calling until she answered, but today she wasn't in the mood. She was probably calling to check whether she needed the driver to fill her car with gas or whether she asked the cook to prepare her dinner or whether she needed her to buy shampoo and conditioner.

It was a habit of her Mama to repeat a question over and over again. In the morning, when she was a child, she would ask: Salma did you brush your teeth? Yes, Mama. Are you sure? Yes, Mama. And at night: Did you brush your teeth? Yes, Mama. Are you sure? Yes, Mama. Her mother repeated questions compulsively, but only saying yes would shut her up. Saying no meant her mother would pressure her, until she had done what her mother was nagging her to do. Her father knew the magic of yes too. *Habibi*, my love, did you give your dirty clothes to Rita? Yes. Are you sure? Yes, my love.

Her mother even repeated herself when it came to the weather. Did you see the dust storm last night? I was asleep, Mama, but I'll see videos of it. Did you see it? It was a wild storm. Mama, I missed it. You didn't see it? Yes, I saw it, Mama. Silence.

In middle school, her mother spoke to her of the benefits of the hijab. She said she didn't have to wear it yet, but she should consider it when she was older. She was devastated when Salma told her she didn't want to wear it. She said she would have a nervous breakdown, until her father intervened and told her not to mention it to Salma again.

Nejoud Al-Yagout

And here she was, a divorcée, with a university degree, and her mother was checking whether she was praying. What was next?

She didn't let her mother's nagging interfere with her awakening. Her lifestyle was changing. She bought healing crystals online, which she kept hidden under her bed. And she used aromatherapy sprays. Her favorites were lavender and cucumber mist. She no longer ate fish, eggs, meat, dairy, or poultry, but she was waiting for the right time to explain this to her mother. Salma expected her mother to oppose the choice, since eating meat was a part of the culture. But one day, Salma summoned up the courage. The cook had prepared a rice dish with lamb for lunch, and Salma had ordered food from a vegan restaurant.

"Are you on a diet?" her mother asked her from across the table.

"No." She licked her fingers, exaggerating the deliciousness of the bland coconut and pumpkin curry and white rice she had ordered.

"Are you ill?"

"No, I'm a vegan."

"What's that?"

"A person who stops eating meat, fish, eggs, dairy."

"What for?"

"Animals are mistreated and I don't want to support the industry. It's too lengthy to discuss now. If you're interested in learning more, let me know. I'll print information out for you."

"Are you crazy? Why would anyone give up Allah's bounties? Why're you denying yourself?" Her mother thanked God by kissing her finger and touching her forehead with it.

Kindness to animals is inherent in the religion, she explained to her mother, and there was no such thing as halal meat these days. It was *makrooh,* an abominable act, to slaughter an animal in front of other animals and Islam emphasized health, whereas today all animals were injected with hormones and antibiotics.

"All the seas are polluted these days. So it's a sacred duty to refrain from eating fish and animals, since fish can be toxic or contaminated," Salma added, shuddering at the sight of the grilled shrimp on the table.

"Who told you all this? Are you brainwashed?"

"I got all this information online. And from Muslim vegans to boot. Even doctors and the medical field would agree. Why do you think we have so many diseases these days? And don't get me started on how eating meat affects the environment."

"*Kaifich*, it's up to you. But I love meat, and I won't give it up. Maybe you should stop reading online."

It took a few weeks for her mother to grasp milk and eggs were not part of a vegan diet, and Salma was touched her mother instructed the cook to prepare vegan dishes for her at every meal.

On most nights, after a light dinner, Salma read poetry. She would get into bed, lean back against her pillows, and search for spiritual verse on the Internet. Although her father told her reading in the dark was bad for her eyesight, she turned off the lights and read books with a flashlight. Salma had never gone camping as a child, since her parents didn't let her spend the night out and were not adventurous, so reading with a flashlight was her way of pretending she was outdoors in a tent. The dim atmosphere enhanced the mystical aura of the poetry.

She devoured the words of Ibn Arabi, Rumi, Hafiz, Sultan Bahu, Bulleh Shah, and Shams Tabrizi. They had transcended dogma and sought connection with Al-Wudood, the Beloved. These poets cherished all of God's creation because they adored God. She read select verses from the Ribhu Gita, the Gospels, and even the Sutras, and grasped a unifying thread in all scriptures.

Salma discovered the Guru Shantiji channel on You-Tube. She watched his retreat sermons in the afternoons while her mother napped. The talks were laden with love for the One, and he welcomed devotees from all faiths and backgrounds. On rare occasions, he would quote mystics like Swami Vivekananda, Ramakrishna, Jesus, and Buddha. She had read once, in an article written by a retreat volunteer, that Guru was reluctant to mention names so nobody could misinterpret what the saints were saying or have their sacred words filtered by the ego. Mostly, he answered his devotees' questions and imparted his own wisdom. Salma held on to each word, and she could tell from the expressions on the faces of his followers, they were all entranced as well. It was time to visit him in Tiruvannamalai.

"Why do you want to travel alone?" her mother asked, suspicious, her brow furrowing.

"Mom, it's a beautiful country. And you know, I don't work, and I'm divorced. I need to get used to being alone."

It was easy to manipulate her mother after her divorce. Any mention of it made her mother sympathetic.

"Listen, Salma. I will think about it, OK? I know divorce isn't easy, but you have to get used to being under our roof again. In our society, you're a single woman once more."

"Yes, but times have changed. I have changed. You don't need to protect me anymore, Mama."

"I don't know why you want to go to India alone. Maybe we can go together."

"You love shopping. I'd go crazy on a trip with you to India."

They both laughed.

A few weeks later, her mother came into her room.

"*Habibti*, I don't think you should go to India alone."

"Why?"

"Salma, if you get married again, you can go on your honeymoon, but I won't let you go there alone. End of story."

"But Baba's fine with it."

"I'm not, and please don't get your father involved again. You don't want to cause tension between us, do you? Don't ask me again."

Don't ask me again. Coming from a woman who repeated her questions in an obsessive-compulsive manner? She sent a letter to the ashram telling them she couldn't make it to the upcoming retreat. Even though her mother had said no, Salma would wait patiently to see what destiny had in store for her. If she were aligned, everything would become accessible to her. So why was she not able to go? Why wasn't she aligned?

Bader was the only other person who would be interested in discussing spirituality. She needed his wisdom now when she was better able to grasp it. Watching videos or reading books was not enough. The reason her mother had said no became clear to her: She was meant to contact him. Being with Bader was her alignment, not the ashram. And his tattoo: O.L. She now understood what the initials meant.

He had said he would never get married. This time, if they rekindled their relationship, they could be husband and wife. After her experience with Bader and her husband's rejection of her, why was she fantasizing about a man who had used her and broken her heart?

Her father was respectful toward her and her mother. It wasn't like she had unresolved issues. Baba flirted with other women in front of her on several occasions, but Salma was certain even if he had an affair, he wouldn't abandon her and her mother. So why was she drawn to men who weren't drawn to her?

As much as she tried to get Bader out of her mind, and as much as she was sure if he loved her he would have chased her ages ago, all she could think about was reigniting their relationship.

When Salma had married Khaled, she had deactivated her social media accounts. And she had changed her cell phone number after her honeymoon, so she had lost his contacts. The best way to get back in touch was through Facebook. She reactivated her account.

He wasn't on Facebook. Had he deleted her? Or did he leave Facebook altogether? She tried to search for him on Instagram. Again, no sign of him. When she tried Google, he had a website. She scrolled through it. He was an author. There were links to interviews and his Youtube channel, but no contact form or social media accounts. He was on a site called LinkedIn though. It was a business site for professionals to network with one another. Though she didn't have a job, she registered for an account and created a page. There was an option to include her relationship status. Salma left it empty. Single might indicate desperation or he would think she was on the lookout for a man. She uploaded a photo.

Bader Essam. Her heart leaped when she saw his profile picture. She had tried to research why women chase bad boys, and none of the theories satisfied her until she came across a spiritual site explaining what she could never put into words since the phrase was new to her: twin flames. Bader was her twin flame. There was usually a runner and a chaser. The runner would not come back until all their issues, from this lifetime or past lifetimes, were resolved. And the chaser would chase after the runner until the roles were reversed. It was evident to her that she was the chaser at this stage.

Twin flames were mirrors for each other, and this could scare partners away if they were unprepared to look inside themselves. Enough time had elapsed, though, to resurrect their sacred union. She remembered the girl he dated after her. Her name hadn't escaped her memory: Maha. It can't have lasted long between them either.

She was spiritual now, so her intuition was getting stronger. Bader must have missed her. How he must have yearned for her throughout the years, and how Bader must have regretted not marrying her. That is why he had avoided her on campus. But he must have left mostly because she was inexperienced and closed-minded when they met.

SHE SCANNED HIS PROFILE PAGE. HE WAS A GRAPHIC designer and published writer. And she was a divorcée with no job and no intention of searching for one. Her father transferred money to her bank account on a monthly basis. She was living in her family's house, and they paid for everything. They bought her a new car after her divorce, and she didn't even have to worry about paying for gas. There was no reason for her to work.

But would Bader disrespect her for not having a career?

No. He was spiritual, not judgmental. He wouldn't care. She acknowledged his credentials but was far more distracted by his photo. Bader was smiling. It must have been a girl who took the photograph. And not any girl. Would he ever smile like that at her? Aisha once told her about "The Last Duchess", a poem by Robert Browning. If her memory served her well, it was about a jealous duke who kills his wife after commissioning a portrait of her. The duchess was smiling seductively and the duke was convinced she had an affair with the artist. His wife had a flirtatious personality and the look on her face in the painting filled him with rage. Salma couldn't recall if he killed the duchess while unveiling the portrait to the public or other specific details of the poem, apart from the title, but it stuck with her.

She navigated the site and typed a private message. It was morning, a respectable time of day to contact him.

Hi Bader. It's me, Salma Yazi. Need to talk to you about something. Please get in touch.

She hit the send button and automatically regretted how she had phrased it. She had watched funny scenes in romantic comedies of men panicking when they received messages from their girlfriends saying they needed to talk. She wasn't his girlfriend, so it didn't matter. But why did she write her last name? Wasn't that formal?

Still, she had done the right thing in contacting him. He would be happy to hear from her. One twin flame had to make a move. Fear is no friend of love, she had once read on a spiritual website. And when he got in touch, she would tell him her main reason for contacting him was to talk about the ashram she wanted to visit.

Had she been allowed to go to India, she wouldn't have

sent the message. It all made sense now. This was destiny. They needed to be separated to grow. And it would have been complicated for him to approach her after they broke up. He was always with Maha and she was always with Khaled back then. It wasn't their time.

But a part of Salma was unsure. Weren't men in love daring? There was a movie where a man crashed his ex's wedding at the last minute and grabbed her out of a church. Wouldn't he have tried to get in touch with her? Was there an option to delete the message? She couldn't find one. Salma spent the whole day checking her LinkedIn inbox. Nothing.

It was evening. She opened her prayer mat and began her self-inquiry. There was no way her mother would enter her room.

2

KHALED

*"What is the name of the beautiful song about
the man who loves a married woman?"*

—Ghanima Marhil

K haled wasn't sure he would complete his university studies. He had barely graduated from high school and taking exams made him nervous. His father told him to try it out for a year, and if he didn't like it, he could enter the family business. A year? That was too long. But he changed his mind on the first day of registration, in the cafeteria, when he met Saadia. She had asked him if he was a freshman. Obviously, he retorted.

His eyes scanned her body. It was difficult for him to stay focused on girls' eyes. He was drawn to breasts, thighs, and bottoms. He didn't understand why girls got offended, especially the ones wearing tight clothes. If they weren't looking for attention, why did they dress provocatively?

And Saadia's shirt revealed her cleavage and the shape of her bosom. How could he not stare?

She glared at him, and his face turned red. You're lucky I believe in love at first sight, she said. Just by that provocative statement, he could tell she was 'easy'. His uncle had taught him the word right after Khaled's high school graduation.

"*Habibi*, you are grown-up now. There'll be many easy girls in university. Have fun with them, but don't marry them."

"What do you mean by easy?"

"Any girl who agrees to be alone with you in a room before marriage. And not just for sex."

Khaled knew what kind of wife he was expected to choose. And he didn't tell his uncle he had met easy girls before. Quite a few of them.

One day, he had stolen one of his father's cars. He waited outside the high school until a girl jumped onto the pavement from a wall. She had dusted off her clothes and got into the car. He took her to his family's beach house and they kissed with tongues. When he tried to go further, she told him she couldn't. But she touched him everywhere, and he was satisfied. A few hours later, he dropped her back at her school and didn't get in touch with her again.

He didn't want to date. He wanted to lose his virginity. But it had been challenging, because all the girls were obsessed with keeping their hymens intact. One girl, Nadia, told him he could penetrate her anally. He was shocked. And she was even more shocked he declined her offer. Nadia had a reputation for being a prude. His best friend had once warned him girls are good at acting. When he told him about her suggestion, he taunted Khaled for weeks. His friend asked him how he could refuse Nadia's offer.

But it didn't appeal to him, and it was against his religion. Premarital sex was too, but that was different, he convinced himself. After Nadia, he stopped trusting girls. He imagined her on her wedding night, feigning a lack of experience, when she had gone further than most: male or female.

After fooling around with countless girls, he was tired. He told his mother he wanted to get married.

"You're too young."

"I'm almost eighteen. I'll be legal soon. And you and dad were eighteen."

"Times have changed."

"I'm entering university in a few months. I'm sure I'll find a wife there."

"I think you should focus on your studies, but if you've made up your mind, I'll support you. But you need our approval. The girls these days are different."

The day after registration, Saadia was sitting alone in Luna.

"Can I sit here?" Khaled asked.

"Do you believe in love at first sight too?"

Khaled couldn't answer. He was afraid his voice would crack. She scribbled on a paper napkin. On it was her number, her name, and her last name.

He called her that night, and they talked until four in the morning. He could not sleep after that, so he took a shower and wrote her a love letter. Was he crazy to write a letter after one phone call? He didn't care. He left it in her locker. Number eleven. When he bumped into her later, she was still holding it.

"This letter is beautiful, Khaled. I've been reading it over and over again. Why don't you come over and have dinner at my place tonight?" He was exhausted but would skip the rest of his classes, go home, then take a nap. He couldn't miss out on this opportunity.

"What about your father?" he asked her. "And your family? Will they be OK with a guy coming over?"

"Oh, my father doesn't live with us. My parents are divorced, and he lives with his new wife. My brother studies abroad."

"And your mother?"

"She can't wait to meet you. She has heard a lot about you."

Khaled was afraid of meeting her mother. He worried she was expecting an engagement. Why else would Saadia have invited him to her house? What was he getting himself into? He could say he was busy tonight, then ignore her until they stopped talking altogether.

He took a deep breath and asked for her address. He had to be with her. It wasn't love at first sight, even though he had written her a letter proclaiming it. Nor was it lust. He liked her. He had never liked a girl before. And his father had once said that love and lust fade, but liking someone is lasting.

THERE WERE MANY BUILDINGS ON THE STREET, ALL cramped together. If Saadia lived in such a place, maybe she would use him for his money. He was a freshman with a custom-made luxury sports car, a wealthy background, and a prestigious family name: Abadi. Many girls would show interest in him when they found out his family name.

He introduced himself as Khaled Abadi to seduce girls. It usually worked.

He got out of his car and walked, continuing to use the navigation system on his phone. It notified him he had arrived. Saadia's car was parked in a lot adjacent to a dilapidated pink building. She drove a secondhand car, an old model. She was a freshman and the same age as him, which meant she had recently obtained a driving license. Her family must be struggling financially if they couldn't afford to buy her a new car.

He had been surprised when she gave him her address earlier. It was an area where blue-collar expatriate workers resided. He had been there once before when his housemaid, Abby, had called him, crying. She had lost her wallet on a day off and was afraid a policeman would stop her because they were cracking down on illegal immigrants. Without her civil ID, he might mistake her for one, she had told him. On the way home, he warned her not to come to such an area again.

"I don't think you lost your wallet. It was stolen."

"No sir. I'm sure I lost it."

"Why don't you spend your day off in the city? It's much safer. What are you doing in this part of town?"

He could tell from her silence she had been with a man. The next day, Abby found her wallet. She told Khaled she left it at her friend's house.

"See, sir. It's not such a bad area. It was my fault."

Khaled had tried many times to get her to stop calling him sir, but she insisted. And when they chatted, Abby would smile at him for no reason. He wasn't sure whether she was flirting with him, but he didn't smile back in case she was. He had heard many stories of employers having affairs with domestic helpers, and though she was attractive, he couldn't do anything with her. He considered her a sister. And his parents informed him Abby would move in with him when he got married, so why create an awkward situation for himself or Abby? Oh, and for his future wife, of course.

And now, here he was in the neighborhood where Abby had left her wallet at a friend's place.

He hadn't expected Saadia to live in an apartment. He debated whether he should go inside or drive back home. You like her, you idiot, he told himself. At least wait until you see her naked.

His phone was vibrating in his pocket.

"Where are you?" Saadia asked.

"Is it the pink building?"

"Yes. We're on the fourth floor."

He was afraid of elevators. When he was eleven, he got stuck in one with his mother. They had left his dentist's office on the twelfth floor, and suddenly the lift stopped. He wasn't scared until he watched his mother wailing and pounding on the doors.

"Help! We can't breathe. Get us out of here! Help!"

His mother pressed one button after another. Then she sat on her knees and pulled him down toward her, and they remained crouched in a corner. She didn't say a word, and her crying stopped. Khaled liked to believe it was his presence beside his mother that had soothed her.

Five minutes later, the elevator shook and made its way to the ground floor. The fear never left Khaled. He still went to the same dentist twice a year for a cleaning, and he walked twelve flights of stairs. Even after being knocked out after a wisdom tooth removal once, Khaled walked down twelve flights of stairs.

According to an online therapist, who had once treated him, but who terminated her services a month later when he sent her an email telling her how beautiful she was, the elevator incident had led to his fear of enclosed spaces. Claustrophobia: that was her diagnosis. He'd become interested in psychology the year before when his sister, Jawa, was diagnosed with anorexia nervosa. Jawa was fifteen then. Khaled's mother told him she had caught her throwing her food in a trashcan, and when she confronted her, Jawa admitted she had a disorder. He stopped going down for family meals after his mother became obsessed with feeding Jawa. She had lost weight, and was gaunt, but he couldn't speak to her about it. His way of dealing with the pain was by pretending everything was normal. His mother could take care of his sister. It wasn't his responsibility.

He walked through the emergency door, which led to the staircase. He stepped over a dead cockroach and continued his way up. Saadia was standing outside apartment 4A. She led him inside, holding his hand. The apartment was small. As he stepped into the flat, he glanced around. The walls were cracked and a chandelier was dangling from the ceiling. Was it going to fall? There was a kitchen to the right, a living room in front of him, a narrow corridor to his left, and three closed doors. Even the quarters of his live-in domestic helpers were more spacious than this. When guests visited his family's estate, the tour took an entire hour.

"I can't believe you walked four flights of stairs," Saadia said.

"I love any opportunity to exercise."

"Hey, Mom. Come say hi to Khaled."

Her mother approached. She was beautiful.

Saadia must have caught him staring because she

turned to him and said people always told them they look like sisters.

"*Salam alaikum khalti.*" He didn't know whether it was appropriate to shake her hand, so he kept both his hands in his pockets. Was it acceptable to have called her aunty?

"*Wa alaikum al salam.* I'm going out for dinner. Make yourself at home Khaled. It was nice to meet you."

You haven't even met me, he almost responded. And how could you leave your daughter alone with a strange man?

When the door slammed shut, Saadia turned around and winked at him. Was she going to kiss him? He couldn't breathe.

"Would you like a drink?"

"Sure, I'll have a glass of water."

"I was thinking more along the lines of beer, or even vodka." Her eyebrow was raised.

"Where do you get alcohol from?" Khaled asked her. It was illegal and expensive on the black market. And though money was no objection to him and he could easily afford it had he been interested in drinking, he wondered how she could afford it.

"My dad's boss is an influential man who has connections, a wasta so to speak. He helps us out with everything."

"Your father knows you drink?"

"Oh yeah. I had my first beer with him when I was fourteen. So? A drink?"

"No thanks. I just want to be with you. I'm drunk on you."

Saadia walked toward the kitchen and returned with a can of beer. She took his hand and led him to the couch.

"Wow. Drunk on me? I like that. Well, I'm drunk on you too, but I still want a beer."

They both laughed.

Khaled had tried alcohol a couple of times with his friends in high school, but he didn't enjoy it. Saadia was still holding his hand, but he removed it gently and took his cell phone out of his pocket, pretending to check it. He had never been this nervous around a girl before. His hands were shaking, so he put the phone on the table in front of them. When he turned to face Saadia, she was smiling at him.

"Tell me about your brother. How old is he?" he asked as he turned his face away.

"He's a year older. Nineteen." As she enunciated each word, the alcohol on her breath made its way to Khaled's nostrils. Was it her first beer of the night?

"Where is he studying exactly?" Khaled moved back a little. Her proximity made him uncomfortable. But he held her gaze, so as to feign confidence.

"In London." Saadia bit her lip. Khaled could not figure out whether it was a cue for him to kiss her, but even if it was, he could not move.

"Why did you choose to stay here?"

"Why did you?" She rested her head on his shoulders. Her hair was curly, thick, long. He kissed her head. He got a whiff of green apples and…

"I want to settle down here."

"Well, I couldn't get a scholarship." He buried his nose in her hair again. Ah yes: candy cane.

They spent the next two hours talking. Khaled learned she had a close relationship with her father. Saadia told him she liked her father's new wife but couldn't tell her mother for fear of hurting her.

A part of him was scared of how forward Saadia was. She bragged about the men she had been with before him and told him she had lost her virginity when she was fifteen. He was angry he wasn't her first but admired her openness with him.

The second time she invited him over, he lost his virginity. Her mother was out, and this time Saadia took him straight to her room. He wouldn't confess she was his first. A couple of thrusts later, Saadia cuddled him and fell asleep on his chest. He must have fooled her. Or she would have asked him, right?

As time passed, he developed strong feelings for her. He could not even look at other women. Wasn't he sick of her yet? Why weren't his feelings waning? He got what he wanted. But it was no longer about sex or pleasure. He kissed her forehead, her eyes, her lips without taking it further. Other nights, he rubbed against her body. And when they went to the cinema, he drove her home without kissing her. Or he would take her to restaurants and they would hold hands. Unlike him, she didn't worry about being in public together. But what worried him more than being caught was he had never dated a girl for company. He was scared. Terrified.

One day, Saadia introduced him to her brother, who was visiting home during his mid-term holiday.

"Hi, love. Meet Marwan."

They shook hands, and Khaled sat next to Saadia on the couch, careful to keep a distance between them, but she crawled into his lap. His face flushed. Her brother was fidgeting with the remote though the television was off. Saadia jumped off him, grabbed his hand, and led him to her room.

"Kiss me now," she said, behind closed doors.

"Saadia, your brother's outside."

"So?"

"I don't feel comfortable. What did you tell him about me?"

"I told him we're dating and are in love."

"Is he gay?" He whispered the last word.

"What the hell are you talking about?"

"How could your brother not be protective of you? A real man would beat me up."

"A real man? What do you mean? That's the most random, ludicrous thing I have ever heard."

"I'm sorry. I didn't mean to insult you or your family, especially not your brother. Please don't tell him what I said."

"How did you insult our family?"

"By implying that he, you know, liked men. That he wasn't a real man."

"He's not gay, if that's what you want to know. But are you saying a gay man is not a real man?"

"You know what I mean."

"No I don't. Look, I find your whole conservative thing endearing, but you need to open your mind. It's not an insult to be gay. Stop being an idiot."

She informed him penguins, dolphins, and even lions were gay or bisexual.

"Dolphins?" he asked.

"Uh-huh. It's nature. They're just urges. What's the big deal?"

"Oh so if someone has the urge to kill or rape, that's natural? Or what about a pedophile? Doesn't he have urges? Sorry, but your rhetoric is screwed. Literally." He snickered.

"Are you serious? Is that all you've got? Murder, rape, and pedophilia involve victims. There's a perpetrator and a victim, silly. When two adults want to hook up and it's consensual, there's no crime. Sorry, but *your* rhetoric is screwed. Don't ever use that argument in public. It's flawed and nonsensical."

"*Astaghfurallah*. Please, let's end this conversation."

"OK, but if we're going to spend the rest of our lives together, you need to change. I'm not raising kids with a homophobe."

It was the first time Saadia had mentioned the future to him. It didn't frighten him. They ordered Japanese food and ate on her bed. When she tried to kiss him after the meal, he told her he was tired and had to go home.

"Is it because I spoke about kids?"

"No."

"Don't tell me it's because of our debate about gays?"

"What? Of course not. I can't do anything with your brother around. That's all."

"Come on baby. Don't be so uptight."

"He'll hear us."

"We'll be extra quiet. Now come here…"

KHALED KNEW IT WAS TIME TO BROACH THE SUBJECT with his father. He wanted to marry Saadia.

"Lathi? Oh no. No, no, no *habibi*. They are Akashis, the lowest of tribes. You'll ruin our lives. Your sister won't get married because of you. How long has this been going on?"

"Since the beginning of the academic year," Khaled responded.

"If you're desperate to get married, your mother can find

you a wife right away or choose a girl yourself. But not this one. Stay away."

"Baba, don't you even want to meet her first and then make a decision?"

"I won't let you do this to the family. Maybe you are too young for marriage. You can't even think straight. You mustn't speak to this girl again. Promise me." His father was trembling.

"I promise, Baba."

He broke his promise and went to Saadia's house that night and the night after that and the night after that until nights became weeks and a month had passed.

On one of the nights, when he returned home, his father was blocking the entrance of the house as he approached the steps outside the front gate. "Are you seeing her?"

"Who, Baba?"

"Answer my question, you fool. The Akashi girl."

"No. What are you talking about? I'm not seeing her. I was out with my friends. Are you kidding? I forgot about her."

His father's facial muscles eased. Khaled watched him as he walked toward him to embrace him.

"Oh, my son. *Alhamdillah.* Thank God. Your mother and I were worried you were with her. Sorry for suspecting you, *habibi.* You look tired. Go rest. *Allah yiwafqik.* May God bless you."

The next day, as soon as he woke up, he called Saadia.

"I can't do this any longer. My father doesn't approve of us. He confronted me last night, and I lied to him. I can't do this to him. It's too much."

"Khaled. Do what?"

"I can't marry you, so there's no need for us to waste each other's time."

"Marriage is a farce. What we have is eternal. Please stay with me. I love you. And I know you love me. Please don't throw away what we have. Please." Her voice was trembling.

"I want to get married. I want to focus on my religion more and be good to my family. Marriage isn't a farce to me. It's a sacred bond. And we come from different backgrounds and tribes. I can't do this."

"Are you breaking up with me?"

"I'm sorry, Saadia. I want to settle down."

"Would you marry me then?"

"You said marriage was a farce."

"I'll say anything to keep us together. But if you want to get married, then fight for me. Your father will come around one day if he sees how serious we are. We don't need to get married now, but let's not break up."

"He won't approve. I know my father well. When he says no it means no. I don't want to drag you into this drama. It's better to call things off now."

"I beg you. Baby, don't do this."

She was sobbing and Khaled was restless to get off the phone. How pathetic of her to beg him. Where was her dignity? Was he heartless? How could he be over her? He had read about sociopaths before. Among the symptoms were being superficially charming and having no remorse or shame. He couldn't be one because his charm hadn't been superficial with Saadia. He had genuinely loved her. But, could people become sociopaths overnight? He would research it later.

"I'm not going to marry you, OK? Your brother sits outside your room while you have a man inside. Your mother has never asked me about my intentions. You and your family are a disgrace to our tradition."

"Don't bring my family into this," she said. "We're a disgrace to you? No, you are. I curse the day I met you."

"I curse the day I met *you*. Why would you defend your family? You're all trash. Don't ever call me again."

Khaled hung up on her and switched his cell off. What a terrible wife she would make. A woman like that was cheap, desperate and wouldn't fit in with his family. And what nerve she had to ask him to marry her.

FOR THE NEXT FEW WEEKS, KHALED LOST HIS APPETITE. He had read eating disorders could be hereditary. He forgot whether the research was conclusive.

He avoided the locker area and would sit alone on a bench between classes. There was a girl sitting on the grass eating a sandwich. He couldn't take his eyes off her. She was a familiar face to him on campus, but he hadn't given her a second glance before. Her hair was long, thick, wavy, brown, and covered with a red baseball cap worn backwards. She was wearing loose acid-washed jeans and a short-sleeved black shirt with olive-green suede army boots. The girl had style.

He had always liked fashion. Once, using his father's car at high school, he picked up a girl. She told him she would kiss him if he bought her a designer bag. His father often let him use his credit card, so he agreed. She was two years younger than him at the time—fifteen. He told her he would buy her two bags if she slept with him, but she refused. Hypocrite, he thought. But she was worth it. She looked like a porn star and quite a few guys at school had made out with her.

He took her shopping and chose an ostrich leather bag for her. His father would kill him if he found out he was spending money on a cheap girl, but he wanted to kiss her. He bought her a scarf and a choker from the same boutique.

He thought maybe a pair of designer shoes would change her mind about not sleeping with him, but she refused. When he paid, she told him she had never been out with a man with such good taste. She then asked him if he was gay. He placed her shopping bags on the ground and told her he wasn't dropping her home and she could take a taxi from the mall. She kept saying sorry over and over again and explained she was not allowed to take taxis. He stopped, looked at her, then said: "Just because I like fashion doesn't mean I'm gay. But you're too low-class to know that most straight rich guys like fashion. And would a gay guy spend all this money on a cheap girl to kiss her?"

And he walked off with the girl trailing behind him begging him not to leave her stranded. A diamond-studded watch caught his eye on his way toward the exit. He went in, charged it to his father's credit card, and walked out. She was waiting outside.

"OK, I'll take you home, but you'll have to do more than just kiss me. Not *that*. I understand. But much more."

She breathed a sigh of relief. "Thank you. Thank you so much. Yes, we can do everything. Except *that*."

Now this girl he was staring at on campus had a unique style. If he ever took her shopping, he wouldn't need to change her taste in clothes. "Your sandwich looks tempting. What is it?"

She got up and left. Then she turned back toward him, told him she had an extra sandwich and asked if he liked tuna. Yes. He took the sandwich from her. It was wrapped in aluminum foil. Thank you.

He found out the next day her name was Salma. Every day, Khaled joined her on the grass. Then, he summoned up the courage to ask for her number two weeks later.

"If you are interested in dating me, your intention should be marriage. Otherwise, what's the point? We might be incompatible, but at least if things end, it was serious," she said.

"I want to get married. Let's try this out."

"We need to tell our families. I'm not starting anything without them knowing."

He agreed. Both families approved and they started seeing each other officially.

He took her to parties, but she left early and, like him, didn't drink alcohol. When they were at university, she sat with him in public places such as the campus coffee shop or her favorite spot on the grass. There were places they could be alone on campus, such as the empty lot behind the auditorium or even parking lot B, where Saadia had straddled him and kissed him in his car, but he would not dare take Salma to those places. When they went out, she met him in her car. She drove a luxury car like him, and he never had trouble parking at her house, with its underground private garage.

He called Salma every day, but their conversations were formal. They had much in common, such as their social status and tribe, but they never had much to say to one another. Still, he was eating properly again, so he took this as a sign she was good for him.

A few weeks later, Salma confessed she wasn't a virgin. What was wrong with women these days? All this time she was avoiding being alone with him and she wasn't a virgin? It didn't matter. She was from a prestigious family. When he tried to spend time alone with her after her confession, she insisted they wait.

Salma bored him. But Khaled's father was proud of his choice, so he was eager to marry her. Could he fall in love with Salma after marriage? She lacked enthusiasm. Was it because she was in love with the man she had been with before him? Or was this her personality? Once, he asked her about her mystery man, and she told him not to bring up the subject again. He could tell she was still affected by this man, but he wasn't jealous. He had asked her about him to feign interest and to steer the subject away from their monotonous discussions about their families and schoolwork.

A YEAR LATER, SALMA AND KHALED WERE MARRIED. On the first night of their honeymoon, he ordered a glass of whiskey with dinner. He asked her if she wanted a drink, but she said sarcastically: Unlike you, I don't turn into a drinker overnight.

One night, when Salma was fast asleep in the master bedroom of their suite, Khaled went to the fridge and took out a can of beer, which he drank quickly. There was another can, but he opened a mini-bottle of whiskey instead, poured it in a tumbler, and added a few ice cubes. Khaled had an urge to call Saadia. But what about his father? He couldn't hurt him. And would Saadia answer the phone? He decided against calling her. Khaled slept on the couch that night.

Once they settled into their new villa, Khaled spent most of his free time away from home drinking. Alcohol numbed the pain. But it also enhanced it somehow.

He resented Salma and approached her only when he was inebriated or horny. He didn't kiss her and his lovemaking was furious. After he ejaculated, he would take a shower and watch television in the living room until he was sure she was asleep.

Khaled never raped her, but he had strong urges, and whenever they were uncontrollable, he needed to release them. He was forceful once inside her, but Salma didn't complain. Why was she submissive? Saadia would have slapped him or thrown him out of bed. He wished Salma would confront him about it, but she remained lifeless in bed. Why couldn't he fall in love with her? A cousin of his had told him the worst thing a man could do is to marry his beloved. It would drive a man crazy, he warned him, because he would be possessive and paranoid, and if she left, he would be scarred forever. But, how could that be true? Had he been with Saadia, they would've both been happy. And even his parents would eventually accept her. His uncle's wife was a Christian, and his parents disowned him until they had a son. After the birth of the baby, they all reconciled.

Salma wasn't in love with him either, but he still wished he could be affectionate toward her. And he had betrayed Saadia by leaving her. He was miserable. Why had he obeyed his father? Why was society so selfish? Wasn't love important? Why did people care about family names and tribes? Wasn't the high divorce rate an indicator something was amiss?

HE STARTED CHEATING ON SALMA. THEY WERE ALL flings. And there was Lana. They dated for two months. He even took her to the opening of a new art gallery. There were photographers there, but he ensured nobody photographed him. It was the first time he had taken a girl out publicly since marrying Salma. When he dropped her home, Lana asked whether he was going to leave his wife.

"What? No. Where did that come from?"

"You were always paranoid about being seen with me in public before, so I thought you were taking this relationship further."

"Our relationship is fine where it is."

"Are you happy in your marriage?"

"Nobody's happy."

"I can make you happy. I can be a second wife. I don't mind."

"I don't want a second wife. Take that idea out of your head. We're seeing each other. That's all. I don't date women, so you should feel special. Let's not ruin what we have with such talk. How about I take you to the Maldives next weekend?"

"The Maldives? Do you have no feelings? You know I can call your wife and ruin your reputation."

Khaled threatened to have her deported. Though he didn't have the power to do so, Khaled must have been convincing because he never crossed paths with her again. Lana was a fixture on the social scene, which was small, and they had bumped into each other at many parties before dating, but she had disappeared. He was happy he had managed to get rid of her. It was best not to check on her.

Nejoud Al-Yagout

One night, Khaled was drunk at a party and had slept with—what was her name?—in the host's guest bedroom. The girl was asleep in his arms. He moved her away gently and tiptoed to the bathroom. Did Saadia have the same number? He dialed it and hung up. He washed his face in the sink and went back to the bed. Should he wake this girl up and tell her it was time to leave? Khaled walked out of the bedroom. If she needed a ride home, she could find one.

Saadia hadn't been a heavy drinker, but she enjoyed the occasional beer and vodka. She held her alcohol well, drinking one or two cans (or glasses). And he preferred it that way, because unlike most people who came alive while inebriated, she fell asleep on the very rare occasions when she had more than two drinks. The next day Khaled was too hung-over to call. But by the following night, his liquid courage propelled him to dial her number.

"I need to see you," he begged, slurring.

"Oh my goodness. Khaled? Perhaps a hello, Saadia, how are you would be a better way to greet me after all this time."

"I miss you, Saadia."

"You sound drunk. You drink now?"

"I'm not drunk."

"Said the drunk person."

How he had missed her wittiness.

"I need to see you now. I love you. I never got over you, dammit."

"I'm married, Khaled."

"I thought you said marriage was a farce."

"I don't remember saying that."

"I remember it well."

"Well then, don't you remember me asking you to marry me?"

"Yes, I remember that too."

Silence.

"Why are you drinking and dialing me?"

"*Wallah*, I swear, I don't care if you're married. I want to be with you."

"Are you crazy? You call me out of the blue after all these years and expect me to drop everything in my life and come back to you? Would you like me to run in slow motion? What soundtrack do you have in mind? Philippe Rombi or how about Luis Bacalov?"

"Oh I remember Bacalov's Il Postino. Your favorite. And Ennio Morricone."

"This is not happening. I'm done with that chapter," she said.

He couldn't breathe. He hung up the phone then called Saadia right back.

"Hello again, Khaled. Aren't we over these games?"

"I'm not playing games. I said I missed you and wanted to be with you. I'm cutting to the chase. There's no point in hiding my feelings and pretending I called to say hello. I can't believe you're married."

"Well, the last I checked, you're married as well."

She had been keeping tabs on him if she knew he was still married. This was a good sign.

"My marriage means nothing. Yours?"

"It means everything to me."

"Don't you miss us? What we had was… There's no word for what we had. It wasn't of this world."

"That's nostalgia speaking. You didn't feel that way when

you were in it. You discarded me like a piece a garbage." She was still upset at him. Another good sign.

"I've changed. People need to get away from each other to grasp the intensity, the beauty."

"I disagree. I don't live that way. Life's too short. If it's love, it's love. Why turn it into hate? If it's beautiful, hold onto it. Why run away? That's fear. I don't want to be with anyone who's scared. I've changed too. I was a sucker for love. But that was back then."

"So you're not in love with your husband?"

"Yes. I am." Saadia sounded defensive to him.

"Then why did you say back then? Aren't you a sucker for love now?" His heart was pounding in his chest. What was she wearing? Would she hang up the phone on him if he asked her? He wished he hadn't left her. It was unnatural begging for love from his soul-mate.

"Stop analyzing everything I say. I meant I'm not a fool anymore. You won't find what you're looking for in my words."

"Where will I find it then?'

"Nowhere."

"When can I see you?" He placed his hand on his rumbling stomach. Even his stomach was calling out to her.

"Didn't you hear a word I said? I moved on from all this, from *you*. You bowed to the system and are now trying to find your way out. But it's too late. I don't love you anymore, but even if I did, I won't cheat on my husband. I don't mind talking to you, but you won't see me. Not even for coffee. Your chance has passed. I'm with Dakhel now."

"Dakhel or Dakheel?"

"Dakhel. His name is Dakhel."

"Dakhel? What the hell? What kind of a name is that?"

"Well, there are random names out there. He's from a rich family like yours. But Dakhel fought for me. I'd rather an uncommon name on a good person than a common name on an evil person."

Khaled cringed. The woman he loved was referring to him as evil but he ignored her comment. "What's his family name?"

"It shouldn't concern you."

How could anyone in their right mind choose a name for their son that means inside? Her husband must have been bullied at school. He asked Saadia, while laughing, whether Dakhel had a twin brother called Barra, outside.

"I'm sorry, babe," he said, after she threatened to hang up if he didn't stop making fun of her husband's name.

"Don't call me babe."

"OK. I'm sorry, but it's a random name. I'm sure you agree."

"Well he's not a local."

"It's random for any Arab. I've been all around the Middle East and the Levant and even North Africa. That's not a name. It's a joke."

"Who said he's an Arab?"

"Where's he from?"

"That's none of your business. Stop asking about him."

Khaled repeated Dakhel and Barra over and over again.

"I told you to stop or I'll hang up. You're so immature." Saadia giggled.

"You never thought of me?" The old feelings of nervousness returned to him. How many men had she been with since him? Did it matter? No. He loved her, with or without the ghosts of her past.

"Of course I have, but just out of curiosity. I wish you could move on. I'm glad you called though. It's great to hear from you, so call me anytime, but don't expect anything to happen between us."

"Do you have children?"

"No."

How he wished he had a son with her. Or even a daughter. He thought of his sperm count. Maybe his body was rejecting having a baby with anyone but Saadia.

He called her every day. And she answered all of his calls.

"Saadia, my love. Are you happy in your life?"

"Yes I am. And stop calling me your love. Do I have to keep reminding you every single frickin' day that I'm married? If you can't handle it, stop calling."

"Then why're you talking to me behind his back?"

"He knows we're in touch."

"He knows? Is he gay?"

"You haven't changed one bit, Khaled."

It upset him the men in her life weren't possessive: her father, her brother, and now her husband. Khaled fantasized about marrying Saadia. He would be the best husband to her, even though he would make sure to check on her whereabouts, because she was the only woman he had ever felt possessive of in his life. Though he would not let her out of his sight if they both got divorced from their respective spouses, he wouldn't ask her to change her style, even if her dresses were short and her cleavage showed. He preferred it to a woman who changed her style to please her man.

HE WOULD BE MUCH HEALTHIER WITH SAADIA IN HIS life. He had gained weight and it was cumbersome to go to work. Abby blamed Salma for his appearance and drinking.

He tried to assure her it wasn't Salma's fault he was miserable, but Abby wouldn't budge. Salma once complained to Khaled about her, saying she had no idea why Abby hated her.

"She doesn't hate you, Salma. Maybe you can be kinder to her."

"I *am* kind to her. She's a part of the family. You should see how hard I try. Our housemaid Rita loves me. So do the drivers and cooks at my house. Your chef and other maids here love me. I don't get it."

Khaled could not tell her what Abby had said about Salma. Instead he said, "Abby misses my mom and my sister. Don't take it personally."

"She isn't unhappy around you, Khaled. She loves to cook for you." Salma's eyebrows were raised and she was glaring at him, head tilted to the side. Her lips were pursed tightly, and she folded her arms against her chest.

"Why are you being sarcastic?"

"You tell me. There must be a reason she doesn't like me. What are you hiding? Was she in love with you? Did you ever have a fling with her?"

"Slow down Salma. Don't put dirty thoughts in your head. I wouldn't go there with a helper."

"With a helper? Why? Is she beneath you? She's a woman, isn't she?"

"What? I didn't mean it like that. Abby's like a sister to me. And the reason she cooks for me is because I don't like our new chef, and you don't cook anything."

Saadia had been a great cook. She had once made him vine leaves cooked with minced lamb soaked in yogurt and garnished with mint leaves and parsley. Inside the dish, there were cubed potatoes.

"What is this? It's delicious."

"I made it up." She fed him directly from the serving platter.

Another time, she made him mashed potatoes.

"How come it's green, Saadia?"

"Oh, I blended the potatoes with zucchinis and pea pureé."

"Another original?" he asked.

"I think so. It might exist in a cookbook, but I found the recipe in my head, just for you, *habibi*."

One night, Saadia had even fed him a concoction in her bed. Was it the eggplants with mashed broccoli and a béchamel dressing or the carrot stew with mushrooms and pickles? He had asked her why she wasn't eating and she said she was on a diet. She had cellulite on her thighs and was terrified because she was too young for it according to her mother, but he assured her every inch of her body was beautiful.

And, now, thinking of her, it didn't matter to him whether she had gained or lost weight. He imagined her when she was much older, with gray hair, saggy breasts, a flabby bottom, bumpy thighs, and wrinkles. Would he be lucky enough to share the aging experience with her? Khaled could be faithful to her for the rest of his life without even struggling to commit. And he would stop drinking. Even if she still drank.

KHALED SPENT THE REST OF HIS MARRIAGE SENDING Saadia love messages and calling her. One day, he begged her to leave her husband, promising he would marry her. She was polite but changed the subject. Her comments from the night before him played over again and again: I'm happy we are friends now. But I think we mistook our connection for love back then. It was evidently lust.

"Don't you love me, Saadia?" he asked her.

"Not like that. You're a buddy now."

Even though he sensed her reluctance to start a new life with him, Khaled's depression lifted. He even cut down on drinking and stopped going to parties. Instead, he would sit on the patio of his house, a glass of wine in his hand, or a can of beer, or a tumbler with whiskey and two cubes of ice, and speak to Saadia for hours.

"Send me a picture of you. I want to see what you look like now."

"No. That would be disrespectful to Dakhel."

"Why didn't you accept my Instagram friend request? And why aren't you on Facebook?"

"Are you cyber-stalking me?"

"I wanted to see your face."

"I'm sure you saw my Instagram profile photo."

"Yes, Saadia. The one with Dakhel written in cursive? Rub it in."

⁂

When Khaled and Salma divorced, his parents were devastated. He had begged Salma not to tell his parents the reason, and she didn't. But his father kept asking if he had misbehaved. Khaled lied and said he neither cheated on her nor treated her badly.

"Baba. It wasn't working out. We fought a lot and couldn't live with each other. There's nothing more to it."

"Your generation is the worst. You get divorced for no reason. Your mother and I struggled, but we stayed together."

You weren't in love with another woman, he wanted to tell his father.

It wouldn't be easy to win Saadia back. She was stubborn and held a grudge against him. Why couldn't she forgive him? Maybe having had many men made it easy for her to fall in and out of love. Whatever her reason, Saadia belonged to him alone. Her words haunted him: Dakhel fought for me.

Maybe he hadn't been a fighter before, but he was prepared to fight now.

3

SAADIA

"It's like a mirror. Once it's cracked, that's it. You can glue it together, but the crack remains."

—Abadia Borido

When Saadia found out Khaled had gotten married, she threw up and vowed she wouldn't let him back into her life. She read the wedding announcement in the local paper. She was haunted for months with flashbacks of him meeting her mother, making love, going to the cinema and holding his head while he fell asleep. And his callous behavior toward her after their break-up plunged her into depression.

"Saadia, you have to move on with your life." Her mother was sitting next to her on the couch. She moved closer and ran her fingers through Saadia's hair.

"Mama, I have," she lied. "Please stop worrying about me." She moved her mom's hand from her hair and nestled her head on her mother's shoulder. Hot tears escaped her eyes, wetting the sleeve of her mother's caftan.

Her mother passed tissues to Saadia and took a couple from the box. Was her mother crying for her or for herself or for all women?

"*Habibti*, why don't you go visit Marwan in London? It'll be a nice change."

Saadia had no energy to travel. She doubted whether things could go back to normal again. No breakup had ever affected her in such a way before, but she was more worried about her mother's pain than her own.

She'd had plenty of boyfriends before Khaled, but how could she be with another man after him? Her mother assured her she would get over him and find the right man. Mom, I've never loved anyone in this way, she had said. To which her mother had replied: The first heartbreak is the worst. She would get married to prove to Khaled she was worthy of being loved. But would she find a husband? What if nobody married her? Why were men complicated?

Like her mother, she had fallen in love with a man who had abandoned her. Her Baba's bride had been nineteen. At the time, Saadia was fourteen, a freshman in high school.

"Where did they meet?" Saadia had asked her mom when she first heard the news.

"He won't talk about it, Saadia. The truth is I haven't been there for your father. When you get married, give your husband attention. Men love women who're wild in bed but ladies in the parlor. I was a lady in bed and wild in the parlor."

"Don't you dare blame yourself. And how could Baba marry a kid? She could be my sister. Sickening."

"She's not a kid. She's an adult. And one day you'll understand men."

Why was her mother letting her father get away with it? She called her father.

"Baba, how did you meet Layla?"

"Who told you her name?"

"Who do you think? So tell me. I want to know."

"It's not important, *habibti.*"

"It's important to me. Please. Oh, and I want to meet her."

"I don't think your mother would like you to meet her yet. We have to respect her wishes."

"I respect her more than you do."

"Saadia, I'm sorry I hurt your mother. I know how much you love her, but our relationship died years ago. We stayed together for you and your brother. Now that you are both older, we decided it was best to separate."

"Baba, we're still young. We need you."

"Nothing's going to change just because I'm not living with you. Even if we don't see each other all the time, I'm still your father."

SAADIA MET HER FATHER'S NEW WIFE A LITTLE MORE than a year after their marriage. She had not expected Layla to be shy. When Saadia greeted her, she bowed her head and blushed. Layla had blue eyes with curled eyelashes and thick eyebrows. Her hair was thick, black, silky, straight and reached down to her tiny waist. Though she was of a petite frame, her breasts were full. Her lips were plump and pink and her skin, golden brown. Saadia's mother was a beauty, but Layla was stunning. She couldn't stop staring at her.

At lunch, Layla didn't say a word. But Saadia sensed her father was in love with her. Her father had never caressed her mother's face the way he touched Layla's. Every time she added more rice on his plate, he would say thank you *habibti*. At one point, her father even winked at Layla.

Saadia went to the bathroom. Since she had been a child, whenever Saadia was tense, she would become nauseated. The reflection staring back at her was pale. Bile rose in her throat as her salivary glands activated. Why didn't the vomit make its way out? She was too scared to put her fingers down her throat. She had tried to once and choked. The nausea would subside. She had to wait a few minutes. Poor Layla. Poor young, uneducated, and beautiful brides everywhere. She would treat her with respect. Women always took their anger out on other women and men got away with everything. It was her father's fault, not Layla's. Still, she would not punish her father either. She loved him. And though her father wasn't available all the time, at least he loved her in return, in his own way.

Layla must be wild in the bedroom and was obviously a lady in the parlor. Whatever her father's reason had been for divorcing her mother and abandoning his family, Saadia had lost faith in men.

SAADIA STARED AT THE WEDDING PHOTO. KHALED WAS handsome in a white robe, headgear, and a transparent, paper-thin black overcoat with a gold trim. There were no pictures of Salma because many local weddings were segregated. She was fortunate to come from a family where weddings included men and women dancing together, drinking, eating, and enjoying each other's company. She couldn't understand society's obsession with keeping men and women apart.

She kept the newspaper clipping of Khaled's wedding in her drawer. At night she would kiss his lips and go to sleep. How could she love a man she hated?

ONE DAY, A FEW WEEKS BEFORE KHALED'S WEDDING announcement, when Khaled and Salma were known as a couple on campus, Saadia followed her home. Saadia had to warn Salma about the man she was dating and tell her how Khaled had broken her heart and would break hers too. Salma's car was slowing down, so Saadia kept a distance. They had entered a neighborhood of lavish mansions with sprawling gardens. It intimidated her Khaled was dating a girl from a wealthy family.

Saadia had found out Salma's prestigious family name from an aunt of hers who worked in administration at the university. She doubted he would marry her, because Khaled wasn't capable of commitment even though he told her he was thinking of marriage while breaking up with her. Saadia parked across the street from the house as she watched Salma drive into an underground garage. Even the apartment building where she lived didn't have a garage. Saadia always had trouble finding parking when she went home.

She waited. It would be best to ring the doorbell and ask for Salma, but she couldn't get out of her car. The garage door opened again. She could make out a man driving a sleek car. Did Salma have a brother? She sped to take a U-turn and followed him. At the traffic light, he was looking at her through his rearview mirror. She lowered her eyes.

He drove for another minute, put his flashers on, and parked to the side. Saadia parked behind him. She had no idea what she was doing. Her heart was racing. The man got out of his car and approached her.

He was tapping her car. Saadia rolled down the window. "How can I help you?" he asked.

"W-w-what do you mean?" Why was she so nervous?

"Well, you've been following me since I left my house. You're not good at trailing people, are you?" His brow was furrowed.

"Are you Salma's brother?"

"Oh, you know Salma?" He frowned.

"Why do you seem upset I might know your sister?"

"She's not my sister. I'm her father. Were you just with her? Oh, and I'm upset because I was hoping you were following me."

His audacity unnerved her. He was flirting with her even after she mentioned the name of his daughter. "You're her father? You're young."

"Good genes." He winked at her.

She put her hair behind her ears and checked her phone. She told him his genes were more than good. How could he have a daughter her age?

"So why were you parked across from our house? Tell me. I want to know."

Saadia's throat tightened. She took a deep breath and tears rolled down her face.

"I f-f-followed Salma home," she sobbed. Saadia blurted everything out, from the way Khaled had left her to how he was now dating his daughter. "You have to be careful. He won't marry her." Saadia waited for his response. What he said next shattered her.

"They're engaged. We know about Khaled. And you're a dangerous woman if you were willing to break them up by telling me about him. What if my daughter wasn't engaged yet? I'm an open-minded man, but I still wouldn't have liked the idea. And what if you had trailed my wife? Salma would've gotten into a lot of trouble. You could've ruined a family. You're messed up."

"No," she whimpered, head in her hands. "I'm not. This is out of character for me. I wasn't even planning this. I wanted to tell Salma, but I panicked. Then I saw you."

"You need serious help. You have major issues. You're sick."

"You're the sick one. You knew I was following you and you stopped your car to talk to me. And you hit on me right away. All you men are sick." She didn't even have the strength to shout at him. Her voice was wavering.

"Stay away from my house and my daughter, or I'll call the police."

"And I'll tell the police you wanted to talk to me. Khaled may marry your daughter, but he'll hurt her. Wait and see. Men like him don't change. He'll come back to me when he's tired of her."

"To you? I don't think so. This isn't normal behavior. I'm sure he left you because he knows you're crazy."

Saadia was confused. If that's how he perceived her, then why was he still standing there talking to her even after calling her crazy and threatening to call the police?

"Khaled didn't see this side of me. I haven't seen this side of me. I'm aware what I'm doing is crazy, but trust me, I've never behaved this irrationally before. I gave him nothing but love. Even if he doesn't come back to me, he is a heartless human being. And he'll hurt your daughter."

"You sound like a jealous young lady." He wiped his forehead and took his headgear off. She watched him walk back to his car, fling it in the car, and come back toward her. It was now obvious this man was interested in her even after insulting her. A car honked as it blared past them. The man yelled for them to get out of the way.

"We're not even blocking the way," she said calmly to Salma's father. "Such jerks on the road today. Such jerks in the world, huh?"

"If you're insinuating Khaled, then I must say all I've seen from him is respectful behavior." She caught him looking at her thighs. He immediately turned his glance away, squinted while looking up at the sky, and said he heard there was a dust storm coming.

"I hope you don't think I'm crazy. I swear I didn't even plan to talk to you. I wanted to talk to Salma." She spoke using a low-pitched voice. It drove men wild. An ex of hers had once insisted she speak to him like that when they were intimate, and Khaled called it her bedroom voice.

"Listen, go home, take a shower, and forget about all of this." His tone had changed as well. He was mirroring her. An ex had told her men and women both mirrored each other as a mode of seduction. It's usually unconscious, he had informed her, but since many have learned about it, some people use it to manipulate others.

"You're not going to report me, are you? Are you going to tell Khaled?"

"I won't tell Khaled."

"Promise?" Saadia asked. Salma's father was staring at her, as though challenging her to stare back. She was used to that look. It preceded a kiss, or even an exchange of numbers. Or, her boyfriends used it before sex when they weren't in the mood for foreplay. At supermarkets, men would even stare when they were with wives or girlfriends. When a man was attractive to her, she would smile flirtingly, unless he was with another woman. How many women, besides their girlfriends or wives, did these men ogle or pine for daily? Her mother had once told her it was easy to catch a man's attention but difficult to keep it. He could easily be distracted by others, she had warned her.

"I promise." His breathing had become shallow.

Saadia's stomach turned at the prospect of what she was about to do. She could taste the bile rising up her throat. She swallowed her saliva and took a deep breath as she leaned over toward the floor of the passenger seat and rummaged through her bag. She found a pen, grabbed his hand, and wrote her number on the back of it. "It's Saadia," she told him.

"Are you serious?" he asked. He rubbed her number off his skin and took his cell phone out of his pocket. "Here, put in your digits."

"Hey, you're pretty avant-garde for an old person." She typed in her number. "Now give me a call."

"I'll call you tonight," he promised. Her phone rang and she saved his number. "Oh, and it's Ali."

He didn't call her that night. But she didn't care. Khaled's engagement was on her mind. Should she call him and tell him he was making a mistake getting married? Should she warn Salma? She couldn't go to classes the next day. After a week of missing classes, she got a call from her aunt who asked her if she was sick. Saadia told her she wasn't in the mood to study, but her aunt said she had to go back to university as the administrative department was in the process of issuing a warning for her absences.

Saadia heard from Ali two weeks later. She was in a taxi, on her way home from a party. She didn't drive when she drank, even though she didn't exceed a glass or two at the most. It was a promise she had made to her father that she kept.

"Hey, stranger," he said.

"Hi Ali."

"I'm at a hotel. Would you like to meet me there?"

"Sure. Send me the location."

"You know the Crystal Palace Hotel?"

"Yes. Of course."

"Come straight to the Orchid Penthouse Suite. Ask reception downstairs. I'll call them now to tell them I'm expecting someone."

"Oh, in a room?"

"Why beat around the bush? Do you want me as much as I want you?"

"Yes." And she meant it.

"Then get your butt over here. I'll send you the address now."

Saadia's stomach rumbled. She apologized to the driver and gave him the new address. They arrived fifteen minutes later. She waited in the car and couldn't get out.

Her heart was thumping. She took out a tissue from her bag and spit into it. The acid reflux was unbearable. She inhaled deeply and closed her eyes. The driver asked her if she was getting out.

"No. Take me back home. I'm sorry. I'll pay you extra."

"It's OK ma'am. You don't have to."

She sent Ali a message saying she wouldn't make it and not to get in touch with her again.

Her phone flashed. It was Ali.

"Come back. I have a surprise for you. Please." His voice was slurring.

"I can't do this. I can't be with a married man. I wouldn't mind having a fling if you were single. But you have a wife."

"It takes two to tango. You're not exactly innocent. Are you a tease?"

"Let's forget about all this. Please. Go home to your wife. It's not worth it. I'm tired of men. Why can't you keep it in your pants? You'd risk shattering your family's life for a lay? How sleazy is that? I feel sorry for Salma. She's marrying a jerk and her father's one too."

Ali hung up on her. The driver was staring at her through the driving mirror. She glared at him. He immediately lowered his gaze. She got a message telling her to go to hell. And she blocked his number in case he called her again. She was attracted to Ali but had managed to resist being physical with him. And the nausea that overcame her outside of the hotel had disappeared. A wave of peace engulfed her. She had scored for womankind.

Saadia had a sudden affinity toward Ali's wife and Salma and every woman on the planet. Women had suffered enough. She was tired of men. And she was tired of women who weren't tired of men.

SAADIA WASN'T ATTRACTED TO WOMEN. KAWTHAR WAS her best friend since middle school, and she was a lesbian. Kawthar was in and out of relationships with women, and Saadia envied her because even Kawthar had managed to find a husband. Saadia suggested they take their friendship further.

"He discovered our messages to one another," Kawthar told her a few weeks into their relationship.

"Oh no. Is he going to divorce you, Kawthar? I don't want to be the cause."

"No, silly. He's got his women on the side, too. We're basically roommates now. He was just surprised it was with you."

"I hope you assured him nothing happened."

"He could tell from our messages nothing did. As long as you're not a man, he doesn't care. And he knows it won't ever be a man, so don't worry about it."

Saadia broke up with her the next day and told her they were better off as friends. Kawthar was devastated. They hadn't even kissed. How could she have not known she wasn't attracted to her? Why was she acting shocked?

"Why do you want to leave me? I told you my husband doesn't care. He won't bring it up again. Why're you freaking out?"

"Kawthar, I'm not freaking out. *You* are. I'm not feeling this. I'm not gay. I can't do this anymore. I like you, but not in that way. I tried."

"You *tried*? Every time I tried to get close, you moved away. And wait, I was a trial? Why? Because you're still in love with Khaled? You're going to end up alone. Nobody wants a woman as cheap as you." Even Kawthar, a friend she had trusted all these years, had no respect for her. Saadia had been in many relationships before Khaled, but she was serious about the men she dated. She would've married any of the men she slept with. They were the cheap ones giving their bodies away easily, not her. At least she was searching for love.

She listened to Kawthar carry on with her monologue.

"I know your kind. You use gay people to feel good about yourselves since men have let you down. Straight men do it too. They sleep with other men in prison when they need sex. It's disgusting. You hold us in low regard. It's unfair."

"Kawthar, how did I use you? We weren't even physical with each other."

"Now I know why. You're not even attracted to me. You used me emotionally. Why would you get involved with me in the first place?"

"I don't know why you're upset. It hasn't even been a month. And what's the big deal about saying I love you to each other and hanging out like we used to? Nothing has changed. Come on, Kawthar. We're best friends."

"You're screwed up. And you're not going to get over Khaled by using people. You were on the verge of having an affair with Salma's dad. You're crazy."

"Stop judging me. I confided in you because I trust you. It's not cool to bring that up and use it against me."

"You've got serious daddy issues. Not all men are like your father. You have to let go of what he did to your mother. You keep throwing yourself on people. I never even thought of you in that way. You came to me. You wanted this. I was happy being your best friend, but you made me fall in love with you."

"I'm sorry, Kawthar," she mumbled. But this apology

82   Nejoud Al-Yagout

came out after Kawthar had hung up on her.

Straightaway, she got a text message from Kawthar telling her not to call her again. She had lost her best friend too.

She blamed Khaled for this mess. If it hadn't been for him, she wouldn't have met Ali or dated Kawthar.

But Kawthar was overreacting. She was being a hypocrite, blaming her for faking a relationship when she was married and gay.

"You're getting married?" Saadia had asked when Kawthar had first broken the news to her, years before.

"My mom found a great guy."

"Kawthar, you're gay."

"Yeah, but I want kids one day. And you know moms. They won't leave us alone until we settle down."

"You can sleep with a man?"

"I've done it before, remember?"

"Yeah, but you hated it."

"No, I hated the guy. I like this one."

"So you're bi?"

"No, I'm gay. But I can sleep with a man. Why do I have to define it for you? A lot of gay people get married and sleep with their spouses. You won't get it. You don't know what it's like to be gay here. I'll give you a hint: it's hell."

When Khaled got in touch with Saadia, years later, after she had given up on him, she lied and told him she was married. She called her faux-husband by the name

Dakhel, her private nickname for Khaled during their years apart. She had been celibate since he left her, and she had chosen the name Dakhel because it was an anagram for Khaled and he lived inside of her and there was no space for another man. She still loved him, but she couldn't let him know. Saadia said they could be friends, but nothing more. Why did it hurt her so much? Wasn't she supposed to feel vindicated?

Then, the moment she had been waiting for arrived. "My wife found out about us," Khaled said. He sounded overjoyed.

"Us? I hope you made it clear there is no us."

"She found out about me being in love with you, OK? She knows we didn't do anything, but she still wanted a divorce. Saadia, listen to me. I'm willing to marry you this time. I'm a free man now. I won't make the same mistake again. Baby, leave your husband. Come on. Let's start a future together."

"I'm not going to marry you."

"Saadia, I beg you," Khaled said.

"Dakhel is the love of my life." She wasn't lying. If only he knew.

She hung up on him. Now they were even. She had continued to speak to him while he was married to keep his hopes up high. Or was it because she was happy hearing his voice? Why did she love him so much? Could she go back to Khaled after he betrayed his wife by professing his undying love to her? Both his wife and her were better off without him. Many women would take back men who hurt them, who came back when it suited them. But not her.

All the memories came flooding back, from how his face would flinch when she mentioned her past to him to the way he glanced over the living room in contempt the first time he walked into the apartment. She recalled his face when her mother left them alone for the first time. He always acted superior to her, as though she were lucky to be dating a man higher than her on the social ladder.

Saadia had stayed with him because she adored him. She had been considerate to him, even as he fumbled around when they had first made love, acting as though he were used to being naked with a woman. She had stayed quiet even when he didn't know the right way to touch her. Being with him was enough for her.

He had left her heart-broken. It was time to let go of Khaled forever. She couldn't forget the way he had insulted her family either. Or the way he had flaunted Salma on campus and ignored her when they crossed paths as though she were a ghost. Well, it was time to become a ghost to him again for the rest of her life, his life, *their* lives.

Or maybe she could return to him in a few months. He would have learned his lesson by then, no? Absolutely not. But what if destiny had brought them back together? Saadia had no idea what to do. She felt her resolve breaking.

Her phone was flashing. It was Khaled.

To hell with dignity, she thought as she answered, hands shaking.

4

BADER

"The most important thing…"
—Laila Naghma Fikh

Bader stared at the message from Salma. Her LinkedIn profile was empty apart from a photograph. It had bothered him she had fallen in love with him when they were at university, but he was more bothered he was still on her mind after all this time. She was insignificant to him. He was curious why she had reached out, but it was best not to respond. She may assume he was interested. He deleted the message.

Salma had been a distraction at a time when he was on a break with Maha. When they had been at university, Bader told Maha all about the girls he was with when they were apart. She was angry but appreciated his transparency.

"Thank you for being honest with me, Bader."

"I won't cheat on you, Maha. But I want to get other women out of my system before I commit to you. If you want to wait, that's great. Otherwise…"

He told Maha she was free to do the same with other men, but Maha stayed faithful to him. He grew tired of his flings.

"It's you and me now."

"Are you sure, babe?" Maha had asked him.

"Maha, I'm done with other girls. All I want is to be with you."

AFTER ALL THESE YEARS, HE WAS COMMITTED AND faithful to Maha. But they were going through a difficult phase. Things had changed after a tense discussion they had about marriage a month earlier on the phone.

"Bader, I'm not pressuring you, but it's been six years," she said.

"Maha, we travel alone together. You spend the night at my place. We're practically married. And we're lucky. Most couples here don't have the freedom to be alone. There's no pressure on us. Is it your family? What are they saying?"

"You know my mom wants us to settle down. She doesn't see why we're taking this long. And my dad gave up on us ages ago. He doesn't want to hear your name unless you want to meet him to discuss marriage. My parents both think you're not serious. And don't you want kids?"

"Now? No way. We're so young. Why would we take on such a responsibility?"

"I want to be a young mother."

"You can have children when you are in your thirties. That's young."

"Oh my God. Are you saying you want to until we're in our thirties? I am not waiting that long. I'm sorry Bader."

"We can get married earlier, but I don't see why we have to have children in our twenties."

"Do you have a timeframe?"

"I haven't thought about it. Why are you pressuring me?"

"If having a mature discussion about marriage after six years of dating is pressure, then we have major issues. You're not serious about me. About us."

"I'm committed. I don't cheat on you. I had my parents build another floor with a private entrance. For you, Maha. So we could be together. Your pajamas are at my place. So is your toothbrush. I used your shampoo when I ran out last night. We spend most of our free time together. Isn't that serious enough for you?"

"We're not living abroad Bader. Spending the night is one thing. Traveling is another thing. But, I can't move in with you without being your wife. You're not going to marry me, are you? Oh my God. I'm such an idiot."

"I am. I told you I would, and I'm a man who keeps his promise, especially to you. But I think it should be when both of us are ready."

"What if you're never ready?"

They remained silent on the phone for a few seconds.

"I can't be with another woman, babe. I love you. Let's not force anything."

"I gotta go. Bye."

A week later, things got worse. They were both drunk at a party. He was horny, but she was on her period.

He confessed he liked it when she had her period or went out of town for business trips or was busy with her family, because he missed her body and looked forward to making love to her again.

"First you tell me you're not ready to get married and now you say you're sick of making love to me?"

"Don't twist things. It's not like that." He was slurring.

"So what's it like, drunken sailor?"

"I dunno. Lemme take you home."

"In that state? No. Sorry."

"I can ask Alex. He doesn't drink, he can take us."

"Who is Alex?"

"A designated driver. A couple of people are going with him. Let me go ask him if he has room for us."

"I don't want to get into a car with a bunch of drunk people."

"You're drunk too, Maha-roo."

"Call us a taxi. Now."

Bader had never been in a local taxi before, but he couldn't argue with Maha. She was in a bad mood. It must be her damn period.

The next morning, he cringed at how drunk he had been and the way he treated her. He would make it up to her and take her out on a fancy date. First, he had to tell her about Salma's message. He called Maha.

"Oh, wow. I remember her. The psycho you dated who wanted to marry you, right?"

"Yeah." Bader laughed.

"What're you going to do?" Maha asked.

"I'm going to ignore her. There's no reason to stay in touch."

"Aren't you curious what she wants to talk about?"

"No. I'm not. Let me treat you to dinner tonight."

"Babe, I'm still recovering from last night. I just want to chill at home."

"OK, *habibti*."

TICK TOCK. SHE WAS EITHER TIRED, NOT IN THE MOOD, would call him back or was busy at work. Maha was avoiding him, and he was avoiding other girls. He wasn't interested. He had fans inviting him out to coffee to discuss his book, and he had politely declined the advances of two female colleagues. One sent him a suggestive email. Another one cornered him in an elevator and tried to kiss him. He didn't want to hurt her by pushing her off him, so he gently moved her away and pointed toward the camera. Her face flushed. She resigned two days later. He didn't know whether it had been her decision or if she was fired because of the footage. If he had done what she did to him, she would have reported him and he would've been legally prosecuted. Why wasn't it harassment when a woman hit on a man? Because men are weak and like it when a woman hits on them? What a generalization.

He spent two hours in meditation that evening. He was accustomed to having visions of Maha. There were lights around her. Bader's energy centers vibrated. But enlightenment eluded him again. The spiritual journey was teaching him patience. He inhaled and exhaled deeply while focusing on the words his guru had once told him: Be in the moment. There is no destination. The words enveloped him in peace.

He dialed Maha's number.

"Do you love me?" Bader asked.

"Do cows fly in the month of July?"

"Sorry to burst your bubble, but I think you mean pigs. So is that a yes? Let me hear a yes."

"Stop being silly."

Bader couldn't bear another moment without her.

He would propose to her. His stomach rumbled. Why was he anxious?

But nothing would change his mind. He was determined to win Maha back even though he hadn't lost her. For them to live with each other officially, they needed a marriage license.

For the first time, he fantasized about having children with Maha. There had been no logical reason to fear marriage. He had private quarters at his family's home. His book sales were lagging, but with his income as a graphic designer and Maha's salary as an advertiser, they could afford a family of their own. His parents would also help him sort his finances. And hospitals and dentists were free of charge. Why was he procrastinating?

He suddenly had the urge to pass by Maha's house. Today, he would meet her parents.

He called her. Maha answered the phone right away.

"Where are you, Maha?"

"I'm taking a walk. The weather is beautiful."

"I want to see you. Where are you exactly? I'll join you."

"Not now. Let's hang out tomorrow."

"OK. What time?"

"I'll call you right after work."

But he wasn't going to wait to see her.

MAHA LIVED TWO STREETS AWAY FROM HIM, A FIVE-minute walk, but he was accustomed to driving everywhere, even short distances. He parked his car across from her house. He turned off his engine and waited.

Twenty minutes later, Maha approached her house. She was wearing the fluorescent yellow sneakers he had bought her a few months back, black spandex leggings, and his gray hoodie that smelled of her skin, a blend of cocoa butter and jasmine, each time she returned it back to him. As he was about to text her, a jeep pulled up beside her. He watched as Maha entered the car and planted a kiss on the cheek of the driver. His first instinct was to get out and confront her, but he repeated a mantra: I am love.

Bader breathed as he watched the automobile speed away. He stayed there for another thirty minutes. He wasn't waiting for Maha to return home, as he did not expect her to be back soon, but he couldn't move. The jeep returned to the same spot and parked outside Maha's house. The man in the driver's seat got out of the car and opened the door for Maha and they walked toward her house together. He hadn't even stepped foot in her house and now this jerk had preceded him. They had vowed to tell each other everything, and Maha had betrayed him. Who was this man? Bader watched her father open the front door and shake hands with the stranger. Then, all three entered the house together.

Maha must be in a serious relationship for her to bring a man home. Was it his first time? He was shocked at the synchronicity of catching her on the day he was going to propose. It was as unbelievable as the number eleven creeping up everywhere. 11:11. Or the number 11 on car plates.

Or on his ticket when he was waiting in line at a bank. Eleven was Maha's number too.

He cried as he started the engine. The universe could not have orchestrated it at a better time. Now, it was clear to Bader why she had been avoiding him. She was not making him miss her. She had found another man.

Do cows fly in the month of July?

No, Maha. They don't. They most certainly don't.

5

MAHA

"There's nothing in writing. It's all in the heart."
—Ahimla Gunwalla

K nock knock.
"Who is it?" Maha asked in a loud voice.

Her mother eased the door open and peered in.

"Come in Mama." She motioned for her to come sit on her bed.

"I'm worried about you. You seem agitated. Is it about Bader?"

"Yes. I'm tired. I don't know what to do. I'm starting to resent him." Tears flowed down her cheeks.

"Oh Mahooy. I can't bear seeing you like this." After a few moments of silence, her mother began crying too.

"Don't cry, Mama. You'll make me feel guilty." Maha walked toward her closet and opened a handbag. She took out a pack of tissues. She handed a tissue to her mother and blew her nose with another one. She sat back on her bed and snuggled next to her mother. Moments later, she lay her head on her mother's lap.

"I don't want you to waste your life with him anymore. Many men would love to be with you, but how can they come close if your heart belongs to him? He obviously doesn't care." Her mother massaged Maha's scalp and stroked her hair.

"He cares about me a lot. I'm not stupid to spend all these years with him if he didn't care, but I don't think he's committed. I mean, it's not like he wants to be with anyone else, but he doesn't want to settle down with me either. I don't want to live apart from him any more though. I want to start a family." Maha didn't tell her mother she suspected Bader was cheating or on the verge of leaving her.

"He's not going to marry you. It's been way too long. He has a job and even wrote a book. He can afford marriage. What's his excuse?"

"He says he's too young."

"If he's too young for marriage, then why's he in a serious relationship? Oh, Maha. Wake up. In university, people may have thought you were classmates, but you have both graduated. If people see you two together now, they will start to talk. This has been going on for too long, *habibti*."

Her mother was right. What her mother didn't know was her entire social circle knew she and Bader were dating.

BADER HAD NOT BEEN TAKING HIS TIME WITH FOREPLAY, nor did he ask her whether she was satisfied or not. She missed making love. Was he no longer attracted to her?

One day, after they had slept together, she broached the subject with him.

"Bader, you seem distracted. I miss taking our time to kiss and touch each other. Are you still attracted to me?"

"There's a lot going on at work lately. Please don't be insecure. I'm tired. It's hard to balance my job with the book tour."

"It's a local book tour. How hard can it be?"

He glared at her. Maha was ashamed she had taunted his success. It was Bader's dream to be appreciated abroad. She leaned over and kissed his forehead. He hugged her. Even when she was rude to him, Bader didn't hold grudges against her. But she was snapping at him a lot more lately, even publicly. It must be sexual frustration.

A friend of Maha's suggested sex toys, but Bader might be insulted. Her friend assured her men liked sex toys in bed too. But, his body, his lips were enough for her. She was still in love with him, so she accepted his advances though she no longer initiated sex.

ONE NIGHT, MAHA AND BADER WERE AT A PARTY, DRUNK, and he told her he liked it when she had her period because he craved her body more. And when she was busy or traveled, he missed her. Maha was offended. Her feelings toward him changed that night. She was afraid he was on the verge of leaving her.

He wouldn't break up with her but she suspected he was being callous toward her so she would leave him. Bader was the calm one, so it frightened her he was more volatile. Was their relationship over? After six years on and off with the same man, it wouldn't be easy to be single again.

"Mama, I'm going to put Bader out of my mind." She was at a supermarket with her mother two weeks after the party and made the decision in the fruits and vegetables section. Her mother was weighing four avocados, and a helper at the supermarket stuck a price on the plastic bag.

Then, she found him: Ahmed. She had met him a year before at a yoga center downtown. He had asked her to go to a coffee shop after a yoga session, but she told him she was in a relationship. They had ignored each other since. That day, however, she eyed him from across the room. Throughout the session he impressed her with his stretches. At one point, during their sun salutations, he turned toward her and smiled. Maha was taken aback, but smiled back politely. When the session was over, she took a shower. When she came out, Ahmed was waiting for her outside the locker room.

"I'm going to try once more, though it has been ages since I last asked you out. I want to explore this connection, and this time I won't take no for an answer. It's obvious you felt it too, today. Can I have your number?"

"Felt what? We were doing yoga poses." She was grinning.

"Give me your digits." He took his phone out of his pocket.

"What do you want from me?" Maha asked. He was staring at her mouth. Bader told her how much he loved her lips. Many of her friends envied her natural pout, and a cousin of hers had even taken a photograph of Maha's mouth to a doctor who injected her lips with fillers. Her cousin showed her the results, crying. It looks like I suffered a severe allergic attack, she lamented. But Maha held her in her arms and said nothing. She didn't have the nerve to tell her it was worse than that. Her lips had ballooned in size. It was clownish.

"I feel people's energies. And I'm drawn to yours.

That's all."

"OK," she said, and she typed her number into his phone. "The name's Maha, in case you're curious."

"I know. But I don't care. Names are just labels."

No, they aren't just labels, Maha wanted to say. Was he trying to impress her by acting spiritually evolved? Maha was turned off by the beads of sweat on his forehead. Was he nervous or sweaty from the yoga workout?

An hour later he called her, and they talked for two hours. Ahmed was thirty-three years old, but the approximately ten-year age gap didn't bother her.

"Mama, I'm seeing him again at the center."

"Be careful, Maha. Don't start the same cycle again. Make sure he's serious."

"Ahmed isn't young, Mom. I'm sure he's looking for marriage."

"For a man, even a hundred is young," her mother warned her.

After the next yoga session, Ahmed took her to a coffee shop. She wasn't used to cologne on a man, and Ahmed did not wear it sparingly. Bader used a spicy, musky deodorant and it was subtle. There were traces of it when they were kissing or he was naked. Why was she comparing Ahmed to Bader?

A few weeks after they began dating, she called Ahmed.

"I've been in a relationship for six years. I'm still in it.

Since I met you, I haven't seen him. He's going to start getting suspicious soon because we don't usually spend much time apart. The thing is, I want to have children and settle down. He doesn't, so I'm going to leave him, but I want to do it in person, out of respect for all we shared. I don't want to get more involved until I know your intentions."

"Maha, I'd love to explore this with you. I know it's crazy, and we barely know each other, but I see myself with you. But I live in the now, and I want you to know that, because if things change after we get married, we don't have to remain stuck with one another."

"So you're saying we might get a divorce even before we get married?"

"I don't see the world the way other people do. I go with the flow. Marriage is an institution, and I honor it. But I bask in the sacred moment. Situations arise beyond our control, but as long as we're together, I'm committed."

Maha was offended by his lackadaisical attitude, but she bore it as a way of silencing the thought of having wasted years on Bader.

"Ahmed, I'm not a virgin," she blurted, almost hoping he would be taken aback. Maybe he would say he didn't want an experienced woman and she could stay with Bader. But Bader wasn't worth her time. He had wasted enough years of her life.

"Neither am I, but that's not important. The truth is, I'm relieved. I don't want a virgin."

"Why?"

"I wouldn't know what to do with one," he laughed.

"I want to wait until we're married. I don't even want to kiss or anything." Maha trusted him, but wasn't attracted to him. She could postpone being physical with him. For a long time.

"Let's wait then."

Maha had waited six years for Bader to propose, and Ahmed was prepared to marry her after less than a month of dating.

"I'll get in touch with Bader this week and end it officially." Was she doing the right thing?

"I know this won't be easy for you. Call me as soon as you talk to him."

He was nonchalant. She couldn't figure him out.

MAHA MADE EXCUSES WHEN BADER ASKED TO MEET UP. It was getting harder to lie to him. And though she was not physically involved with Ahmed, guilt gnawed at her. But she had no choice, because she no longer trusted Bader. Why else would he have been aggressive with her at the party unless he wanted to end the relationship?

He had even mentioned Salma, a girl he had briefly dated at university who recently got in touch with him. When they were still at university, Bader told her the girl was obsessed with him and wanted to marry him. Though he said he wouldn't get in touch with Salma, Maha sensed he was lying. Suspecting Bader of cheating on her with Salma or any other girl justified her relationship with Ahmed, but it still consumed her with jealousy.

WHENEVER AHMED SPOKE TO HER, SHE ACHED FOR Bader. But each time she had an urge to call Bader, she would call Ahmed instead. Ahmed was a rebound, but couldn't rebounds become love? What would Bader do if he found out? He would be devastated, wouldn't he?

A few days had passed since her conversation with Ahmed, but she was still avoiding Bader.

"Ahmed, pick me up outside my house at seven. Let's go for a short drive before you come over."

"Is everything OK?"

"Yes, I'm still on my walk, but I want to talk to you before we go inside."

It was the first time Ahmed was coming over for dinner. He had spoken to Maha's father two nights earlier. And though Maha hadn't met Ahmed's parents yet, since they were out of town for a vacation, his mother had phoned Maha's mother to ask for her hand in marriage. Both families were happy.

Bader had called her to meet, but she promised she would meet him the following day. Maha couldn't wait any longer to tell him it was over. The official engagement to Ahmed was to take place the following week.

Maha carried a small bottle of perfume with her to spray behind her ears and on her neck right before Ahmed picked her up. Not too much. Just a little. When she was a little girl, her grandmother had taught her how to do it.

Spritz the perfume twice on one wrist, then rub both wrists until it dissolves. Then, dab both wrists on either side of your neck and behind each ear.

When she arrived home and got into Ahmed's car, she told him she hadn't told Bader yet, but she promised to tell him the following day. He said it didn't matter to him.

"I know we're meant for each other, Maha. Even if you decide to tell him after we get married, I know your body, your mind, and your heart belong to me now."

"Why do you keep saying now, Ahmed? It frightens me. Isn't marriage forever?"

"Nothing's forever. We're all going to die."

"Come on. You know what I mean. I want to be with you for the rest of my life."

"So do I, Maha. But life's unpredictable. I love you but am detached."

"Detached? I don't understand."

"But you're still here. Maybe on an unconscious level, you know what I'm saying."

AFTER THE FAMILY DINNER, SHE WALKED AHMED TO THE door and kissed him on his cheek. She recoiled at the saltiness of his skin beneath his cologne. She was relieved the dinner was over and she could be alone. Goodnight, she said. She closed the door on him faster than she should have. He would text her when he got home. Even his predictability annoyed her. She walked over to hug her mother, then kissed her father on his forehead and went up to her room. After taking a shower, she checked the time. It was 11:11 p.m. Her and Bader's number.

Bader would be awake. He didn't sleep before midnight. She had to call him and set an exact time and place to meet. No need to wait until work the next day to set up an appointment. Otherwise, she wouldn't get around to breaking up with him.

Bader didn't reply. She tried calling again. Maha sent him a text asking him if he was awake. He came online and two blue ticks indicated he had read her message. But he didn't respond. Where was he? Who was he with? She fell asleep on a wet pillow. The next morning, she had a response from him: Check your email. She didn't like reading emails on her phone. She opened her laptop.

Hey Maha,
I cannot do this anymore. I have fallen out of love with you. I think we are better off apart. It is best we do not contact each other. I will never marry you. Maybe you can find a man who will. I know how much you want to be a mother, but I do not see that in my future either. Please do not reply to this. I am now blocking you from my email, my phone, and social media.

She was shocked by how formal his writing was in the email. It sounded robotic. And he didn't even sign off with his name. There was his account photograph. She had taken that photograph of him a year before. They were out of town and about to make love and she asked if she could capture his love in real time. He told her she was crazy. She jumped out of bed, naked, and told him to put on clothes. Then, Maha wrapped her body in a bathrobe and they went out to the balcony of their hotel room. Bader, I want you to remember this moment every time you look at this photograph of yourself, she had said to him. Here we are, so in love. And I want this photograph to be on all your accounts, so this moment is our seal in time. Put it on Facebook, LinkedIn, Instagram, every account you have. So that whenever you're distracted online, you have a visual reminder of how happy you are with me. And every couple of years, I'll take a new one to capture our enduring love. He held her in his arms. When he let go, she took photographs of him with her cell phone. They both chose the one that reflected the depth of his love for her. The one where he was smiling in a way only a man in love could.

———————————

Maha's lips quivered. She got down on her knees and prostrated. Please God please, ease this pain. Tears streamed down her cheeks, and her chest was hurting. It was over now. She had been expecting this. Now it was official. Bader was over her. But why did she need more closure?

She called Ahmed and told him what had happened. She made sure to conceal her pain.

"Wow. The guy sounds like a real jerk. But his loss is my gain. Let's do this, Maha. It's you and me now."

"Yes, my love. You and me." My love. The words felt artificial. He wasn't Bader. And her next thought frightened her more: Nobody ever would be.

That night she couldn't sleep properly. She kept waking up to use the bathroom, and whenever she managed to nod off, she had nightmares of Bader with Salma. She needed Bader. She had to end it with Ahmed. She called him.

"Yeah. Cool."

Cool? She was breaking off her engagement with Ahmed and all he could muster up was Yeah. Cool.

"I want you to be happy. I knew you weren't invested in this. All you talk about is Bader, by the way. Intuitively, I stayed detached, though I wanted to be with you."

"It makes no difference to you whether or not I'm in your life? I thought you loved me."

"Love? This wasn't a love story. It was barely a story. Let's call it a transitional chapter. Come on, Maha. I could tell you weren't in it. I've had many traumas in my life, and what helped me recover was detachment. And I had to detach myself from you in case you'd leave me."

"I don't know if I can grasp this detachment thing."

"Don't you want your freedom? You are breaking up with me. I'm letting you go. Why are you locking yourself up in a self-made prison? Do you want me to suffer so you can suffer more? You released me. Now release yourself."

"I'm sorry. I don't know why I got you involved in my mess."

"I was a rebound. That was obvious to me, but I thought I could help you get over him. I was wrong. Now go live your life. And align it with what or who you want."

AHMED AND BADER WERE OUT OF HER LIFE FOREVER, and she wasn't looking forward to being single. She had to talk to Bader. But how could she get in touch if he had blocked her on all his devices? She drove to his house. It was nearing five p.m. and he wouldn't be back for an hour, but she was too restless to wait at home. She climbed up the flight of stairs to his private entrance and sat outside his door. She put on her headphones and watched a documentary about yoga and its benefits. Less than an hour later, Bader walked up the stairs.

"What are you doing here?"

"Why're you angry if you fell out of love with me? I'm the one who should be angry with you. How can you ditch me after six years of stringing me along?"

"Are you kidding me? Coming from a cheat and a liar? Why didn't you tell me you were with another man?"

"W-w-what are talking about?"

"I came over to your house that day, right after I called and you were taking a walk. I saw you guys drive off, and I was there when you came back. Your father knows him. What the hell is going on?"

"Oh my goodness. I thought you left me because you didn't want to commit. And I thought you were cheating on me." Maha put her hands in her head and sobbed. Then she looked up at him.

Bader motioned for her to move so he could open the door. Maha got out of the way and followed him inside to the kitchen. He sat at the kitchen table, and she sat facing him.

"You cheated on me," Bader said.

"That was the first time he came over. I didn't sleep with him. I didn't even kiss him. We didn't even hold hands. It's not what it looks like. I was desperate. I thought you were going to leave me."

"Leave you? What the hell? Where did that come from?"

"Remember that night at the party when you said you liked it when I have my period or when I travel because you miss me? What kind of a thing is that to say? And when we spoke about marriage and kids, you said you felt pressured."

"So you cheat on me to get me back?" Bader had tears in his eyes.

"It wasn't physical. I was going to get married, but I couldn't. He's not you. I broke up with him even when I thought it was over between you and me."

"Marriage? You were planning on marrying him? How long have you known him?"

"We rushed into it. It started after our fight at the party. He's in my yoga class."

"Is that what you do? Run into another guy's arms

because of a stupid fight? You should've told me you were upset. That's the mature thing to do. How can you handle a marriage? Please leave. I can't even look at you now." Bader's lips were trembling. She moved toward him, but he jolted out of his chair. "Don't touch me. Don't you dare."

"Bader, please. We can't throw what we have away. I don't give a damn if we don't get married. I just want to be with you."

"I can feel him on you. Get the hell away from me."

"I didn't let him touch me."

"Leave me. Go. Just go."

FOR THE NEXT THREE WEEKS, MAHA WAITED FOR HIM outside his door a little while before he came home from work. They fought constantly. When she had tried to hold his hand once, he humiliated her by asking what the hell she was doing. Her face turned red. Still, he kept calling her and messaging her. Did he love her or were they friends?

Though he didn't initiate dates or try to touch her, they would meet at his place every evening at six. Bader cooked dinner for them most nights, and though Maha didn't like to cook, she enjoyed the sight of Bader stirring curries, checking if more salt was needed by dipping a wooden spoon in the boiling pot and pouring a tiny amount on his hand and tasting it. He would ask her to set the table. They were living as a married couple, without rings, without intimacy and without cohabiting. Bader would change the subject when Maha asked if he loved her or whether they would ever go back to being in a relationship. Time is a healer. She would have to wait. But what if he never changed his mind?

ONE NIGHT, SIX MONTHS AFTER SHE FIRST WAITED FOR him outside his door, she told him she loved him. Bader was silent.

"Well? Please say something."

"I can't. I'm sorry, Maha. I care about you, but things have changed. I don't trust you anymore."

"You're punishing me for something I didn't do."

"You were practically engaged to the guy."

"I told you it's because I thought you were going to leave me. I even thought you were with that Salma chick at one point."

"Salma? What the hell? She means nothing to me. I'm an open book with you. If I didn't want us to be together, I would've left. Stop trying to put this on me. You were going to get married."

"But I didn't. I easily could've. Don't you miss me? Don't you feel our connection? This? In this moment, don't you love me?"

"If you're going to keep bringing this up, maybe we shouldn't even be friends."

Bader was biting the skin around his index finger.

"OK. I won't bring it up again, as long as I can be around you. I waited six years to marry you. I can wait the rest of my life for you to stop seeing me as a friend and realize we can't be apart." Maha fell to her knees, bawling. Bader came toward her and held her head in his hands. He told her to get up. She obeyed.

"Maha. Don't. Please." He wiped away her tears and kissed her forehead, her cheeks, her neck, her mouth. "Oh, I missed your mouth."

Bader grabbed her shoulders and pulled her toward him. He was crying. She kissed his lips. They were salty and his cheeks were warm, wet. "I adore you," he said. "I adore you. I adore you."

Maha spent the night at his house and woke up to find Bader pacing around the room.

"Oh, thank God you're awake Maha. I couldn't sleep."

"What's wrong, love?"

"I figured out why all this happened. You've never been with another man. Ever. Maybe you should explore it. I have no right to possess or punish you. The way I'm treating you is against my spiritual practice. I know your heart belongs to me, but maybe you need to share your body with other men."

"Are you insane? I don't want anyone else."

"But it's obvious you did, subconsciously. You almost married another guy. What does that mean? And who am I to stop you? This was a test of my jealousy and attachment. I can't love you while I'm attached to you. I need to learn about detachment. We need to learn to live without each other. I think we're standing in each other's way."

He sounded like Ahmed. The detachment aspect of spirituality irritated her, but Bader's guru had once told her whatever triggered her was the key to her personal growth. Perhaps she had to let go of her attachment to being part of a couple. Was it a sign that she kept hearing the word detachment? But she liked being in a relationship. And she liked that Bader was jealous. It meant he cared. Didn't he care about her anymore?

"I don't want anyone but you," she insisted.

"Let's take time apart. If we still feel the same way about each other in the future, we'll come back together."

"You were outraged by the whole Ahmed situation. And

now you're practically throwing me on other men. You've moved on from me, right?"

"I don't know what I'm feeling. I had an epiphany. I'm even over the whole Ahmed thing. I feel so calm. It's strange. I want to be alone. We've had an intense relationship and six years is a long time to have not taken it to another level."

"What are you saying?"

"You need to learn to be alone, and so do I. We can't hang out like this. It's not healthy. We're not friends or lovers. It's weird. I think we need time apart."

"For how long?"

"I don't know. A year? Let's see."

"A year? Are you crazy?"

"It's better than this limbo."

"I don't think you can wait for me."

"If I don't, or you don't, then it wasn't meant to be. And we would have learned how to live without each other. Maybe you can find the husband you're so desperately seeking."

"I can't do this."

"Maha, we have to."

"I'd rather be alone. Nobody is you."

"That's your ego talking. You were almost with another guy. Remember?"

"And I left him. Remember?"

"Well maybe in a year's time you can get over your fixation on a man-made institution."

"Why are you doing this?"

"I want to see what a year can do."

One month later, Maha was on a flight to Nepal. She was looking forward to living in a retreat for two months.

She turned to the passenger sitting next to her.

"Excuse me, sir. Why're you staring at me like that?"

"This is a public plane. Are you going to have me arrested?"

"No, but I can call the hostess to have you moved."

"Go for it."

She pressed the button and a light went on overhead. Two minutes later, a hostess arrived.

"May I help you?"

"Yes, can you get this gentleman a glass of water? And I'd like a cup of tea."

"Right away ma'am."

"Are you happy?" the passenger next to her asked.

"Do cows fly?"

"Pigs, Maha. Pigs."

"I knew we couldn't wait a year." She kissed his cheek.

"We couldn't wait a day. And we waited almost seven years for this." He lifted her hand toward his lips and kissed the wedding ring on her finger.

6

AISHA

"You are (and will always remain) my favorite."
—Sue Adele Rand

"Are you a fag? What is this?" Aisha asked Hussam. She had found the magazine under their toilet sink. It could only be his. Aisha waited for a response but Hussam was silent. She could barely touch the magazine, so she flung it on the bed where her husband sat with his head in his hands.

"Aisha, please don't call me that." Hussam was now upright on the edge of the bed. He was trembling.

Why wasn't he telling her it was all in her imagination? She held back tears while pacing the room.

"Why? Aren't you a fag?"

"It's called gay, Aisha."

Aisha watched her husband bite his knuckles.

"So, you're gay?" Aisha was in utter shock. How could

he have blindsided her? She liked Hussam. And though she wasn't in love with her husband, she was attracted to him and enjoyed being married to him. Hussam was a hands-on father to Dania, who had turned three. When Dania was a baby, though they had hired three nannies for her, Hussam changed her diapers and put her to sleep. The son of Abdul-Aziz Salama, one of the richest men in the world, fed his baby and took her to the park when she learned to walk. Someone must have envied her for having such an ideal husband who was a great dad and extremely wealthy to boot.

"I seek refuge in you, oh Allah, from the evil eye."

"Aisha, please sit down. Let's talk. I wanted to tell you a long time ago, but I was uncomfortable. There's something about my past I need to discuss with you."

"Your past? How long has this been going on? It's not something new?"

"No, I mean there's something I have been hiding."

"Oh my God. No. This can't be happening."

"Sit down. Let me tell you—"

"I don't want you to tell me anything. You aren't a friend. You're my husband. The past is in the past. Please tell me you aren't sleeping with men. We have a daughter!" Aisha screamed. Hussam cupped his ears with his hands.

"Please don't scream. I beg you." Hussam stood up and approached her. He tried to touch her face, but Aisha pushed his hand away.

Though she was dizzy, she couldn't sit down.

"Oh so I'm supposed to be calm? If it were a magazine with naked women, I would still be angry. But men? I don't know what to say. Were you pretending to be attracted to me? How could you sleep with other men and be with me? What if you have a disease?"

"Stop being backward. Straight men bring diseases too. So do straight women. I haven't touched a man since we were married. Adultery is haram."

"Oh, and being gay is not?"

"No. It's not. Adultery is a sin. Acting on pure lust without regard for another is a sin. Casual sex. Orgies. Those are haram. But not being gay."

"Are you out of your mind? *Astaghfurallah*, Hussam. What you're saying is blasphemy. I know you come from a modern family, but these ideas are dangerous."

"Trust me, Aisha. Even my so-called modern family is against homosexuality."

"Well, they're right to be against it. Oh my God. What did I do to deserve this? Why aren't you normal?" Tears welled up in her eyes as she spoke. She could never give Dania a sibling. How could she raise more children with a gay man? But divorce wasn't an option. She had heard how separation traumatizes children, and she was willing to sacrifice her pride for Dania.

"Why does everything have to be defined as normal or abnormal? Why is what's mainstream a barometer for normalcy? Have you seen our world? It's messed up. And that's considered normal."

"Religion defines what is normal or not for our guidance. You can't claim to be religious and think that way. You know it's a sin."

"I've done my research. I've come to my own conclusions. I may be wrong, but that's how I interpret the verses. They talk about raping men in desire."

"Stop, please. I can't hear such insanity. Don't use sacred words to justify your perversion."

"I'm not asking you to change your beliefs. But we are

both God-fearing and see things differently. Why can't you accept that? OK, you're straight, but imagine if you were born into a world where women had to marry women and sleep with them? How would you feel?"

"So marriage and sex with me is repulsive? Is that what you're saying?"

"This isn't about *you*. Put yourself in my shoes. Being gay isn't easy. Nobody would choose to be gay in our world. And I'm not talking about experimentation. I mean really being gay. The judgment is unbearable, especially when it's backed up by dogma. You don't think I'm terrified every day of eternal punishment?"

"You don't seem terrified. You're justifying it."

"Maybe I'm trying to find love in the verses because I can't fathom a deity who would condemn me for my nature. Where's your compassion?"

"Compassion after betrayal? I would've had compassion if you had mentioned it to me during our engagement. But after getting married and having a child? You cheated me out of an authentic life."

"I know I did," Hussam said, his voice quivering. "I'm sorry, Aisha. I've been living with the guilt this whole time. But being around you and having a child was easy until my past haunted me. I wish you could understand I cheated myself out of an authentic life as well."

"If you don't think being gay is wrong, then why aren't you open about it?"

"Why do you think? Our society would condemn me. When my father found out I had a boyfriend, he beat the crap out of me. My father was sobbing. He kept calling me a dirty fag over and over again. Nobody had ever called me that before. And now hearing it from you..." His voice trailed off.

Hussam sat down on the bed again, tears in his eyes. Aisha walked over to him. She had to bring this to a close so Hussam wouldn't utter the word divorce out of frustration.

"So you've been faithful? Swear to me."

"*Wallahul Atheem.* I'm in touch with this guy, but we aren't physical. I swear to you."

"What's your boyfriend's name?" Aisha asked.

"Dhari. And he's not my boyfriend. He's an ex."

"From when?"

"We were together before we got married, but I broke up with him so I could settle down."

Her husband's lips were twitching.

"You aren't with him now?"

"I swore to you. Believe me. I chose this life with you, and I'll stay in it. I speak to him all the time, yes, but I broke up with him to get married."

"You don't even meet him?" Though she was angry, she was relieved her husband wasn't with another woman. That would have been more humiliating for her. But what about when Dania was older? Wouldn't she be less humiliated if her father were with another woman?

"No. Dhari and I vowed not to see each other as long as I was married."

"As long as? Are you planning on leaving me?"

"I don't want a divorce."

He was lying. She sensed it. But she needed another lie to assuage her shock, so she asked if he loved her.

"Yes. Of course I do."

But her need for a dose of truth pushed its way to the surface.

"In a different way, though. Right? Not in the way you love him."

"Please don't do this."

"Are you still in love with him?"

"Aisha. I beg you."

"Are. You. In. Love. With. Him?"

"Yes."

"And is he?"

"Mm-hmm."

"Uff. This is too much. I'm such a fool."

"Aisha, we didn't do anything. I swear."

"It's still a relationship though, isn't it? You can't be just friends, no matter what. Even if you don't do anything, even if you don't see each other. You love him. There are people who don't speak to the ones they love. They move on in their lives, but they don't move on from the person. I know a girl who's still in love with an ex, but she settled down. She thinks about him every frickin' day but she never calls him."

Aisha couldn't reveal to Hussam she was that girl.

"I didn't cheat."

"You kept him a secret. That's cheating."

"I'm sorry. I don't know what to do."

Aisha left the room and went to check on Dania. She was fast asleep. Then she went to the bathroom, locked the door, crawled into the bathtub, and cried. Hussam knocked, but she asked him to leave her alone.

She took her phone out of her jacket pocket and sent a text to Salma asking her to meet the following day. From then on, every time she spoke to Salma or met up with her, all she discussed was Hussam and their failed marriage. When Salma told Aisha she was divorcing Khaled, Aisha was shocked. How selfish she had been to speak of Hussam and not bother to ask how Salma was doing in her own marriage.

THE SAME DAY SALMA WAS LEGALLY SEPARATED FROM her husband, Aisha went out for coffee with her.

"Aisha, you look haggard. I'm worried about you."

How could Salma be more concerned with her situation with Hussam than her divorce from Khaled?

"Please don't worry about me. A part of me knows I can no longer live with him. I just don't know what to do next. I don't want a divorce. Don't judge me." She rubbed her eyes with her fingertips. Salma grabbed her hand and told her she would get premature wrinkles.

"You're old enough to make your own decisions, but let me tell you this: Leaving him will be the best thing you do. I mean look at me. I feel like I've lifted a huge weight off my shoulders. And Khaled said it wasn't a good idea we stayed in touch. Not that I want him to, but how rude is he? Anyway, I feel free now. Isn't it strange we're going through this at the same time?"

WHEN SHE DROPPED OFF HER DIVORCED FRIEND AT home, Aisha went upstairs with her to the private family quarters. Salma's mother was watching stand-up comedy in the living room. Her father shook hands with Aisha, then grabbed Salma's hand and waltzed her around the room, singing a song Aisha hadn't heard before about life and happiness, until her mother shouted for him to be quiet. Nobody was affected by the divorce. Maybe her parents were masking their pain. There was no other explanation.

In Salma's room, Aisha asked Salma if she hated her ex-husband.

"Of course not. I resent him though. He's sleazy, and I'm glad I'm out of his life. My situation sucks, but it's not as bad as your..."

Aisha stared at her. Then, there was an awkward silence.

"Look, I know you think I'm an idiot for staying with him, but I like him, and I got used to having him around the house. He's such a good father. Dania adores him. Plus he's religious, so he won't cheat on me. He's just friends with his ex."

"How about a religious straight guy who won't cheat on you instead?" Salma retorted.

Aisha was conflicted, but she couldn't confess to Salma the main reason she hadn't divorced Hussam. Though Aisha came from a wealthy family, Hussam's family upheld a much higher standard of wealth. She didn't worry about the price of anything. Aisha's mother-in-law lavished her with gifts. And Hussam's family spoiled Dania.

Aisha and Hussam owned a fleet of luxury cars, two yachts—one with her name inscribed on it—and they traveled often. They lived in a white brick mansion with a red roof that boasted two guesthouses, an underground garage, a private marina with boats and jet-skis, and a sprawling garden overlooking the sea. Her in-laws had built the house for Hussam. It was across the street from where they lived. It was a dream home for Aisha.

Her parents and Hussam would continue to spoil her if she got a divorce, but it wouldn't be the same. Money was more important to her than happiness. She had left the love of her life because he wasn't rich.

But she was paying the price. Aisha wasn't over him,

and he was on her mind every single day, but she'd blocked him from getting in touch. She used to call him PLG. How she yearned for him, but she put her husband and daughter first. Where was he now? Did he think of her? Did he miss her? Or was he over her? Should she call him? Maybe her and Hussam could stay married, raise Dania together, and live separate lives with Dhari and PLG. But Aisha couldn't live that way. He could have an affair with Dhari, but she would stay with Hussam and remain faithful to him. Yet could she bear this situation any longer? She would give it a year. Maybe then she could call PLG…

AISHA HAD ALWAYS FLOWN FIRST-CLASS WITH HER family, but now she no longer flew commercial. Instead, Hussam would take her to locations around the world in a private plane with large leather seats embossed with the family emblem. They attracted attention everywhere they went. They arrived at the entrance of restaurants or museums or even bookstores in one car and security trailed them in another car. Hussam's chauffeurs around the world had access to areas forbidden to all but diplomats and taxi drivers. They stayed in suites and, on business trips, Hussam reserved an entire floor for his staff: private secretaries, bodyguards, and sycophants, as Aisha called them. Hussam asked her on more than one occasion not to use the word, but Aisha said he should be more careful, and that many people were around him for his money.

Hussam spent plenty of money on others. There was a friend of his whose mother was not well. Hussam paid for her surgery. Then there was a colleague who needed money to send his son to university, a secretary who asked for a deposit for her mortgage, and all the others who came begging for money. Hussam helped them all. Aisha couldn't complain. He spoiled her more than anyone.

Two years into their marriage, Hussam had built her a library. He flew in architects to work closely with her on an extravagant design to ensure she could call it a real library. And, of course, like the Olympic-size pool she swam in once or twice since her wedding, she barely went down to the library once it was completed. She preferred reading in bed. He also built her a private gym, and hired a personal trainer who came to the house three times a week. Every couple of months, she flew to London to treat her acne with laser technology. And she had a private Thai masseuse who massaged her body every Saturday morning with lavender aromatherapy oil. Life was good.

But Aisha became guarded. She wore her most unattractive nightgowns to bed. If Hussam craved intimacy, he would have to initiate. In retrospect, it made sense why she made all the moves. And now, he would come to bed, kiss her forehead and fall asleep. Was she destined for a life of conjugal celibacy?

She read articles online to learn if it was possible for a gay man to become straight. Most of what she glossed over was not promising, apart from stories of conversion camps.

Aisha downloaded books about homosexuality and exorcism. She was waiting for Hussam to ask what she was reading, so she could tell him. But he didn't ask. One day, while they were sitting in their living room upstairs, she turned off the TV and faced him.

"Hussam. Let's call Imam Yaseen."

"What for?"

She played with his hair. "I think if he reads scripture on you, maybe you could get better."

He moved away from her. "Better? Oh, Aisha. I'm not sick. You think my father didn't do that? After he beat me up, he took me on pilgrimage. And every evening, he called a man to recite holy verses in my room with *bukhoor*. And it wasn't the normal incense. It was that weird kind with the white crystals."

"OK then, just give him a call."

"Are you out of your mind? I don't want any Imam reading on me."

"I don't mean the Imam. Call Dhari. And tell him I don't mind if you guys have an affair."

"I won't cheat on you."

"It's not cheating if I know."

"No Aisha. As long as we're married, I'll stay faithful."

"Would you quit already? It's like you're waiting for me to leave you. I won't. If you want a divorce, have the courage to do it yourself." She got up and walked toward their bedroom door. She slammed the door shut and locked it. She waited for Hussam to knock on the door but he didn't. Half an hour later, she opened the door and peered outside. He was in the living room, texting. When he saw her approach, he put his phone away.

"I want to go to the opening of a spa in Phuket next week. I need to get away for a while. For a week," Aisha said, arms folded around her chest.

"Just a week?" He looked at her. His eyebrow was twitching.

"Oh you want to get rid of me, so you can be with your boyfriend?"

"That's not cool, Aisha. You know I won't see him. I just think time alone would be good for you baby."

"Baby? I'm not your baby. And I don't want to go alone. I'll take my mother and Dania with me."

"Dania? To a spa? She's three. What's wrong with you?"

"My mom and Dania can stay at the resort, and I'll be at the spa alone for a weekend, then join them for the rest of the holiday. And I want you to be with Dhari."

"I told you I won't be with him."

"Anyway, I'll check the dates with my mom and let you know."

"OK. As soon as you do, I'll ask my secretary to call our travel agent."

"What about the private plane?"

"Baba's using it. He's in Switzerland now."

"When's he coming back?"

"In a couple of weeks."

"I can wait."

"Isn't the opening next week?"

"I don't have to go to the opening."

AISHA COULD NO LONGER STAND WHO SHE HAD BECOME. She was a compulsive shopper and spent all her time at restaurants and cafés. She and Hussam barely spoke to each other. She prayed more, beseeching Allah for guidance. Then, on a trip with her mother to Mecca, she chose to fly commercial. First-class, yes, but commercial nonetheless.

On the airplane, on the way back, she fell asleep with the Koran on her breast and tears on her pillow.

When she got home, she walked straight to her bedroom. Hussam was changing out of his clothes. She craved his body.

"I love you, Hussam."

"I love you too, *hayati*," he whispered. Aisha had thought when he whispered terms of endearment it was an act of seduction. Now she understood. He was just a soft-spoken man, shy to express emotions. Or worse, maybe he couldn't say it louder because he was uncomfortable and did not mean it. She cringed for all the times she had assumed otherwise.

"I've been doing a lot of research, *habibi*. I read about gay imams and reformists. They say the same thing you do. I'm not going to lie. I don't accept what they're saying, but I care for you. And I know where you get your perspective from now. And I don't want to be a part of the collective hatred. I want to learn more, accept more."

"Oh I love your mind."

"I also read about these undercover gay movements supporting gay rights now in our region. It's coming to our neighborhood." She walked to her cupboard and took out her favorite purse. She fished through the contents and handed him a crumpled piece of paper. "These are the names of the initiatives."

"For a well-read person, you sure don't know much about current events," Hussam said, laughing.

Hussam took the paper from her and squinted. He looked around the room. He was searching for his eyeglasses again. It frustrated Aisha that he didn't wear contacts because he was constantly losing and buying new pairs of designer eyeglasses.

Aisha fluffed the bedcovers and Hussam's glasses fell to the floor. She picked them up and handed them to him. His fingers touched hers as he took the glasses from her, and electricity ran through her spine. She took a deep breath, dismayed by her attraction toward him. Hussam was reading the names of the initiatives.

"Yeah, I've heard of most of these."

"Well, I'm a bit behind on all this, but these initiatives are not exactly mainstream in our part of the world. Oh, and I read homosexuality was nature's method of birth control, to keep overpopulation at bay. I can accept that theory. But it doesn't mean I think it's OK for people to be gay."

His eyes welled up with tears. She approached him and kissed his forehead.

"What are we going to do Aisha?"

"Let's get a divorce, Hussam. Not because you're gay, but because we don't belong together. You love a man, and we're both living a lie. I'm with you for the money. And you're with me to please your father and society. Now you can be with Dhari openly. Or secretly. But without marriage in the way."

He sighed. "I was wondering why you stayed. It was for the money? I don't get it. Your father's a millionaire."

"Well yours is a billionaire."

They laughed.

"I adore you, Aisha. Please don't take Dania away from me."

"Well, by law she stays with me until she is eighteen, but you're her father. You can see her whenever you want. And our families don't need to know the reason."

A big part of her life was over. But now they could both lead authentic lives. Don't cry, she said. These are tears of gratitude, Hussam responded. They hugged. She rested her head on his shoulder as he stroked her hair.

"Can you hold me while we sleep tonight?" Aisha asked him.

"Yes *habibti*."

Throughout the night, she had a recurring dream of an angel singing *Al-Rahman, Al-Raheem*. The Compassionate, the Merciful.

7

HUSSAM

"I let you go to make my country proud.
I let you go but our love was too loud.
This is a song about losing control.
This is a song about regaining one's soul."

—Marginal Hookahs

Hussam had taken a risk by inviting Dhari to spend the night at their farmhouse. A member of staff must have reported him because on their second afternoon together, while sitting on the sofa, chatting, a safe distance away from each other, his father barged into the living room and dragged him by his arm out of the house. He didn't acknowledge Dhari's presence. It was as though he didn't exist. Hussam's father was sobbing. The whole hour-long ride back to their house, he cursed Hussam, shouted at him, and kept calling him a fag. Hussam didn't say a word. When they got home, his father slapped him, punched him, then whipped him with a belt, until his mother came in and begged him to stop.

"If you ever see that man again, I'll put you in jail myself, you sick bastard," his father had said, before he left the room, panting, heaving.

That evening, Hussam went to a hotel his family owned in the city. The manager rushed toward him and held his head in his hands. Hussam's right eye was bruised and his upper lip was swollen.

"Hussam? What happened? I'm calling the police."

"Don't. My father did this to me. Don't ask why."

"Should I get a doctor, sir?"

"No please, Sami."

"I'll get the keys to the suite."

"I don't want the suite. I'll take an ordinary room."

"This is your hotel. Your suite is always available to you."

"You know what? Give me a junior suite."

"Yes sir. Are you expecting anyone?"

"No. I'm alone tonight. I want to be alone."

Sami knew about Dhari, and the hotel had been their haven. But Hussam could no longer disappoint his father. It was time to grow up, settle down, and have children. Enough of this gay business. The time had come to break things off with Dhari. He filled the bath with hot water and salt crystals. He got in, relaxed in the tub and got out right away when the salt burned the lash on his upper back. When he got out of the bath, he wiped the mirror and stared at his swollen face and bruised body in the mirror. He turned around and rotated his neck halfway. His back was filled with red belt-marks. One of them was bleeding. He wondered whether he should have waited to take a bath. Wasn't he supposed to have used ice instead of heat? He would sleep on his stomach tonight.

And he would ask Sami to bring him painkillers.

Hussam's father had hit him before, but never with a belt. The only way to rectify matters was to get married. He ordered room service: avocado toast and tomato soup. Though he usually ate heavy dinners, he was too nervous to eat much. He left his tray outside the room and dialed Dhari's number. He was still in his bathrobe.

"You can't break up with me," Dhari protested. "When are you going to stop living in your father's shadow?"

"I'm his son. I have responsibilities. You know who he is. I can't ruin his reputation."

"By being gay? Everyone has a relative, a sibling or uncle or aunt, who is gay. So everyone's reputation is ruined by your logic."

"My dad was a wreck."

"I'm sorry about what happened with your dad. I thought he was going to beat you up."

"He did. As soon as we got home."

"Oh man. I'm sorry, *habibi*. But we have to fight for our love. Everyone thinks of us as perverts. If you leave me, then you must think we are too."

"I don't, but my family comes first. My dad broke my heart. I can't be selfish and think of myself all the time. I'm sorry." The side of his face twitched. Hadn't he outgrown this tic? Why was it back?

"Are you kidding me? Oh my God. I knew you'd do this. I knew you'd give in to society. I wish your father could hang out with my parents so they could teach him what it means to love your kids."

"Dhari, please. We talked about this before. You know my family. Your family is the exception." Hussam's mouth was dry. He swallowed a few times to catch his breath.

"Why are you doing this?" Dhari's voice cracked. Was he crying? Was his forehead crinkled now? Was he biting his bottom lip until it bled? He had told Dhari on several occasions not to, but Dhari said he wasn't conscious of doing it until he tasted his blood. "I understand your compassion for your father, Hussam, but what about you?"

"I want to obey my father. There's nothing more to add."

"I respect that, and I'll wait for you to come around."

"Don't wait for me. I can't do this anymore. I want to get married, and once I do, I won't cheat on my wife." While he spoke, tears rolled down his face, but his voice remained firm and resolute. He removed his eyeglasses and wiped the tears flowing from his eyes.

"Pardon me for saying this, but you're living a lie." Dhari didn't even sound angry. He heard him take a deep breath and continue. "Before we met, you felt something was wrong with you. I was the one who told you there was nothing wrong with being gay. You amended your beliefs and adjusted them to your new mindset. But it was all a lie, huh?"

"Dhari, I still don't see anything wrong with it. This has nothing to do with being gay. I have a responsibility toward my father, and I want a family. Let's be realistic. We can't have that." Hussam could hear Dhari crying, and his resolve broke. He cried aloud too. They stayed on the phone for another hour, sobbing and talking, and decided to remain friends so the separation wouldn't hurt. After Hussam hung up, he called his father.

"Baba, find me a woman. I want to settle down and have a family. I spoke to my friend and ended it. I'm sorry. It was a phase, and it's over."

"I'll speak to your mother to search for a suitable wife.

This is a good thing you have done. I'm proud of you. Where are you?"

"At the hotel."

"Come home son."

"OK Baba," Hussam said.

After hanging up the phone, he called the reception and told Sami he was checking out.

"Already?"

"Yeah, I just needed a little time by myself."

He walked to the bathroom and looked at himself in the mirror. You're a coward, he said to his reflection. He washed his face and wiped it with the monogrammed hand-towel. Where were his eyeglasses? He had taken them off while talking to Dhari. He went back to the bedside table. There they were. He put them on and walked out the door.

WHAT HAD DRAWN HUSSAM TO AISHA DURING THEIR short, arranged engagement was her wit and intelligence. And he liked that she was open-minded but didn't drink alcohol. His mother, who was against the hijab, hadn't known Aisha was veiled on the night she laid eyes on her, since it was at a wedding and there were no men present. But when they went over to Aisha's house the first time, his mother and Hussam agreed Aisha was the right match for him. On their first date, they went out with her friend, Salma, and Hussam enjoyed their company.

They went to an Indian restaurant Salma had chosen. Hussam liked Salma immediately. He had heard more than once that birds of a feather flock together, and he could tell Salma was authentic and kind, so Aisha must be too. It wouldn't have changed his mind if Aisha had introduced him to an indecent friend. He would marry anyone his mother chose, so his father wouldn't bring up what had happened.

He asked Aisha if they could go out alone the next time so they would get to know each other better, but she refused, saying she wouldn't date him alone until they were married. He argued they were engaged, but she told him to wait.

THE WEDDING LASTED UNTIL THREE IN THE MORNING. When he walked toward the altar, he was shocked by her appearance. He wouldn't have recognized her on the streets. Aisha was wearing heavy make-up, long fake eyelashes and blue contact lenses. Her new veneers were gleaming white. She had on a lace dress and a loose silk, embroidered white turban to keep her hair hidden from the men who had dropped him to the altar.

Throughout the ceremony, Hussam was anxious. His heart was beating fast, and he kept breathing heavily. At one point, Aisha even turned around and asked him, whispering in his ear, if he was all right. He stared ahead, unable to answer. He was sweating and at one point, the room turned black. He wanted to massage his throbbing head, but there were video cameras everywhere, so he sat still to conceal his agony.

When it was time to leave, he walked hand in hand with his wife to the limousine waiting for them outside the hotel lobby, and Hussam scrunched his eyes tightly so he wouldn't faint. When they arrived at his home, Aisha told him she was going to shower. By the time she came to bed, it was four-thirty in the morning. She was wearing a transparent baby-doll dress with a red bra and matching underpants. Hussam was repulsed by her appearance and overwhelmed with guilt his new wife was a virgin. He couldn't undress her and was shaking. She got under the covers, seductively eyeing him, and removed the dress and flung it on the floor. Next, he watched her remove her underpants and bra without revealing her body to him, still under the covers. Then she motioned for him to come to her. How did she have the confidence to make the first move?

Hussam fumbled while touching her. He closed his eyes and kissed her lips, imagining she was Dhari. He kept whispering, "I love you. I love you." He managed to keep his erection while inside her, but it took him a long time to ejaculate.

After it was over, he went to take a shower and couldn't stop bawling. He was trapped. There was no way out now.

The unbearable lovemaking went on for a couple of months until Aisha was pregnant. He had never been happier in his life, apart from the time he had spent with Dhari before getting married. Being a father had been a dream of his since he was five. When he was ten, he was sitting in his cousin Fatma's bedroom. She was holding a lifelike baby doll. He asked if he could change her nappies. When Fatma told him dolls were for girls, he told her boys raise babies too and he had to practice becoming a father. In retrospect, he realized he was not just feminine early on in his life but precocious. Who spoke like that at such a young age? And now, his dream was coming true. A baby.

Aisha couldn't sleep with him during most of her pregnancy because of her severe morning sickness. The family doctor diagnosed her with hyperemesis gravidarum. She could barely eat, and during her second term, she spent two months in the hospital. Hussam was relieved to take a break from physical intimacy. Aisha was a nymphomaniac. She initiated sex all the time, and more than once a day when the mood struck her. He would feign exhaustion, but most days he had to comply with her needs because of his fear that she would suspect he was gay.

THE YEARS PASSED, AND HIS PHONE CONVERSATIONS with Dhari became more frequent than in the early days of his marriage. Still, Hussam couldn't profess his love to Dhari.

"How much longer can we keep up this façade, Hussam?"

"What are you talking about?"

"This whole friendship thing you have going on with me. Do you want to stay like this for the rest of our lives? Can you?"

"What else can we do?"

"We can do so much."

"Why can't you let go of the past? I have."

"You've let go of the past, but I'm your present and future and you know that. How would you feel if I were in a relationship?"

"It would kill me."

"And it's OK that you're still with her?"

"She's a woman. And she's my wife. If you got married, I would understand. But I would be broken if you were with another man."

"I'm dying here. I couldn't be with anyone else, man or woman. Can you continue this way? Are you OK with this arrangement? Should I give up on us? Tell me."

"I'm dying here too, Dhari, but I see no way out. I mean I love Aisha and Dania. I adore them. But I don't know how much longer I can pretend to be straight."

"Get out of the marriage. I beg you. For your sanity. For us. You tried to do what your family wanted. It's not working."

"How *habibi*? How?"

"Confess to her."

"No way. I can't."

"You know what? I'll send you love messages, and leave the phone where she can read them."

"You don't want Aisha to think we cheated when we didn't."

"Well, even discussing this is cheating."

"No it's not. We're not doing anything."

"Hey, I know. Leave a dirty magazine under the sink or in your cupboard. She'll think she accidentally found it. Then, once it's out in the open, tell her you're in love with me. I'm sure she'll divorce you right away."

"Where'll I find a dirty magazine?"

"I'll send one to you."

"What're you doing with dirty magazines?"

"I'll throw them all away when we're back together."

"You better."

HE DID AS HE WAS TOLD AND LEFT THE COPY BENEATH the bathroom sink, behind Aisha's extra stock of deodorants and toiletries. He was trembling when he laid the magazine down, but he trusted Aisha wouldn't expose him to her family. She was a kind person, and he trusted her. Apart from the physical intimacy, Hussam enjoyed being married to her. He admired his wife for being a prolific reader and looked forward to her discussions of novels and literary articles. And her body was beautiful and fit. He appreciated the aesthetics of her curves and muscles. But Hussam dreaded seeing her naked because it meant he had to perform, and he was tired of acting.

It took Aisha two weeks to discover the magazine.

She shouted at him, but instead of fear, Hussam imagined his new life with Dhari. The door to a cage had opened. He was free. Fag. The word bothered him, but he was willing to take it if it meant Aisha would divorce him. His wife's body and mannerisms morphed into his father's. And all of society—mullahs, mothers, brothers, teachers, grandparents—one by one were condemning him through her mouth.

"So that's why you never initiated sex with me? I thought it was strange, but I had no idea you were gay."

Hussam waited for her to say she was leaving, but to his dismay, Aisha chose to stay with him. Some time later, she even suggested Hussam have an affair with Dhari. Hussam refused, telling her it would be unethical since they were married. Why wouldn't she take the hint and ask for a separation? Why was she holding on? Why was he still afraid of his father?

Dhari was not religious at all. He told Hussam he couldn't be a part of anything that ostracized people. With Dhari's influence, even Hussam's views evolved. Once, Hussam tried to share his newfound interpretation regarding the verses, and how they applied to heterosexual men with extreme lust who raped men even though they were not attracted to them.

Nejoud Al-Yagout

"Justify it how you want, Hussam. It's haram. All scholars say so."

"Not all scholars."

"Trust me. The ones who defend us are considered astray. They call them reformists, as though it were an insult. And it's not just that. What about this whole divide between believers and disbelievers? Why is it our way or the highway to hell? Haven't you seen the way non-Muslims are treated here? We talk about Islamophobia, but we have everything here: Sikh-phobia, Buddhist-phobia, Judeo-phobia, Christo-phobia, Jain-phobia, agnostic-phobia, atheist-phobia. Isn't it strange we have mosques on every corner and just a handful of churches? And nothing else. No temples. No synagogues. No ashrams. No gurdwaras. Come on, Hussam. Wake up. If we want respect, we have to give it to others. I'm done."

"Islam wasn't like this before. This is politics. Read history. Jews, Muslims, and Christians coexisted peacefully for centuries."

"OK, let's suppose it's politics, for the sake of an argument. If things tone down in this region, do you think temples will be allowed? Why were only the Abrahamic religions respected? They'd call me an infidel. But, I love God, not religion. Why does that take away my special relationship with the Creator?"

"You don't understand religion the way I do. I don't know how you can leave Islam."

"I haven't left anything. There are parts that will always resonate for me, the beautiful parts, the esoteric parts, the mystical parts. But I can't confine myself to one ideology. I guess you could say I'm Muslim once a month. The rest of the month I'm Jewish, Hindu, Sikh, Christian, Jain, Buddhist, Baha'i, agnostic, and the list goes on. Oh, and I take the best and leave the rest." Dhari laughed.

Hussam remained silent. It bored him to debate religion. Dhari called it a discussion, but to Hussam, it was an argument with one person trying to change another person's mind. That was what everyone did. He didn't want to be like everyone.

"Let's change the subject. I don't care what you are or aren't."

Aisha's character transformed. Whenever Hussam came home from work, she was out. She spent all her time shopping and at spas. Aisha still read a lot, but she was becoming more obsessed with her looks. She wore multicolored veils, which was not her style, and she wore fake eyelashes with blue contact lenses every day. It reminded him of his wedding night. Was she trying to seduce him or was it because he had hurt her dignity? Her appearance and spending habits didn't bother Hussam. What scared him was she could be trying to look good for him. This meant she'd never leave him.

"Why don't you leave her?" Dhari asked him. Hussam was in the bathtub, fully clothed.

"Are you kidding? After what I've inflicted on her? I need more time. Can you wait?" He was whispering so Aisha couldn't eavesdrop on him, even though she had encouraged him to be with Dhari. He wasn't sure how she would react. Her mood swings since the day she had discovered the magazine terrified him. One day, she ordered pistachio ice-cream, his favorite flavor, and fed him; the next day, she ignored him when he said *Salam Alaikum*. He was tired of her bringing religion to the discussion, because it was a losing battle. She always had an intellectual argument prepared or a verse to quote when he spoke to her of God's mercy.

"Do I have a choice?"

"Dhari, if you want to live your life, I'm not stopping you."

"The choice is not mine. It's my heart's and it has made up its mind."

AND THE DAY CAME. AISHA ASKED FOR A DIVORCE.

"You won't regret this," Dhari said on the other end of the phone.

"No I won't. And the best part is Aisha gives us her blessings."

"That's wonderful babe."

Hussam paced his bedroom. He sat on the bed and got up again. He walked toward the window and pressed a button on the wall. The sound of the shutters soothed him, because it preceded the revelation of the view of the ocean from his bedroom. Once the shutters were up, he opened the glass door and walked out onto the balcony. It was dusty, but he stayed outdoors and his elbows cracked as he stretched his arms. He put the phone back to his ear. Dhari yawned. Then, he yawned. A strong gust of wind carrying sand with it blew on his face. He coughed and spit out a couple of grains. Dhari asked if he was alright. He said it was just dust.

The sea was choppy and gray. And the sky turned orange. He'd read in the papers a dust storm was coming. Dust storms were romantic. There's nothing romantic about a storm that gives people allergies and asthma, Dhari had said to him once. All storms are dangerous but peaceful beneath the surface, Hussam replied. It wasn't just Dhari who complained about dust storms. The whole country did.

Dhari sighed, as though waiting for Hussam to speak. For years, it had been a habit for Hussam to speak then remain silent for a while on the phone. Dhari didn't interrupt what he called Hussam's cell spells. Aisha would hang up on him and wait for him to call her back, and his father communicated with him via messages or in person, unless Hussam called him. Once, his mother crossed paths with him while he was on the phone. She told him to hang up if the other person was not answering. He pointed toward his cell phone to indicate someone was already on the line, but she didn't understand him, so he held the phone away from his ear and whispered that he was on the phone, and his mother walked away, perplexed.

"I heard a dust storm is coming."

"You're the only idiot who loves them," Dhari replied. "So what about your father? Do you think he'll get suspicious?"

"Aisha and I agreed we would say we were no longer compatible. What do they call it? Irreconcilable differences?"

"Yes. Irreconcilable."

Hussam walked back into his room and closed the door, but he left the shutters up. He wanted to hear the thunder and see the lightning.

"You waited for me baby."

"It was torture. But you're worth it. I love you so much it hurts. Don't leave me again."

"Are you kidding me? I'll never leave you. And even though we can't get married, you're my husband."

"I know you well. You're the son of Abdul-Aziz Salama. You'll cave in to his demands. And trust me, he's going to want sons. But I don't care. I'm the idiot who's going to stick around and trail you like a shadow."

"I would've stayed with Aisha if that were the case. Marriage was torture. I could never put us through that again. You're my eternity."

"Yes I am. But you'll have non-eternal marriages here and there. I see it. There'll be a Fatma, then a Dana, then a Ghalia. And I'll wait for you each time you get off the hamster wheel again."

"I think you've lost it Dhari."

"Give it a year or two and you'll get sucked right back in. Mark my words. And one of your wives will expose you one day and then what?"

8

MOHAMMED

*"Each day is a themed episode. All incidents
and conversations are linked."*

—Ranima Al-Jaruni

"Maryam, calm down," Mohammed said.
He couldn't understand what his sister was saying between her sobs.

Before coming over, she said she had something important to discuss about Salma and needed to see him right away. He asked if Salma was ill, but she said it was a personal matter.

His earliest memory of Maryam crying was when he was eight, and she was seven years old. His mother was trying to calm Maryam down because she had fallen off a bike.

"That's your brother's bike, Maryam. Girls shouldn't ride bikes. See what happens when girls don't obey their parents?"

Mohammed had been too young to understand why girls could not ride bicycles, but when he was older, he heard girls could lose their virginity from riding one. If he ever had girls, they would not be allowed to play any sports.

There was another time when Maryam had come to him for help, bawling.

"Our parents are taking me out of school because it's time for me to wear the hijab now."

He cringed his sister was hinting she got her period. How disgusting.

"Why're you crying about it? You always wanted to wear the hijab. I remember you saying it for years."

"It's not that. I'm happy I can wear it. But I want to continue going to school. Please talk to Baba. I beg you."

Then, Mohammed had been going to a religious center for boys. He was planning to become a scholar. Though he secretly agreed with his parents regarding protecting women in the tribe from temptation and veiling them, he was prepared to defend Maryam in regards to her education. Why were his parents keeping her from studying if she only had two more years to graduate? He went straight to his father's room and confronted him.

"Baba, it's unfair to take Maryam out of school."

"She's a woman now, so it's better to keep her at home. Women go crazy at this age, as do boys. We know stories of boys picking up girls at school."

Mohammed watched his father scratching his beard. He couldn't wait to grow one like his father's. He would wait until he was married, in case his future wife was averse to facial hair. Even if she didn't like it, she would have no choice in the matter after marriage.

"Maryam isn't that type of girl. Nobody takes their daughters out of school just like that. It doesn't make sense. If you're that worried, then let Mama ask the principal to keep an eye on her."

"And ruin our reputation? No way. The principal will suspect something about her that isn't even true."

"What's she going to do at home?"

"Your mother's going to teach her how to be a mistress of a house." His father cracked his knuckles.

"But she'll have staff running the house when she gets married."

"Maryam has to learn everything to train her staff."

"Baba, you promise you won't get her married before she turns eighteen?"

"I swear, son. I won't. And the law wouldn't allow it, so don't worry."

Shortly after Maryam turned eighteen, they had found her a husband: Ali. Mohammed didn't like him. Ali debated matters of religion with him. Mohammed was appalled Maryam's husband didn't consider the hijab a requirement and spoke of the benefits of secularism. When Mohammed tried to broach the subject of Ali's lack of religious fervor with his father, he told him to stay out of it.

Throughout the years, Mohammed watched his sister's daughter grow into a young beauty. Maryam had called him when Salma got her period. He told her it was none of his business, but he was secretly happy she told him. It was now his duty as an uncle to preserve Salma's honor since she had reached puberty, since her own father was unconcerned. He waited for the right time to broach the subject with his sister. One day, when his wife, Zayna, was spending the day at their beach house with their sons, he called Maryam to have lunch with him. He insisted she come alone.

They settled in the entrance parlor. He had intentionally picked the room farthest away from the dining room, because his domestic helpers spoke Arabic and two of them were prone to gossip, as the chef had once warned him. He told a maid to call them when the food was on the table and asked her to leave. "Maryam, are you going to take off your hijab?"

"What a silly thing to say, Mohammed."

"Your husband is against it."

"He's not against it. He doesn't believe in it. There's a difference."

"Ali never asked you to take it off?"

"He said I could take it off if I wanted. He didn't tell me I had to. That's as bad as telling a woman to wear it. And I'm not wearing it for a man in my life or for you. I can easily remove it now, and Ali would support me. In fact, he would welcome it. I'm wearing it for Allah and because I believe in it. What's come over you?"

"Women are brainwashed these days. They think it's backward and repressive. I'm worried you will be swayed."

"You must remember how badly I wanted to wear it growing up. And I would've worn it much earlier if Mama had let me. It wasn't pressure for me."

"Well there are women who take it off even after wearing it for a long time."

"Well, I can assure you I won't."

"OK. Good to know. Praise be to Allah. So what about Salma? She's fourteen now. What about her?"

"Oh, of course. How stupid of me. That's why you asked me. You can't interfere with my family. I told her it was a duty, and Ali told her it wasn't, so it's entirely her choice. And to be honest, she's too young."

"Too young? You wore it when you were just a year older than her. This is terrible. Ali's a devil. He's a bad influence on you. How can you allow this?"

"Mohammed, this is not your issue. Salma is my daughter, not yours. And allow what? I did my duty. Now it's up to her. Of course I want her to wear it one day, but I won't impose it on her."

He waited for Salma to wear the hijab, but the moment never arrived. So, when she had called him to say she couldn't come to a family lunch one week because she was ill, he lectured her on the benefits of wearing the hijab and how it was an obligation, but Salma told her mother. Maryam was at his house less than an hour later. The maid told Mohammed his sister was downstairs waiting for him and crying.

"Mohammed. How dare you speak to Salma about the hijab. I told you not to interfere. You made her uncomfortable. If she tells her father, he'll throw a fit." She was blubbering. It hurt him to see her cry. He didn't know what to do. Was he supposed to hug her? But they didn't do that. It would be strange to start being physically affectionate now. And maybe hugging her would mean he agreed with her.

"I wanted her to know not all men are sissies like your husband."

She slapped him. He glared at her.

"Get out of my house, Maryam."

Though they were used to meeting at least once a week, it took him three months to call his sister to make peace. He promised Maryam he wouldn't broach the subject to Salma again. And she apologized for slapping him.

And he kept his promise. Salma went to university, married, and divorced, and he didn't mention the hijab to her again.

———

AND NOW, MARYAM WAS FACING HIM ON THE DIVAN, ready to discuss a personal matter with him regarding Salma. What had she done? Had she brought shame to the family? Maryam was embracing a cushion on her lap and fidgeting with the tassels. He was waiting for her to speak.

"Salma. I don't know. I can't. It's too much."

"Get the words out. I don't have all day. What has Salma done?" His face turned red with rage. He clenched his fists. It must be serious if Maryam couldn't even tell him.

"S-s-since Salma's divorce, she has changed. A-a-and now she wants to travel alone to India. I don't know w-w-what to do."

"What do you mean?"

"I mean what I said. She wants to travel alone."

"*Wallah*? You came all the way here to tell me this? Are you serious? That's it? I thought she was talking to a man."

"Salma? No way."

She repeated how Salma wanted to go to India over and over again to him. Why was she crying? It was simple: tell Salma not to go. He told her it was her lack of productivity, and because she only had one child, that gave her such an incentive to, as Mama would say, make a mountain out of a molehill.

"I thought there was a scandal involved. You scared me on the phone."

"Mohammed, her father spoils her, and Salma makes me feel guilty when I say no."

"What did the devil do now?"

"Please stop calling my husband that. He approves of her going to India. I don't. The good thing with Salma is she won't go unless we both agree, so she's begging me."

"Women shouldn't travel alone. Our country's spinning out of control. There's no regard for our customs. If she wants to go to India, why don't you take her?"

"I told her I would, but she said we have different interests."

"What are her interests exactly?"

"I don't know."

"And what does she think yours are?"

"Shopping."

"Well, she got that right."

His sister wiped her nose on her *abaya*. A strand of hair was sticking out of her hijab. He leaned over and pushed it inside her veil.

"So what should I do?"

"What you should do is tell your daughter to wear the hijab. She's a divorced woman. Men will flock to her like bees to honey."

"You promised not to bring that up again. Why're you obsessed with the hijab?"

"I promised not to bring it up to Salma. But you're my sister. Even you agree she should wear it. God knows what men think of her when she goes out."

"*Astaghfurallah*, Mohammed. I don't care what men think. Most of them have dirty minds. I know my daughter. She's not the type of girl. And since her divorce, she barely leaves the house. She spends her time reading."

"She should be living with me. I would raise her the right way."

"You're insulting me. Are you saying I didn't raise her well?"

"Letting your daughter go out of the house naked is not exactly raising her well."

"Naked? Have you seen the way she dresses? She's conservative."

"Any woman who leaves the house with her hair showing is naked to me."

Maryam was crying again.

"What do I do, Mohammed?"

"This is all your fault. The freedom you gave Salma. And you let her go to a mixed university. She married a man who drinks alcohol."

"She's a good girl."

"Does she pray? I don't see her pray at our family lunches anymore. But you won't let me interfere, so maybe you should. Those who do not pray stray away from the faith. Keep a close eye on her and forbid her from traveling alone. May Allah shower you with a thousand blessings, my sister."

When Maryam left his house, he prostrated and thanked Allah he had three sons. But his eldest son, Raed, was proving to be a challenge. Mohammed had trouble waking him up on Fridays to go to the mosque, and during the previous Ramadan, when a housemaid was taking a tray to Raed's room during fasting hours, he took the tray from her, set it down and knocked on his son's door.

"Come in."

The room reeked of cigarette smoke. Raed's eyes were red, and he was glaring at his father.

"Are you sick, son?"

"No. Why?"

"It's Ramadan. Why aren't you fasting? There's a tray of food I left outside. The maid was bringing it to you."

"Oh Baba, I'm hungry."

"Do you smoke?"

"No way. A friend of mine was over. He's not Muslim. He had a cigarette in my bathroom."

"I didn't waste my life studying religion to bring up a son like you. Go take a shower, and make sure not to eat during fasting hours in this house again. Do you understand?"

"Yes Baba."

"And tell your friend to respect our religion and smoke at his own home."

"*Inshallah.*"

ANOTHER TIME, MOHAMMED HAD TRIED TO BROACH THE subject of marriage to Raed. He suggested Zayna's niece, Lubna.

"You got to be kidding me, Baba. It's too early for me to get married."

"Not now. I mean in the future, when it's time. Young marriages are the best. They will keep you away from temptation. Five years, even six years from now, you should settle down."

"So why're we discussing this now?"

"I was wondering if you ever thought of her in that way. We don't have to mention anything yet."

"She's my cousin."

"So? Marrying a cousin is halal and legal."

"Just because it's legal doesn't mean I have to do it. Lubna's like a sister to me."

Nejoud Al-Yagout

Raed's untraditional side was even clearer to Mohammed when he told his son to keep an eye on Salma after her divorce.

"She's a grown woman. Leave her alone. She can do what she wants."

"Are you out of your mind? She's our responsibility. What she wants? You're not my son."

"Baba, I don't care what she does, or what anyone does. I'm the wrong person to ask. I think Salma should have as much freedom as you give me. She's older. Why do you let me stay out late? What's the difference?"

"You are crazy."

"You're spitting on me again." Raed wiped his cheek with his sleeve.

"You should be ashamed of yourself, protecting the rights of a woman."

"You're a caveman Baba. Get with the times."

"Respect me. I'm your father. You have no right to speak to me like this."

"What? Are you going to hit me? You got away with it when we were young, but I'd like to see you try now. I'll leave the house and you won't ever see me again."

Mohammed left his son's room holding his chest. He walked up the stairs and sat down on a step. Everything around him was spinning. He checked his pulse with his fingers. How dare his son speak to him in such a rude manner! What was wrong with young men these days? Giving freedom to a woman? If Salma were his daughter, he would have made her wear the *niqab*, so only her eyes showed, even though it was not compulsory.

Mohammed went to the bathroom and performed his ablutions and the sunnah prayers before and after the night prayer along with the witr, the extra prayer. Then he combed his hair to the side to cover the part that was balding and went to his bedroom.

His wife, Zayna, was waiting for him. She was in the mood for sex lately and even initiated it. It had been so long since they were regularly intimate, and her appetite had become insatiable. Ever since he married his young secretary, Lina, Zayna's competitive streak emerged and she lavished him with attention, inside and outside the bedroom.

Zayna was thirty-eight and young-looking, but Mohammed had grown tired of her. And yet, his attraction toward her returned as soon as he married Lina. He had discovered the secret to a healthy marriage: marry another woman.

THOUGH ZAYNA WORE A HIJAB AND ABAYA, MOHAMMED observed many men staring at her. How could it be the older she got, the more men paid attention to her? It became a source of fascination for him. And though he was proud she belonged to him, it angered him.

His mother had chosen Zayna because she was from a religious and conservative family. Looks don't matter, she had told him. And Mohammed respected her because she was shy and kept her eyes on the floor while speaking. He didn't understand why men were drawn to her if she was plain-looking and when no one had looked at her before.

Mohammed imagined he was a sultan with his own private harem. If his attraction toward Lina waned, he could, by Sharia law, marry a third or fourth wife. How exciting. He was proud to be a man.

Mohammed used the sultan fantasy whenever his wives were in the mood for sex and he wasn't. Tonight, Zayna was more excitable than ever. He imagined she was Lina and closed his eyes while he kissed her.

After making love to her, Mohammed took a shower and went to his friend Basil's *diwaniya*. He looked forward to attending the all-male gatherings held either in reception halls or a specially built section of the house. Most families had one, but Mohammed hadn't built one because it gave him an excuse to leave the house as much as he could. The men often debated politics, but most of the time, they needed a place to unwind after a long day at work, away from women. Basil's *diwaniya* was spacious, and, unlike most, it was built as an extension into the backyard, not visible from the front entrance.

Basil told him he was trying to marry off his eldest daughter.

"She's getting old, Mohammed," Basil whispered so nobody could overhear.

"Buthayna? How old is she now?" Mohammed said, glancing around the room. He'd had a habit since he was a teenager of counting people at gatherings and events. There were fifteen men so far. But within an hour, more would arrive. Basil's *diwaniya* was attended by more than thirty men.

"Twenty-nine."

He asked Basil if she wore the hijab now. The last time he had invited Basil and his veiled wife for lunch was four years prior, when they brought Buthayna with them. Mohammed was sitting across from her and couldn't wait for the meal to be over. Women without the hijab made him uncomfortable.

"No. She doesn't."

"That's the problem right there."

"We don't want to force her."

"You have to force her, Basil. You have the right."

"Where do you get your information from? You're mixing tradition with your own interpretation of religion. No compulsion in religion. It's a holy verse."

"So you admit it is part of religion, then?"

"No. It's your interpretation."

Though he had knowledge discussing religious matters, he was self-conscious when debating, so he glanced around to make sure nobody was eavesdropping. Not everyone understood religion the way he did, which made him uncomfortable. Why were people moving toward progressive thinking? Basil's views were dangerous, and he noticed many men and women who shared his perspectives lately.

"All scholars agree it is *fard*, an obligation. These reformists are corrupting your minds. Buthayna has to wear it. And if you mistakenly think it's not a religious command, what about our culture? No man will marry her without a veil unless you want her to marry a liberal, God forbid."

"What? Even religious men get married to unveiled women. And many religious women are unveiled. Where have you been hiding? It's a blessing you don't have daughters."

"I'm just obeying my religion."

"I obey my religion too. But I know it gives women the freedom to choose. If my wife tells me she wants to remove hers, I'll ask her why she needs to tell me. I'm neither for nor against the hijab. It doesn't concern me, since I'm not a woman. But if I were, I would hate it if a man forced it on me. Wouldn't you?"

Mohammed glared at his friend. Basil's ideas frightened him. It was difficult for Mohammed to accept there were women who didn't want to wear it or were taking it off. What was happening to his country? Was it gearing toward liberalism? It had been liberal in the sixties. In all the photos, women were unveiled and wore short skirts and sleeveless tops. His aunts, who were now veiled, were among those women. Were they going back to those days? Was his blood pressure high? He checked his pulse, but removed his hand quickly so Basil wouldn't notice. It seemed stable.

"I don't care what women think about wearing it. We are responsible for protecting them. You're my friend, and my duty is to advise you."

Mohammed watched Basil wipe the spit off his face. Zayna did that often. Mohammed was aware when he was excited or angry his saliva would fly out of his mouth, but he couldn't help it. He asked Allah for refuge from the whispering of the evil one seven times. It helped calm him down. He learned repeating the phrase from his father. But, unlike his father, Mohammed didn't say it aloud.

"I feel sorry for you, Mohammed. It's people like you who are destroying our faith. I won't force my daughter into the hijab, and I don't care if she ever wears it. What's important to me is her happiness, and no piece of cloth can preserve her honor. Many veiled women wear tight clothes, the shape of their breasts show, and they walk in high heels with bright lipstick. I'm not saying they're doing anything wrong, but the hijab won't stop anyone who is seeking attention. Women are women, and they have their style."

"Those girls you speak of are exceptions. Many people are serious about their hijab."

"And many people aren't serious. Those girls who you say are exceptions are a symptom of the pressure we place on women to look good and cover up at the same time. They are a product of our obsession with beauty and guarding honor. And many people are serious about their honor, whether they wear it or not. What happened to lowering your gaze, like the Koran told us to do, brother?"

"So you're saying men shouldn't guard women's honor? And you don't seem to be lowering your gaze if you notice those women."

"This has nothing to do with men or women. No person, in general, should guard another's honor, Mohammed. And I notice these women because I don't need to look away. My urges are under control. I don't get a sexual feeling each time I look at a woman. I would only lower my gaze when the person I'm looking at becomes a source of temptation."

"Most men aren't like that. The hijab is there to protect women."

"Covering up women means men aren't willing to work on inner purification. That's laziness. We can't have that woman, so cover her up. It's like when they close restaurants here in Ramadan. We can't eat, so close down all the restaurants. Or we can't drink alcohol, so don't allow bars."

"At least come up with a logical argument. You're not even making sense."

"Think about what I'm saying. It doesn't make sense because you don't want it to. Why can't we face temptation instead of hiding it under a table? Mohammed, you know I don't drink alcohol, but many people do. Why is it our way or nothing? Live and let live. And why are men weak when it comes to women?"

"It's our biology. Laws were created to protect women from certain predators."

"In that case, why don't we stay at home? We're dangerous, aren't we? We can't handle ourselves when we see a woman, right? We should be locked up like animals in a zoo and let our women go out. At night, they come back to us. They'll be safer. No rape, no sexual assault, no harassment."

"This is insanity. I don't know who you are. You've made up your own philosophy. It's your own religion. This is blasphemy."

"Whatever I adhere to is between God and me."

"I can't stay here another moment and listen to your ranting."

Mohammed got up and left. He'd had enough of this nonsense. First Salma, now Buthayna. Why were these girls averse to the hijab? And why were men like Basil and Raed defending women? He was angry and he wanted Lina. And he wanted Zayna to know. Her jealousy excited him. Basil had humiliated him, and to put his injured pride aside, Mohammed would humiliate Zayna.

––––––

MOHAMMED WALKED INTO HIS BEDROOM AND PACKED his little suitcase in front of Zayna.

"*Habibi*, don't leave. Let's sit with the boys."

Pride welled up inside of him, but Mohammed wanted Lina's skin against his. In the meantime, he could use Zayna's desperation to fuel him up for Lina.

"I can't *habibti*. You can sit with them. I have to see Lina. She has needs too. You have to get used to it. Why do you give me a hard time when I want to see her?"

He turned around to make sure she was pouting. She was. He could leave now. Mohammed was excited by the idea of her sleeping lonely, dreaming about him. He couldn't wait to return home so Zayna could lavish him with attention and praise.

LINA WASN'T EXPECTING MOHAMMED. AND HER GRATI-tude would guarantee a long night of reward and pleasure.

He walked into the house he had rented for her and climbed the stairs. Mohammed had chosen to be with her on a weeknight. How excited she would be.

He turned the knob. She was in bed, reading a magazine. Hello Mohammed, she said. Then, she continued reading. Mohammed walked toward her and sat facing her on the bed. There were tears in her eyes.

"Lina, *habibti*. What's wrong?" He kissed her cheek.

"What're you doing here?" She wiped the spot he kissed. He glared at her.

"You don't want your husband to kiss you?"

"Aren't weeknights for her?"

"Baby, don't be bitter. I'm here. Aren't you happy to see me? Come, show me how much you love me."

"I want a divorce."

"What? Lina, what's wrong with you?" He cracked his knuckles.

"I can't live like this, being your second wife. And who knows if you will marry a third or a fourth?"

"I don't want another wife." He grimaced. Could she tell he was lying?

"You think I trust you? What guarantee do I have? I'm still young. I can start a family with a man who loves me."

"And I don't love you? Have you lost your mind? You should feel lucky I married you. I can get you citizenship."

"I don't want citizenship anymore. I want to go home."

There was a jug of water on her bedside table. He poured a glass for himself. He took a few sips, then handed her the glass. She shook her head. He gulped the rest.

"Listen, you're feeling emotional. What happened? Tell me. Come here." Mohammed was still facing her, and he held her head and leaned toward her mouth. She pushed him away by his shoulders.

"See your arrogance? I'm upset, and you want to kiss me?"

He got up from the bed and paced the room. Mohammed stood for a while, with his back to her, contemplating what he should say. He wanted to make love to her. He turned back toward her and sat on the bed.

"Don't come close to me, you sick man." She jolted out of the bed.

Was she playing hard to get? Why was she angry?

"I transfer money to your account every month. Last month you wanted your family's roof fixed. Then you wanted me to pay your sister's medical fees. Did I complain? No. It made me feel like a man to help you."

"Feel like a man? Is that what defines you? Your masculinity? Maybe if you stopped trying to be a man and acted more like a human being, people would like you. Being a man has turned you into a filthy person. You see women as sex objects to cover up and please you."

"Please don't insult me." Mohammed stared at her. She was disheveled. Is this what she looked like when he wasn't around? She was either impeccably dressed when they went out, or lounged about in silk nightgowns or caftans at home. Her natural look was pale and her face was puffy. There were dark circles under her hazel eyes. And the roots of her blonde hair were black. She had never worn pajamas before, but she was still sexy to him. And though he didn't like her attitude toward him, he respected her defiance. Wasn't he supposed to be angry?

Mohammed got up from the bed and approached her.

"What are you going to do? Hit me?" She sounded like she was challenging him.

"How could I hit you? Our prophet said the best of us are those who are best to their wives." He sat down on the bed again. She looked at him, turned away from his gaze and paced the room.

"Listen to yourself. It's as though you are on autopilot. Who are you? Who are you beyond this role you're playing?"

"Role? What role? You're not making any sense. What are you saying?"

"Oh, you won't get it. You're too busy trying to make people hate religion."

This was the second time in one night he'd been told he could make people hate religion. "If you people studied religion better these days, then you would not utter such nonsense about me."

"I'm not people. You have such a distorted view of religion. All that matters to you are appearances. What about your heart? Has religion ever entered your heart? Did you ever try to connect to Allah for the sake of Allah alone? You hide behind religion to suit yourself. If you were following religion, you would've only married another wife if your first one couldn't get pregnant or was sick, or if she agreed. Your wife bore you three sons and is healthy, as far as I know, and she hates me. You married me for sex."

"And what did you marry me for? Love? Come on. Be honest."

"I feel sorry for your wife."

"You didn't think of her when you wanted to marry me. I knew you were attracted to me for my money, but to discard me after I spent so much on you and your family?

How could you be so cheap?"

"You said men are responsible for their wives. Is religion not suiting you now? You use quotes when they suit you. The Koran is not a book to use for your benefit. It was given to us to get closer to God."

"Don't teach me religion. I'm a scholar."

"Well, whoever taught you needs a refresher course."

"Stop mocking me. Didn't I give you everything you want?"

"I didn't want this!" Lina wailed as she walked to the cupboard, took out her headscarves, one by one, and flung them on the bed beside him. She sat on the floor sobbing. "I wore the hijab for you. When you met me, I was my own woman, but you made me a prisoner. I stopped working and I have to wait for weekends to see if you'll even show up, and when you do come to see me, all you care about is sex. I can't even go out on my own. You aren't like this with Zayna. She goes out alone. She drives."

"Lina, please, let's stop this. I love you. I'll give you freedom. You want to work again? Go ahead. You want a car? I'll buy one for you."

"No. You're the worst thing that ever happened to me. I'll never wear a veil again nor let you touch me."

"Is this about the veil? Is that it? I'm sorry. I'll accept anything but you removing it. You'll make a fool of me."

"The veil is for God. Not you."

"Well the sin is on you for removing it."

"You pressured me to wear it, so it doesn't count. And you have no say in that. As of tomorrow, I am no longer a hijabi."

"I divorce you," he repeated three times, as per the religious stipulation. It was strange that it had to be uttered three times and not two or four or even five, but he silenced that recurring thought by repenting to Allah. Now all he needed was to make the divorce official in court. Why had he betrayed Zayna and taken another wife? He wouldn't marry another woman as long as Zayna was alive. Polygamy, though halal, was not for him.

"Oh no Mohammed. *I* divorce *you*. And I'll only say it once. Now get out of my sight."

9

LINA

"The lights came on without me planning."
—Alana Tougray

When Lina's boss would pass by her, or call her into the office, he would mutter *Salam Alaikum*, peace be upon you. Mohammed wouldn't look at her while greeting her. Once, when Lina was taking notes for him in his office, Mohammed glanced at her, then looked away in disgust and asked for God's forgiveness: *Astaghfurallah*.

Lina turned to make sure the door was open. When Mohammed had hired her, he required that Lina keep the door open when she was inside and close it on her way out.

"Our prophet said that no man is present with a woman without the devil being the third party," Mohammed reminded her.

Lina had heard the hadith from her father, growing up.

And she recalled a conversation with her cousin Talal, who was like a brother to her. It was two weeks prior to his wedding. It was an arranged marriage with a girl, Ruba, from another village.

"Lina, I have to break off my engagement. I can't get married."

"What happened?"

"I'm gay."

"What do you mean?"

"Why do people always ask what I mean? It's simple. I love men. I don't know what to do with a woman, and I don't want to learn."

"Oh." Lina blushed. "Will you tell your parents?"

"No. But I'll spend time with girls after I end it with Ruba so they don't suspect. Maybe they can catch me alone with one?" Lina was staring at him confused, so he added, "Not like that, silly girl. I mean sitting in a room talking."

"How can they allow you to be alone with a woman? My father says the shaytan is present—"

"I'm a man," he interrupted. "They don't care what I do, as long as I'm not with another man."

Lina asked Talal why the devil wasn't present with two men or two women alone in a room when most people regard homosexuality as a sin. He said he would use her rhetoric in the future to justify being alone with a man. They both laughed.

———

THE DOOR WAS NOT CLOSED, SO LINA WAS CONFUSED AS to why Mohammed had a need to ask for God's forgiveness.

"Excuse me, sir?"

"Lina, you're a young lady far from home. Why aren't you married?" Mohammed was speaking in a confident tone, but he was fidgeting with his pen, his gaze averted.

She had grown accustomed to being asked whether she was married during interviews. But nobody had ever asked her why she *wasn't* married. Lina was aware from her first boss, Emad Jasri, a renowned businessman, that employers preferred single women since married women were a burden on the economy. Emad had even explained to her why. "All my previous secretaries were married. They're not only absent when they're not feeling well. They take leave when their son or daughter has a fever, or if their husband leaves on a business trip, or if they have a parent-teacher conference."

"Why would they be absent if their husband leaves the country?"

"Because they don't want to leave their children at home without a parent present, even though they have nannies. Any excuse to sleep, travel, or go shopping."

Lina had been comfortable at her job until Emad sexually harassed her. She was approaching her car in the underground parking lot when his car drove by. She watched, stunned, as he reversed at quick speed, tires screeching, and rolled down the window. He told her to get in the car with him.

"What for, sir?'

"I need to talk to you. It's urgent." He was breathing heavily.

"You have my contact details. Please get in touch with me via email or phone," Lina said, speaking to him as she would a client. He looked at her legs. She adjusted her skirt. Then he stared at her cleavage and she buttoned the top of her shirt.

"I need to talk to you now. It's too personal for a phone call or an email."

"Go ahead. Tell me. But not in your car."

Lina's heart raced and she had trouble breathing. Her legs were shaking. Her boss got out of the car and walked toward her. Nobody was in the parking lot. There were no cameras either.

"You're beautiful." He touched her face. She moved his hand away.

Lina turned away from him and opened her car door, trembling. He pushed the car door and asked her why she was scared. She ran away, heels clicking on the pavement and turned around to see where he was. He was standing outside her car, blocking it. If you don't move from my car, I will call the police, she said. She fumbled inside her purse and took out her phone. I'll take a photo of you standing there, she added. She warned him to move right away. He covered his face and walked sheepishly, hurriedly, to his car. He drove off in a fury and she stayed there for a while, leaning on a column, frozen, terrified he would reappear. She didn't want to stay there alone, in case he came back, so she ran back to her car, locked the doors, and started the engine.

The next day, her boss ignored her. An hour before the end of the workday, he asked her to stay after work in front of an employee. She tried to come up with an excuse but was flustered.

"Why're you afraid of me?" he asked her when she entered his office and they were alone.

"Sir, what do you want to discuss? My looks? I cannot work here if you are interested in me. You have a wife and three children. Please respect them and me." Lina glared at him as he stared at her cleavage. She folded her arms across her chest defensively.

"I said you're beautiful. That's all. Anyway, I wanted to clear things up between us. You can go home now." He was smirking.

Lina was frustrated by his callous apology. She had to speak up, but words escaped her. She nodded.

A few weeks later, as she left her boss's office, he trailed behind her and touched her back.

"I want you, Lina. Please let me kiss you. I beg you. I need you now."

"I'll submit my resignation tomorrow," she said as she opened the door and left the room.

Emad was her first boss, and the experience had traumatized her, so when Lina applied to Mohammed's firm and he required she keep the door open, she was relieved.

Lina was conservative, but she wore short skirts, and when it was hot outside, she would take off her jacket and walk around in a sleeveless shirt. It drove men wild and they couldn't take their eyes off her. But Mohammed wouldn't look at her. He spoke to the space above her forehead. Or he would stare to her right when he addressed her. After her experience with Emad, it soothed Lina not all men were infatuated with women's breasts or calves.

She had once told a local co-worker that in her country nobody cared about what a woman was wearing. "Society only judges you by your honor as a woman," she added.

"Oh, here they'll judge you for both your honor and what you wear," her colleague had retorted.

Mohammed didn't flirt with her and she was sure he wouldn't harass her, so his question about her marital status had startled her.

"What's come over you? I can't focus. Let's get back to

work right away. Can I go for my lunch break?" Lina asked.

"Slow down, Lina, slow down," Mohammed said looking directly at her for the first time. It unnerved her. "How can we get back to work if you are asking to go on your lunch break? You don't know what you're saying. Why are you flustered?"

For a religious man, he knows how to talk to women. What should she do? What should she say?

"Sir, I'm going for my break. We can continue this later."

"Marry me."

"What?" Lina grimaced, pretending to be appalled. But she was overjoyed, not because she was in love with Mohammed, but because she had waited years for a local to propose to her. Even before she moved to this country, she had heard there were many wealthy men and they were generous with their money. Lina hadn't expected a proposal from Mohammed since he was married, but visions of her new, luxurious life floated before her, and she couldn't wait to tell her family back home.

HER MOTHER WAS THE SECOND WIFE OF HER FATHER. Lina grew up in the same house with her mother, sister, father, and his first wife, Aida. And her mother had a room of her own for when Baba had sex with her. Aida shared the master bedroom with her father. Her father was not allowed to stay overnight in her mother's room. Lina shared a room with her sister, and they would hear the sound of their father's footsteps as he walked the short distance from the master bedroom to their mother's room. And then back to Aida's. When the moaning was loud through the thin adjacent walls of the tiny house, they would sleep with the covers over their heads.

Once, when Lina was thirteen and her sister was nine, Aida banged on their mother's door and yelled: Open up you whore! Years later, when Lina was eighteen, old enough to ask intimate questions, she asked her mother why Aida had done that. Her mother said her father had fallen asleep by mistake, and she cradled him in her arms and watched him breathe instead of urging him to go back to Aida.

"Why didn't you wake him up, Mama?"

"I couldn't bear him going back to her. I thought maybe I could keep him for just one night. As the hours went by, I thought maybe because Aida was sick and contagious, she might have permitted him."

"Baba never slept in your room before?"

"Never before and never again."

"So what happened?"

"I couldn't stay asleep from the excitement. I knew I was supposed to wake your father up or at least ask him whether Aida had allowed him to stay the night with me. But I didn't."

"And?"

"I would sleep, then wake up, sleep, then wake up. I needed to use the bathroom, but I thought Aida would hear me through the walls, or your father would wake up. In the morning, Aida banged on the door. Baba jolted out of bed. She came to me, pulled my hair, and scratched my cheeks. Your father tried to intervene, but we were rolling on the floor." Her mother paused.

"And?"

"Your father shouted for us to stop, but we kept going. Then, at the top of his lungs, he threatened to divorce both of us and marry another woman. We stopped immediately.

He turned to Aida and said it was her fault for not waking him up the night before."

"Had Aida fallen asleep?"

"No. She had taken prescription medicine for her virus. One tablet had a sedative, so she passed out. Aida should've been angry with your father for falling asleep, but women always take it out on each other."

"What happened next?"

"I ran to the bathroom. I needed to go!" Mama laughed. "I'll never be a man's second wife."

Lina had resented her father, but now, faced with the same situation as her mother, she welcomed the opportunity.

LINA HAD BEEN IN THE COUNTRY FOR FOUR YEARS, AND no local man had been interested in making her his wife yet. Lina had many prospects back home, set up by her mother and the other women in the village. A few of the men were even willing to move to where she was, but she refused them all. She insisted on a local.

Whenever any man approached her, she would ask him immediately about his intentions. Her boldness scared many away, but this method would weed out any suitors with evil intentions. Men asked how they could marry her if they did not know her.

"In my village, men and women get to know each other with their families as chaperones. I won't go out with you alone or talk to you on the phone without you speaking to my father first."

Not one man accepted the challenge. But Lina was willing to wait, even if she remained single. Her mom said men with good intentions don't try to meet women on the streets. She hadn't dated a man before or even spoken to a suitor on the phone. And no man would be an exception.

Mohammed must have sensed her purity, or he wouldn't have proposed. She was sad she waited this long to end up with a man who already had a wife. Lina remembered telling her mother she would never be a second wife. But every decision she made was filtered through the words of her grandmother: Don't let any opportunity pass. And here was an opportunity to get married and escape the stigma of being a spinster. Though she was only twenty-four, Lina was considered old for marriage in her village back home. And would she ever find another local who was prepared to marry her? Or any man as wealthy as Mohammed?

There was no way she could decline his offer. It was evident to Lina he would spoil her. She was always ordering flowers from Mohammed for his wife, or booking first-class tickets for him and his family. Lina was attracted to his lifestyle but not to him. He was her boss. Lina asked Mohammed how long he had been thinking of marrying her.

"Since the day I interviewed you," he told her.

"Call my father."

ON THEIR WEDDING NIGHT, MOHAMMED TOOK HER virginity and went to take a shower. She watched as he put on his clothes.

"Where are you going?"

"Home."

"Isn't this your home too now? Please don't leave on our first night together."

"I have to go, Lina. I'll see you tomorrow. I'll bring you a resignation letter to sign. You don't need to work again. I'll also transfer twice your salary amount on a monthly basis to your account. And that doesn't include your provisions and clothes. Please don't ever leave the house without telling me. OK, my love?"

He kissed Lina on her forehead. She felt cheapened by the way he was subjugating her with financial rewards, but she acquiesced. She didn't enjoy working and was excited by the prospect of more money in the bank and a local man spoiling her.

But the excitement didn't take away the pain of how much she missed her mother. She wished she'd had a proper wedding. Mohammed would've invited her family and paid for everything, even though it was the custom for the woman's family to pay for the ceremony. He had insisted on a Sharia-compliant marriage without guests. Because of his connections in the financial sector, his wedding would be covered in the papers, he told her. He didn't want to humiliate Zayna.

As soon as Mohammed left, she called her mother.

"Remember how lucky you are, Lina. He's a wealthy man. I live in a small house with your father and his wife. I can hear everything through the walls. You have your own home. Your father could've divorced me, but I was a wise woman. I know how to keep him. Don't show him you are jealous of his first wife, and don't nag him. When he comes to you, treat him like a king."

"But this is our honeymoon night, Mama."

"It was the same on my honeymoon night. You know your Baba only slept in my room that one time when Aida had taken a sedative. I accepted a long time ago your father wouldn't be mine exclusively. It's the price we pay for being the second wife. Or the third or the fourth."

"What about the first wives? They're the lucky ones, aren't they?"

"That's what I used to think. But now I know they're the most humiliated of us all. The second wife chooses to be with a man who is married, but the first wife usually doesn't have a choice."

"Shouldn't the first wife agree?"

"She should, but no man does what he should, Lina. He does what he wants."

"I thought you said Aida personally picked you."

"Yes, she did. But she resents me to this day."

"Why did she pick a beautiful woman, Mama? You're known as the village rose."

"Your father told me the story. He rejected five, or maybe six, women before me, and he realized after a while she was picking women he wouldn't like on purpose. He threatened her with divorce. She found me right away."

The next day, Mohammed phoned her and said he was taking her to Ribzi's.

Every day on the bus ride to Mohammed's office, Lina had passed by Ribzi's. When she went for a walk, she would stare inside the window. Lina was intimidated to enter the boutique because the prices were expensive. And now Mohammed was taking her there. Her mother had been right: She should treat him like a king.

Lina waited for him in the parlor. The doorbell rang. She went to hug him.

"What're you doing downstairs?"

Lina was confused. "What do you mean? I thought we were going shopping."

"Yes, but maybe you can show your husband a little affection first, no?" Mohammed winked at her.

After they made love, Mohammed took a shower, and when he came out and changed, he kissed Lina and pressed his body against hers. He whispered that he wanted her. But she wanted to take a shower and was restless to go to Ribzi's. The thought of him on top of her, heaving and sweating and moaning and salivating on her, filled her with nausea. How could he be in the mood for sex again?

"I want you. What are you doing to me, woman?" He was panting.

Lina was turned off by his insatiable desire for her. Maybe he was like all other men, after all. Her mother had advised her to always say yes when her husband wanted to make love.

The second session didn't last long, much to Lina's relief, and after it, they both showered and went to Ribzi's.

***

"CHECK OUT ALL THESE BEAUTIFUL SHOES, MY LOVE. Which ones do you want?"

"I can't afford this place," she whispered feebly. Lina wanted Mohammed to assure her he was going to pay even though she had no doubt he would.

"Men are responsible for women. It says so in the Koran, *habibti*. Buy whatever you want. And forget about the prices."

After they browsed the shoe section, Mohammed and

Lina moved to the clothing area. There were a few skirts that caught her attention, but her joy vanished when Mohammed told the sales lady his wife was preparing to wear the hijab and to bring out headscarves and abayas in subdued colors. And he said it loudly.

"Mohammed, can I have a word with you?"

"Sure, my love."

But there was nowhere private to talk to him. The sales lady must have understood because she walked away.

"How could you do this to me, and in front of the sales lady?"

"You know how religious I am. And my family is religious. It's our tradition."

"My parents are religious too, but my Mama doesn't wear it and neither does my Baba's first wife. My mother's sister is the only one in the family who wears it and it was her choice."

"Are you against it?"

"Not at all, but it's a personal decision. If a religious woman wants to wear it because she is sure God stipulated it, then it's her right, but if a woman doesn't want to wear it, that's her right too and doesn't take her away from religion, Mohammed."

"I'm not going to get into an argument about that with you. But you have to wear it for me. I'm prepared to spend a fortune on you. I'll buy you anything you want: designer bags, jewelry, you name it. The sky's the limit. But I won't walk around with an uncovered wife. You hear me? You are my family now, and I protect all the women in my family."

"What about your niece who came to your office a couple of months ago? Salma? You're not protecting her."

"She's not my responsibility."

"She's family, isn't she?"

"Salma is neither my daughter nor my wife. But if I ever hear anything about her, I'll fight my sister tooth and nail to be her guardian. Anyway, this has nothing to do with Salma. Please keep her out of this."

"Why didn't you tell me this before we got married? And why did you wait until after our wedding to tell me not to work?"

"You want to work?"

"No. I don't. But would you mind if I did?"

"Yes. I would. But you don't want to work, so it is a win-win for both of us."

"No, it's not. You're trying to control me. It sounds like this is a win for you. I'm not controlling you. It just so happens I don't want to work, but if I did, you wouldn't let me."

"I love you, Lina. And I don't want any man looking at you now that you belong to me. I'm a religious man. And it shows. Look at my short *dishdasha* and my long beard. It'll be shameful for me to walk around with an uncovered wife looking like this. You can buy revealing clothes to wear under the abaya, but I don't want anyone else to see them. Don't you want to be a dutiful wife to your husband? This shop is filled with clothes and shoes and bags. I told you I'm willing to buy whatever you want. Why do you want to insult me by wearing revealing clothes or uncovering your hair? Can't you do this for me?"

Mohammed spoke softly, and Lina was surprisingly endeared by his possessiveness. And all around her were designer clothes, shoes, and bags lined up on racks. Maybe if she wore the hijab, he would fall in love with her and leave Zayna. He was kind and generous to her. It was the least she could do. She squeezed his hand.

Her husband motioned for the sales lady to come back. She raised an eyebrow and looked at him in a flirtatious manner, but Mohammed turned away as she approached them. Lina was about to confront the woman but didn't. She was a newlywed. How would Mohammed react to her making a scene publicly? Besides, Mohammed had ignored the woman. And he would've asked for God's forgiveness aloud if he was attracted to any woman apart from his wife. *Wives.*

The sales lady brought her hijabs in every color and design. Lina picked a yellow one, but her husband frowned.

"I don't like the color yellow. It'll attract too much attention. Is it all right with you if I choose?"

"Of course. Go ahead."

After handpicking her new wardrobe, Mohammed gave the sales lady the delivery address for Lina's new clothes, shoes, bags, headscarves, and cloaks. Her husband held her hand all the way to their car. She was sure he was falling in love with her.

When he dropped her home, she phoned her mother.

"Are you wearing it now, Lina?"

"No, tomorrow."

"You're making a big mistake. The veil is a decision you make by yourself. Nobody should influence you."

"Mom, you told me to treat him like a king."

"Yes, but you're his queen, not his subject. I told you not to nag him when he spends time with his first wife, but I didn't think you'd allow a man to dictate what you wear."

"Aunty Yusra wears it and she's happy."

"She chose to wear it. I'm disappointed in you."

As the months passed, it became obvious to Lina her husband was using her for sex. When they were together, he ate, watched television, and made love, usually not in that order.

Mohammed's code word for sex was ready. Lina had to wax, then shower with an orange and bergamot body wash, scrub her hair with jojoba shampoo and a gardenia-flavored conditioner, spritz rose-scented perfume, and massage jasmine body oil all over her body. He chose and ordered all her cosmetics from abroad. Mohammed was picky, but she enjoyed pampering herself with the exclusive products. She couldn't even pronounce some of the brand names.

"Are you ready? I'm coming to see you tomorrow," he would say.

And most weekends, he would stay a few hours or a night. She couldn't remember the last time he stayed for an entire weekend.

One night, as Mohammed was making love to Lina, he moaned Zayna's name. Lina threw him off of her.

"You dog!" She jolted out of bed naked. Lina had never stood before him without her clothes on, because she was still shy in bed. She undressed under the covers and wrapped a sheet around her whenever she went to the bathroom. She was not insecure about her body, because of the way men looked at her in the streets and the way Mohammed moaned when he touched her. But she hadn't been able to relax in bed. She was too angry to care she was nude for the first time in front of her husband.

"Dog, Lina? You have the nerve to call me a dog?"

He was talking to her breasts.

"A dog is more honorable than you. At least dogs are loyal." She walked to the bathroom and put on a bathrobe.

Nejoud Al-Yagout

When she came back, Mohammed, who was sitting on the edge of the bed with his head in his hands, got up, picked up his clothes from the floor, and walked to the bathroom. Less than a minute later, he walked out, fully clothed, and left the room without showering and without saying a word. She called him right away to apologize, but Mohammed had switched off his phone. He ignored all of Lina's attempts to get in touch with him for the next week. He would be furious if she went to his office because she had vowed not to leave the house unaccompanied by him, so she waited for him to call.

When Mohammed called two weeks later, Lina didn't pick up the phone. She had to punish him for neglecting her, but she couldn't wait to be with Mohammed. She called him back five minutes later.

"Hi, Lina. Ready for me?"

She showered, blow-dried her hair, waxed her legs and bikini area, and spritzed perfume all over her body. When Mohammed came over, he fell asleep, exhausted, on her breasts.

When he woke up an hour later, Lina confronted him.

"Did you make love to Zayna right before coming to see me?"

"Please, Lina. I have to go home soon. I want to be inside you now. Let's not talk."

When Mohammed left, she fantasized about divorcing him. Lina no longer cared whether or not she ever remarried. In her village, divorced women were no longer frowned upon as they had been in the past. She recalled her Aunty Yusra saying it was better to be divorced than not to have been married. When she told her mother she was divorcing Mohammed, she supported Lina.

"What about Baba?"

"Call back tomorrow afternoon. I'll speak to your father in the morning."

SHE DIALED HER MOTHER'S NUMBER ON SPEAKER AND finished applying silver glitter nail polish on her toes.

"Come home, Lina," her mother told her. "Leave him. Your father wants you to divorce the dog."

"Oh, I'm so glad he approved. I will divorce him." She twisted the lid of the bottle shut and kept it in the drawer beside her bed. She massaged her temples.

"Those men think they can buy our women because they're rich. Don't fall into his trap. Do it right away or you'll be stuck with him."

"There's no way I can spend another moment with him. I have to wait until the weekend for His Excellency to grace me with a visit." She pressed the speaker button again to turn it off and picked up the receiver.

"Keep me updated. He won't beat you or refuse a divorce, will he?"

"He couldn't harm a fly. I've heard him on the phone with his other wife. He's all talk and no action." She twirled a strand of hair around her finger.

"He got you to wear the hijab. Sounds like more than talk to me."

"This is different. I know his character. He's weak. If I had fought harder not to wear the hijab, he would've agreed." She checked the time on her expensive watch. Her favorite talk show was about to start.

"I doubt it."

"OK, he would've given me more time at least."

"What if he postpones the divorce?"

"I'll fight him so hard, he'll give me one right away. I have to go Mama. I'll call you tomorrow. I want to speak to Baba too."

She opened the drawer beside her and took out the remote and turned on the curved flat-screen television. Channel eleven. She looked at her watch again. One minute left.

AND THE NIGHT ARRIVED. LINA DIDN'T HAVE TO PUT UP much of a fight. After rebuking him, he divorced her three times. He left the house and called her the next day, saying he couldn't take her to court because Zayna was divorcing him. He begged her to reconsider, but she cried and said she wanted to go home. She pleaded with him not to use his power to keep her from a divorce.

The next week, Lina was on a plane back home, a newly divorced young lady. She would never leave her country again.

10

ZAYNA

"I could make myself free."
—Ahmed Moh'd El-Barcemy

M en didn't look at Zayna in the streets. Lately, she would walk in front of her husband and glance at them seductively, eyebrows raised and duck pout so they would stare back at her. Her husband would look at the men in contempt, and when he caught up to her, they would walk away, embarrassed, if not confused. Then, he would come close to her and whisper in her ear how much he loved her. Or, he would be angry and ignore her. If a man is possessive he loves you, her mother had said. And though she left the house alone without him asking where she was, whenever they were out together, he was protective. Her trick had been working in her favor. So it came as a shock to her when he told her he was taking another wife. They had just had lunch in the dining room. She glared at him. The house-helpers were clearing the dishes and Maryam asked them to go to the kitchen. She would ring the bell for them later.

"How could you say that in front of the staff?" she asked when they were out of earshot.

"I wasn't planning to. It just came out. I'm sorry. They're going to know eventually. There's no point in keeping it a secret. I don't care what they think."

"Are you divorcing me?"

"Of course not. You're my number one."

"Who is she?"

"My secretary."

"Which one?"

"Lina."

"That slut at work who wears short skirts?"

"Zayna. Behave yourself. That's no way to speak about her."

"I knew she was bad news. You can't do this to me."

"I've made up my mind. We're getting married in a few days."

"You discussed it with the whore before telling me?"

"Don't use such filthy language."

"I'm in such shock. This can't be happening. Is this because we don't make love anymore? I can make an effort." She hit her forehead with her palms repeatedly. He walked over to her and grabbed her by the wrists.

"I love you. But a man has needs." He let go of her hands and kissed her forehead.

"Needs? Whatever you want from her, I can provide for you. Please, Mohammed."

"I feel sorry for her. She's poor, single, far away from home. I'm going to take care of her."

He had made up his mind. There was nothing she could do. "This is an insult to me. To our sons."

"Our sons know. They're happy for me."

"They know? You told them before me? And they're happy?"

"Except for that rascal Raed. All he spoke of was women's rights and how I could do this to you. His ideas frighten me. What about my rights as a man?" Saliva was shooting out of his mouth.

"Raed's the only one in this house who cares about me." Her scalp was itching beneath her headscarf. She removed it and threw it on chair beside her.

"Put it back on. What if a houseboy comes in?"

"You should care about what your wife thinks."

"I don't care about you? Are you serious, Zayna? After all these years?" He picked up her hijab. "Here you go," he said, handing it to her.

She put her headscarf back on and got up, facing him. "Well after all these years you're betraying me by taking another wife, aren't you? Is that caring for me?"

"I have a right to enjoy myself, don't I?"

"You don't enjoy being with me? Don't I make you feel loved? I thought you were marrying her because she was poor, single, far away from home." She had her hands on her hips.

"I thought you should know. Many husbands hide it from their wives. I don't want to be like them. And I'm not asking for permission," he said, as he returned to the seat across from her.

"Will you be living with her?" Zayna sat back down again. This was going to be a long conversation.

"I'll spend weekends with her. But I promise nothing will change. You're my first wife, and I respect you more."

They spent the next hour arguing, until Zayna rang the bell and walked to her room.

On the night of Mohammed's marriage, Zayna sent him a text message telling him what she wanted to do to his body. Mohammed fled home. He was easy to seduce. Perhaps if she made love to him every day, he would divorce Lina. Beneath her husband's religious exterior, Mohammed was an ordinary man with raging testosterone. Though he couldn't perform that night, Zayna was satisfied he had left Lina alone on the night of their wedding.

She would make life difficult for Lina. The next morning she pounced on her husband with her new lingerie. He moaned Lina's name while they were making love, but she didn't confront him. The last thing Zayna would do was to alienate her husband and make him go back to Lina. After they were done, he took a shower.

"Where are you going?"

"I'm taking Lina shopping."

"Why today?"

"*Habibti*, I haven't bought her anything, and I want her to switch to a more conservative style, so I have to get her a new wardrobe."

"Good idea, my love. You shouldn't encourage her to walk around naked like that. It's strange she's uncovered, Mohammed, don't you think?"

"Soon enough, I'll make sure she wears the hijab, but not yet."

"Soon enough? The truth is, she needs to wear the hijab right away. Doesn't she have any shame? Even if she dresses conservatively, how can she walk around with her hair showing?"

"Lina shares our religious beliefs, but the poor girl comes

from a different culture, and I want to ease her into ours."

"The longer you wait, the more she'll get used to not wearing it. How can she walk around with you looking like that?" She pointed at his beard. "People will think you're a hypocrite. And they'll mock you behind your back. You're a scholar. What example are you setting for other men?"

"Oh dear. You're right. It's been bothering me, but I guess I was waiting for the right time to broach the subject."

"There's no right time. She needs to wear the hijab right away."

"I'm glad you brought this up. I might as well do it now. Why wait?"

"Go, *habibi*. Tell Lina she needs to wear the veil. Don't wait another day. You know this kind of a woman. She's used to being without it, so it's your job to get her used to wearing it. Best to let her know right away who's in charge."

"You're truly a God-fearing devout woman. You shall have a reward for this."

As she watched Mohammed walk away, she snickered. Lina would resent him, and they would either fight or get divorced over the issue. Nobody likes to be pressured into wearing it. When Zayna was a young girl, she thought all women of her faith and country covered their hair, so she accepted her fate. She had been raised in a conservative neighborhood, about an hour's drive from the city center, and it was when she married Mohammed and moved to the suburbs and became acquainted with many local girls who dressed liberally that her conservative background bothered her. And even the ones who were covered were independent and were given plenty of freedom. Mohammed let her drive and leave the house alone, but she wasn't allowed to work.

Though she was used to wearing the hijab, Zayna wondered whether she would have chosen it had her mother not imposed it on her. She often had fantasies about a life without the veil. But when Mohammed proposed to her, all her ideas of living without a hijab vanished, and she surrendered to being a covered housewife. Zayna was jealous Lina could roam around freely and had still managed to capture Mohammed's attention.

Now Lina would be subjugated. This would be the perfect revenge on the secretary who had seduced her husband.

THE NEXT DAY, MOHAMMED TOLD HER LINA HAD accepted the hijab. "And she agreed not to leave the house without me. Good woman."

"Are you saying I'm not a good woman because I leave the house without you? You're not jealous when it comes to me?"

"Zayna, of course not. I'm not comparing the two of you. We've been married for a long time. We have three sons. It's different. She's young."

Mohammed kissed her forehead. It was the second time in their marriage Zayna was repulsed by him. The first time had been during their first year of marriage, when Mohammed had asked her to massage his feet in a commanding tone. He taunted her further by moaning harder near the heel area.

"Yes, right there. Harder, Zayna."

Then Mohammed fell back, laughing. "Silly woman, I'm teasing you. Now let me return the favor and massage your feet."

She smiled. He was a good man.

On a Friday, Mohammed had informed her he would be spending the night with Lina. Maybe she should divorce him? How hadn't she thought of that before? If he ends his marriage to Lina or the other way around, she would leave him on the same day to humiliate him.

Zayna brushed her long hair, tied it in a bun, and wore her hijab. She wore loose jeans and a T-shirt and walked toward the entrance of the house. She grabbed her car keys from the key holder on the wall, put on her abaya, and drove to Amy's house.

Amy was her youngest son's English literature teacher. Zayna had met her at a parent-teacher conference, and they bonded immediately. Mohammed didn't accompany her to any of the meetings. He wasn't interested in their studies. Zayna often tutored Raed, Faisal, and Isa. Her English was impeccable. As a newlywed, Zayna had hired a private English tutor and learned how to speak it fluently in seven years.

"Amy, I have no say. He decided to marry her against my wishes."

"Do you love Mohammed?"

"I did. But I hate him now."

"Then why're you staying with him?"

"I don't know. Both love and hate have a hold on us, no?"

"Um, not really."

"What I mean is I hate him because I love him. It's not the love of television series, but I got used to him. And now he's no longer there for me. He seems restless and distracted since he married her."

"Well," Amy sighed, shaking her head. "I'm here for you. Anytime."

"I know. That's why I'm here. He's such a hypocrite. He speaks of this vision he has for a segregated country, but he puts his sons in schools with girls. He wants a society that subjugates women but gives men freedom."

Amy squeezed Zayna's hand. "Keep venting. It's good for you."

"I can't complain much because Mohammed is kind to me. He has never hit me, not once. He buys me flowers throughout the year. Mohammed curses Valentine's Day. He calls it the festival of pagans. But he loves pampering me with gifts otherwise."

"That's hilarious. A pagan festival? And not hitting you should be a given, not an indication of kindness."

"Yes, you're right. I mean he can raise his voice. And when he gets excited, I have to wipe his saliva off my face."

"OK, that's gross. I know a guy who has sloppy kisses."

"Oh." Zayna raised an eyebrow.

"Not like that. He's a friend. He licks his lips all the time, then kisses my cheeks."

"Ew. Gross."

Amy and Zayna laughed.

THE FOLLOWING WEEKEND, ZAYNA WENT TO AMY'S again. And the weekend after that. She was beginning to enjoy time spent away from Mohammed and welcomed her curious friend's questions.

"You're not allowed to travel by yourself?" Amy asked.

"No. But I can travel with my sons. And my husband lets me drive alone, and I can go out by myself. See? I'm here. And he hasn't called once."

"Lets you? I don't get it. Why should he have to let you?"

On one occasion, their conversation became bolder.

"Zayna, can I ask you a personal question?"

"Of course."

"I mean, I don't want to offend you, but I'm kind of curious. Did you wear the hijab before marrying Mohammed?"

"Yes."

Amy stayed quiet.

"Why do you ask?" Zayna was confused by Amy's silence.

"Well, I have a friend who's doing her thesis on gender studies, and she's focusing on young girls and the veil."

"Oh, OK."

"When did you wear it, if I may ask?"

"I was a teenager."

"Did you choose to wear the hijab? Don't worry. I'm not interrogating you for her thesis. I'm just curious. I don't see a lot of teenagers covered up at school, so I'm confused about the culture. When is the right age to wear it?"

"There is no right age. Some people say girls should wear it when they begin menstruating, but that's not the case with the majority these days. It all depends on the family, since the government doesn't impose the hijab, thankfully. Most people in this part of town decide to wear it in college or even after university. It's not the norm around here for teens, but I grew up in a conservative part of town. My mom forced me to wear it."

"That must have been hard."

"I was lucky because the popular girls at my school wore it, so I was suddenly cool. I now envy the ones who like wearing it, because they don't have to struggle like I do. I don't know why it is still hard for me."

"It's just who you are. It's the same everywhere. Some

Nejoud Al-Yagout

of us don't belong in the place where we're from. I mean I wish I knew why we were born where we were in the first place, but that's a whole other discussion. So? You still don't like wearing it?"

"No. But I got used to it. Mohammed would throw a fit if he knew I have moments when I want to take it off."

"That sucks you're scared of your husband."

"I was more scared of my mother. As I said earlier, everything depends on your family. It's like a lucky draw, or an unlucky one in my case. Still, I'm blessed I didn't have daughters with Mohammed. Can you imagine how he would have raised them?"

"Well, there's your lucky draw then."

"If it were his choice, he'd veil every single woman, including you. He has a niece called Salma who's liberal. Her mother is Mohammed's sister. And he's upset she's unveiled." Zayna rolled her eyes.

"How did she get away with it? Is Mohammed's sister less conservative than your husband?" Amy poured water from a jug. She handed a glass to Zayna who gulped it. Amy poured her another glass.

"Oh, no. She's conservative, but Salma's father is open-minded. Mohammed hates him because he thinks he's corrupt and it's his fault Salma is free." Zayna sipped the water.

"What do you mean by free?"

"Well, according to Mohammed, free means any girl who doesn't wear the hijab. Imagine that. But free here also means loose. I like Salma. Maybe one day I'll introduce you to each other."

"Sounds good."

"What do you think about women who wear the hijab?"

"Well, to be honest, before I moved here I thought it

was oppressive. But living here helped me understand the religion, so I think if a woman's doing it for God, then it's spiritual and beautiful. But if it's about society, or for a man, or in your case, for a mother, it's upsetting. And like all religions, there are more followers than sincere devotees, you know? It's rare to find a person who isn't selfish when it comes to faith. But when you do, it's mesmerizing to be around them."

"Have you been around anyone like that?" Zayna's eyes widened with interest.

"No, but I've read about them. And you can feel their energy. I mean Rumi, St. Francis of Assisi. Those guys were stars. They had that spiritual *je ne sais quoi*. If there were more religious people like that, there'd be no wars. Oh well..." Amy was staring at the ceiling.

"What does *je ne sais quoi* mean?"

"It's French for I don't know what. You can use the phrase to refer to something that is hard to describe."

"Hmm. Interesting. I wonder how many woman wear it for God. You got me thinking now."

"Who are we to judge why? We're all complicated."

"True. It's hard when I travel. The looks I get sometimes." Zayna hit her forehead.

"It's sad, but I get it. It's easier to judge other cultures, so we don't have to face our own hypocrisies, you know?"

"Yes, but it's tougher for women." Her second glass was now empty. She was still thirsty, but was embarrassed to ask for more water.

"Yeah women are suffering everywhere. Even if we have rights, the patriarchy is still alive," Amy said.

Zayna let out a sigh.

Amy was looking at Zayna. It was the same look Zayna

gave her children when they fell down, or were bullied at school, or had a fever.

"Amy, please don't look at me that way. I don't want you to feel sorry for me. I feel humiliated."

"Oh no. Please don't ever feel awkward around me. I'm just sad you had to go through all you did. It's unfair. I'm sorry. I didn't mean to embarrass you."

"No, don't apologize. I think you brought up feelings I've been suppressing," Zayna admitted. "I'm upset at my mother. By now, yes, I'm used to the hijab, but I feel it's not fair it was imposed on me. You know what kept me going? The attention I got. My aunts and uncles congratulated me, and I felt special. Oh, and the sense of honor I felt when Mohammed came to propose to me. You know what thought kills me? The question of what kind of person I would be if I had not been forced to wear it. What if I were born into a different family? Am I who I am because of my culture?" Zayna took a deep breath. Talking to Amy about her feelings released a heavy burden. She hadn't even been aware of how much pain was stored within her.

"That's profound, Zayna. I guess it's a question we all need to ask ourselves."

"Yes. I can't let go of my roots. But I know I should. In cases like mine, roots can make you unhappy."

"What're you going to do?"

"I don't know. It's the struggle that's torturing me. I don't think my anger at his betrayal will ever leave me. If his second marriage ever breaks down, I'll leave him."

"Why wait? What if he stays with her forever? Would you stay with him?"

"I'm not sure yet. For now, I'm still consumed with this desire to compete against her. And in a strange way, it's keeping me in the marriage. I can't explain it. It hardly makes sense to me. If their relationship ends, he'll expect me to be over the moon. But my reaction will shatter him. Don't they say revenge is a dish best served cold? I want to humiliate him when he least expects it."

"OK, you're officially scaring me now," Amy said. "But I get it. He's a jerk. He doesn't deserve you at all. I mean, your logic's a bit warped with your whole revenge plot, but to each his own. I mean *her* own."

"Don't get me wrong. I know it sounds sick, but I care about him deeply. It's kind of like a love and hate tug-of-war. I guess I'm conflicted and want a way out but I'm still too much of a coward to leave him, so I've set this target moment in my mind, a moment that may never come. Who knows?"

"I think you're better off without him, but the way you're planning on leaving him is messed up."

The doorbell rang.

"Oh, that must be your friend." Amy had mentioned a coworker, Mike, who was coming over. "OK, I'll head out. Enjoy yourselves."

"We're going to a barbecue together. Want to come with us?"

"Oh. I can't. I have to go home."

Amy opened the door and said hello to Mike. He hugged her and walked toward Zayna.

"Hey there. I'm Mike." He extended his hand.

Zayna lowered her gaze, and though she didn't shake his hand, she reveled in the electricity running up and down her spine.

"Oops, sorry. I keep forgetting to wait for the woman to shake hands first, and I've lived here for ages." He grinned.

"Amy, I must go." She blushed. "I'll call you."

"You sure you don't want to join us? It might be a nice change."

"No, thank you. Go ahead. Have fun."

She kissed Amy on the cheeks, walked by Mike, and got into her car. She looked at them from the rearview mirror. They were outside Amy's apartment. Zayna walked straight back to where they were standing.

"You know, I think I'll join you guys. Just for a little bit."

"Zayna, that's great. OK, let's do this," Amy said.

"Wait, I need to use the ladies' room. I'll be right back."

Zayna locked the bathroom door. She removed her hijab and abaya and took her hair out of the bun and finger-brushed it. She straightened her T-shirt and rolled up the hems of her jeans. When she came out, Mike and Amy were staring at her, dumbfounded. She placed her hands in her pockets and scratched her upper thighs. What were they thinking? Did Mike find her attractive? Was Amy shocked? Confused?

"Oh my goodness, Z. I wasn't expecting that. Are you sure about this?" Amy's mouth was open.

"Let's go before I change my mind."

"Our taxi is on the way."

"I can drive. Cancel the taxi."

"Oh, I can't. Iqbal will be here any second. He's already ten minutes late."

"I can go with Zayna," Mike offered. "Amy, I'll still split the cost of the taxi with you, but I'll show Z how to get there." Zayna was shocked by his forwardness. And only Amy called her Z. They just met. It must be because she had removed her hijab. Men treat unveiled woman with less respect, her mother had once told her.

In the car, neither of them said a word. Mike spoke only to tell her to turn left, right, take a U-turn, slow down when a road bump came out of nowhere, or drive to the end of the road and park outside the pink building with the palm trees and blue-gazed windows.

When they got to the barbecue, all around her were women who were scantily dressed or wearing bathing suits. A couple was kissing on a terrace. She was both appalled and exhilarated.

"Amy, I have to leave. There are local men and women here. If anyone here knows me or my family, I'll be in big trouble."

"Z. I've been meaning to ask you. Did you remove your hijab because of our conversation? I don't want to influence you in any way."

"It was a spur-of-the-moment thing. It has nothing to do with you. When you mentioned a barbecue, I couldn't picture myself walking in with a hijab."

"Are you sure? It was literally right after our conversation."

"It might have triggered something, but it wasn't you. This is my battle."

"I hope this won't cause a further rift between you and Mohammed."

"Are you crazy? He won't even know about this. I'm putting it back on in the car." Zayna pointed at her uncovered head.

"OK. Well are you sure you want to leave? You just got here. I'm sure it'll be fine." But the look on her face must have changed Amy's mind. "OK. I understand. Text me when you get home."

Zayna walked toward the front gate. She glanced over her shoulder. Mike was approaching her. .

"Not having fun?"

"I have to go," Zayna said.

"So soon?" He was licking his lips. Did this mean he was attracted to her or were his lips chapped? Or was this the guy Amy had once referred to who licked his lips and kissed her cheeks? She wouldn't mind kissing his wet lips.

"Yes."

"Well, can I have your number?" His eyebrows were raised.

"I'm married. I have three sons." She gave him a suggestive look so he would insist.

"So? I want to get to know you better. Give me your number."

"Give me yours."

As he told her his number, she typed it on her cell phone and called him. His phone vibrated in his pocket. He took it out, asked how she spelled her name and saved her information.

"Listen, don't call me, OK? I'll get in trouble. Wait for me to call," Zayna said.

He put his phone back in his pocket. "I won't call. Promise. But don't make me wait too long."

ZAYNA CALLED HIM THE NEXT MORNING WHEN MOHAM-med went to work, and mornings soon became a routine for them. On the rare nights her husband spent with Lina, Zayna stayed on the phone with him all night long. She reiterated to Mike not to call her, even if he was sure Mohammed wasn't in the house. Messages were allowed in the morning, but only after they had spoken first.

Fantasizing about Mike made her more aroused with Mohammed. Zayna was afraid she would say Mike's name while her husband was making love to her, the way Mohammed had moaned Lina's. So, during sex, she kept her mouth closed, unless Mohammed would force it open with his lips and darting tongue.

After meeting Mike, Zayna changed. She had a new-found confidence. Mohammed had never spoken to her the way Mike did. Though both men were polite and respectful to her, Mike, unlike Mohammed, asked her about her childhood, her fears, her ambitions, even her failures. Is this what men were like? Or was it because Mike was not from here?

Zayna was still waiting for Mohammed and Lina to divorce so she could leave him, but she was scared. How would it be when she and Mohammed were no longer together? She wavered between her disgust and desire for him. When he would go to Lina's, she would feign illness or wear lingerie to seduce him. Her ploys to keep him at home were working. He was spending less time with Lina. But there was a part of her that no longer wanted him around. The idea of another woman pleasing him in bed had changed the dynamics of their marriage. Was she that unworthy that he needed another woman?

Mike, however, made her feel attractive, and he hadn't even touched her yet. One day, he begged her to meet him for coffee. She resisted. Zayna had vowed to God she wouldn't date him until she got divorced. And she wouldn't sleep with him unless she was married to him.

"Mike, I told you I wouldn't meet you while I was married."

"Are you going to stay with him? He humiliated you by taking a second wife. And now you're with me."

"I have three sons."

"You keep saying that. I don't care if you have ten kids. I want to be with you. I haven't felt this way for a woman in a long time."

It was not Mohammed's feelings she cared for, but her reputation. If she were from another country, she would have had an affair with Mike. But she would be shamed for the rest of her life if anyone found out about her in her country.

A brother of hers had a mistress once, but less than half a year later people had moved on to other family headlines: a cousin's nanny, married with five children, had attempted suicide because she was pregnant with the cook's baby; an uncle of hers was guilty of fraud and in prison; and the most salacious gossip was her lesbian aunt who was having an affair with her sister-in-law. Because Zayna was a woman, she would be talked about for the rest of her life. An affair with a woman was one thing, but an affair with a man? She could be killed.

Zayna had heard about honor killings. Though they were not common locally, there was a law in place that if men caught women relatives in a sexual act and killed them, they were only sentenced to three years in jail and had to pay a minute fine not worth mentioning. She had watched an interview on television with a local woman who was fighting to abolish this patriarchal legislation that treated honor killings merely as a misdemeanor. Zayna had admired the woman's eloquence and elegance, and her insistence that this mindset had nothing to do with religion but was rooted in tradition. From the interview, Zayna discovered this woman was one of five local female activists who spoke to Members of Parliament and traveled around the globe to raise awareness for this initiative. Their mission, known as Abolish Article 153, is an effort to have honor killings recognized as murder, a crime in the eyes of the law.

"*Astaghfurallah*," her husband scoffed. He turned off the television. "What is this world coming to? Women are trying to get away with adultery?"

"*Habibi*, turn it back on. That was not what she's saying. The Koran doesn't even mention honor killings. The punishment for both adulterous women and men is lashes. When did culture get mixed up in religion?"

"See, you're brainwashed, just by watching a small part of this interview. Adulterous women should be killed. I don't want to discuss this."

"What about adulterous men? Would you be OK with men getting killed for adultery?"

"Zayna. What nonsense."

"Give me the remote." She extended her hand.

Mohammed gave her the remote and left the room. She was tired of the way he tried to control her and the way he looked down on women.

―――――――――

"MIKE, WHAT DO YOU WANT FROM ME?" SHE ASKED HIM one night when Mohammed was spending the night at Lina's.

"I haven't thought about it, Z. I like you. And I told you I want to be with you. We have a connection. It's kind of hard to define this while you're still married."

There were footsteps outside the bedroom door. She hung up the phone. Mike wouldn't call her back, but she still turned off her cell phone just in case.

"What're you doing here, Mohammed?" She got up.

"I divorced her, Zayna. I can't be with anyone but you. I told her I want you and you alone. I love you."

"Are you serious? Just like that. No other reason?"

"No. What other reason?"

He fidgeted with his headgear and stroked his beard. Mohammed avoided her gaze.

"You're lying. You wouldn't leave that whore so soon after marrying her."

"You're calling me a liar?" She watched his saliva fly out of his mouth. She was standing far enough away from him not to feel it on her cheek.

"Yes. I am. Swear by Allah you divorced her."

"I divorced her. Three times."

"Who instigated it? You or her?"

Mohammed's silence confirmed her suspicion.

"I want a divorce too. You humiliated me and married another woman just because you were attracted to her. Tomorrow, take me to the divorce court."

"What's come over you, woman?"

"I've come to my senses. It's over between us, and there's nothing you can say or do that'll change my mind. I've been waiting for this moment to punish you for the way you disregarded my feelings and married that bitch of yours."

"Please mind your language."

"I want a divorce." She said it while looking straight into his teary eyes. Zayna wondered where his masculinity was when he needed it the most. And what would happen to him now that he lost two women on the same night? Would he learn his lesson?

"I refuse to divorce you. Listen to yourself. Be wise." His voice was trembling, and he was shivering. He removed his headgear and threw it on the floor.

"I've never felt wiser. What an idiot I was. I would have stayed with you forever, but ever since you married her, things have changed for me. I have no feelings for you anymore."

"You seem to have more feelings for me lately."

"Why? Because I sleep with you more? You know why I seduce you? To keep you away from Lina. Feelings are not defined only by sex, Mohammed. But you wouldn't understand that."

"You accepted my marriage. And your father married and divorced more women than we can count."

"I never accepted anything. I had no choice. You didn't ask for my permission. You knew I was against it, but you had made up your mind. I can't break the curse of being born to a polygamous father, but I have the choice to break the curse of marrying a polygamous husband."

"No, Zayna. You're emotional now. I refuse. You know our religion states divorce isn't favorable."

"Yes, but it's permissible. And how funny coming from a man who just got a divorce."

"You're the mother of my children. We can't do this to our sons. You won't forgive yourself."

"What you've done to me is unforgivable. Have you forgotten our religion says to marry more than one if you can deal with them justly? Or do you pick and choose verses and the sayings of the prophet, peace be upon him, conveniently?"

"I treated you both justly."

"Then why are we both divorcing you?"

"Zayna, please. I beg you. I'll never marry another woman again."

"Take that back. You're going to have to marry another woman or you'll be alone."

She watched as Mohammed held tightly to the side of an armchair to gain his balance. He became dizzy when he was emotional. She watched him check his pulse with his fingers. Even though she had been waiting for this moment, his fear filled her with compassion.

Zayna still cared for him even after he had betrayed her. She didn't want to hurt him. But this was no longer about him, it was about her. She couldn't stay with a man who didn't appreciate her. Nor did she want her sons to marry more than one woman. Her strength would teach them it wasn't acceptable to hurt their spouses in that way. She knew Raed wouldn't, but her other sons were conservative, though younger. Raed promised her their mindsets would transform one day. Give them time. They're still young. Impressionable. You'll see. They're bound to change, he had told her.

Mohammed had tears in his eyes and was pleading for a second chance. She was no longer leaving him to punish him. She was leaving to be free. She was leaving to be with Mike.

"Is there anything I can do to change your mind? Can we at least wait?"

"Wait for what? It's over. It has been for a while. I'm calling my father now."

She watched Mohammed's forehead crinkle at the mention of her father. Mohammed was terrified of him. She went over to where he was and hugged him. In all their years of marriage they had never hugged without it leading to sex. He kissed her forehead when he came home from work, but anything else, including holding hands, was considered foreplay. During dry spells they would sit next to each other without touching. If he was in the mood and she wasn't, Zayna would feign a headache. If she was in the mood and he wasn't, he'd feign a stomachache.

Now, she held him as a mother would her baby. All her anger subsided as he bawled on her shoulder. She was embarrassed to admit she was relieved. Was she normal? There was compassion for him, yes, but no pain. Maybe she was in shock. Or maybe it was, dare she admit, excitement.

That night, after her prayer, she thanked Allah. She promised she would be responsible with this new freedom that had been bestowed upon her and wouldn't be physically involved with Mike unless they got married.

THE NEXT MORNING, THEY WERE DIVORCED. ZAYNA would keep the house with their three sons, and Mohammed would live in the house he bought for Lina, but without Lina.

Though she was terrified of what would come next, she couldn't wait to tell Mike. A new beginning awaited her.

11

MIKE

*"For now it's live for today. Don't speak of
the future or past. That's a good exercise."*
—Agatha Doug Lay

M ike was fascinated with local women, especially
veiled ones. He was intrigued by what was beneath
the abaya. Mike had been in the country for ten years and
had dated three veiled women. But love came once in a
lifetime, as his mother had said at his parents' fortieth
anniversary the year before.

For Mike, love arrived, uninvited, with the second of
the veiled ladies he dated. She was terrified of being in
public with him, so whenever they went out to cultural
events or art galleries, they would walk in separately, and
his girlfriend would sit or stand away from him. And she
wouldn't attend parties with him as his girlfriend.

To spend time alone, they would meet at Mike's apartment. One day they were watching a movie at his place. She asked if he had alcohol. He walked to the fridge and poured her a glass and handed it to her.

"What's this?" she asked, sniffing the glass.

"Red wine, babe."

"This isn't wine. This smells like vinegar. I'm scared to even taste it."

"Oh, it's homemade wine. My colleague made it. I can't buy booze on the black market. It's too expensive."

"Let me get the alcohol next time. And we'll keep it in your apartment since I can't keep it at my parents' home." The next weekend, she came over with her driver and a houseboy, who stocked Mike's cupboards with Château Latour Pauillac, Ornellaia, and Brunello di Montalcino. And they filled his fridge with Chablis and Gavi di Gavi. He had never heard of these wines before, but Aisha educated him. She prepared cheese platters for dinner on weekends and taught him which wine went best with which cheese.

She even paid for his gym membership.

"I know the girl who owns it. She's willing to charge us as a married couple so we can get a discount. But don't talk to me inside the gym. She thinks I don't know you. I told her I met you at a lecture and you were complaining about gym prices and I was doing this as a favor for you."

Mike was embarrassed he couldn't afford it, so he saved up and gave her his share in an envelope six months later.

"What's this?"

"It's my share for the gym membership."

"Oh, you didn't have to, *habibi*." She handed the envelope back to him, but he insisted until she said it would make her upset. He took the money back from her, more ashamed than before.

Nejoud Al-Yagout

MIKE ATTENDED A LECTURE IN WHICH HIS GIRLFRIEND spoke about women's rights. He asked her how she could be a feminist and wear the hijab.

"Look, I chose this. My family didn't make me wear it or anything like that. I don't know why the hijab and feminism have to be mutually exclusive. What a shallow way of looking at things."

"OK, I'll give you the benefit of the doubt, even though I beg to differ. But why do you sleep with me? Why do you drink alcohol? Doesn't that conflict with the whole veil thing?"

"No. It doesn't. I mean, not for me. I love my religion and my freedom. And that's all I have to say about it."

THINGS WERE GOING GREAT BETWEEN THEM. THEY didn't argue and were together whenever Aisha was free. But a year later, she broke up with him.

"What about our plans to get married in the future?"

"You won't fit in. My family would ask you to convert."

"Honey, I'll convert for you."

"No, I mean real conversion. All the pillars," Aisha said.

He licked his chapped lips. His mother had advised him to use chapstick because licking them would make his lips drier. But a woman at a party told him her friend had wanted to approach him but thought he was gay when she saw him applying lip balm. It's not lip balm, it's chapstick, he insisted. Then he asked where her friend was. Oh she went home, but I'm here, the girl said. He took his chapstick out of his pocket and threw it in the nearest trash can. He asked whether she was now convinced he was straight. Oh it'll take more than throwing away your lip balm, I mean chapstick, to convince me. What was her name again?

"Teach me Aisha. I know a marine here who converted. He went to this center and learned all about Islam. If that's what it'll take to marry you, I'll do the same."

"The truth is it's what I want. I don't want to marry someone who converted for my sake. You'll resent me one day."

"I could never resent you. I can do it. It can't be that different. I can start praying your way."

"It's not my way, Mike. And it is different. Very. You'll have to pray in another language and five times a day."

"I'll learn."

"You'll have to be circumcised."

"Baby, anything for you. Let's just get married now. We can't keep talking about it and running in circles."

She kept bringing one challenge after another, and Mike kept telling her he would do anything for her. Then, boom. It hit him she didn't want to marry him. She was trying to make it difficult because she hadn't expected him to comply with all her demands. It couldn't be their age difference. You're mature, she had told him. That's sexy. It couldn't be his personality. She said she loved his character and integrity. What was it?

Mike tried calling her for weeks after she left him, but she never picked up her phone. Then, a couple of months later, she blocked him from all her devices and social media.

HE READ ABOUT ISLAM. MIKE QUIT DRINKING AND TWO years later converted officially. He still slept around, but didn't neglect the obligatory prayers. Not drinking alcohol enhanced his sex life and helped him concentrate at work. Mike even had more energy at the gym. He still attended the same one he had gone to with her. It was an extravagant splurge to keep renewing his membership as a single man, but he kept hoping she would walk in one day.

He dated one short-term mistake after another. And he initiated all the break-ups. Whether he was with these women for a week or a couple of months, he couldn't fall in love with any of them.

When he wasn't teaching, exercising, or going to house parties, Mike studied his new religion. He went to Mecca and fasted. After one week of fasting, he complained to a local friend.

"How do you do it? It's difficult."

"It's just a month, Mike. And between you and me, I know a couple of people who drink coffee or water while fasting. Maybe that'll help you."

"No. I want to do it the right way. You're right. One month is nothing."

It wasn't hard for Mike to refrain from eating or drinking. It was his impatience that made it difficult. Time passed slowly. It was easier to fast without checking his devices. Praying was easy, but ablutions were challenging. Sometimes, he was in a dirty bathroom and it was difficult to raise his feet and wash them in a filthy sink. Other times, he couldn't remember whether he needed to do them again. He stopped going to the center where he had announced his new faith because the scholars were more concerned with appearances than spirituality. The founder, Mustafa, recommended he grow a beard, pray more than the required five prayers, and change his name.

"Why would I change my name?"

"So people know you are of this religion."

"I'm not doing this for people."

Mustafa walked away.

Mike was aware he had initially done it for *her*, but he now embraced his new faith. The more he studied it, the more he connected to it. But it wasn't only religion that helped him deal with loneliness. It was also women. He couldn't give them up no matter how much he adored his religion. Women numbed his pain and kept him in the moment. There was Lucille, Brandi, Lulwa, and Warda. And there was Zayna.

MIKE LIVED TWO STREETS DOWN FROM AMY. THEY would cut costs by splitting the bill of a taxi whenever they were invited to a party. They used Iqbal regularly, and he gave them a discount, so they went everywhere with him.

He met Zayna at Amy's house. She reminded him of an older version of the woman he had loved, nay adored. She even used the same word as her: roohi, my spirit. Nobody could ever replace her though. There was a song he had once heard called "Only A Few" by a singer named Kirtala Issouna. It became his anthem when the love of his life left him. He listened to the song over and over on replay, and when it played at restaurants, malls, or on taxi radio stations, it gave him goosebumps. There was a verse in particular that resonated for him:

> *There's a kind of love that comes once, only once*
> *And only a few of us get to experience it*
> *But if it leaves, if it has to go*
> *Then only a few truly know grief*

The simplicity of the words, the depth of feeling, and the way it resurrected her in his mind made him miss her more, if possible. But mostly, it reminded him he would never be with her again, something he had learned to accept. Mike had gotten used to her absence. What scared him was losing his yearning for her, because holding onto the pain meant she still lived inside him, where she belonged.

Nobody had been able to distract him from missing her, apart from Zayna. She was a blessing. He enjoyed her company, and it helped they were both attracted to each other. Zayna's husband had married a second wife. Mike couldn't do that to a woman, even if it was halal.

"Can we meet?" Zayna asked him.

"For real? What about your husband?"

"It's over. I divorced him. I'm single. He has no other wife either. We ruined him. On the same night."

"Hey, slow down. I don't know what you're saying." He listened as she explained everything to him. "You both divorced him on the same night? How twisted. I still can't get over how easy it is to get a divorce here."

"It's easy if the man agrees. And I made sure he took me to the divorce court first. He can take her later this week for all I care."

"This makes no sense to me. You've been married for ages. You have three sons. And you got divorced in one day? He didn't even put up a fight or use his power as a man to make you wait?"

"He tried his best, but had no choice. He knew I was serious. We stayed awake the entire night. Not one wink of sleep. When I spoke to my father, Mohammed knew it was over."

"What about your sons? Weren't they shocked?" He had heard about how easy it was to get a divorce here, but didn't that apply to couples without children? Though he was happy she'd left her husband, it scared Mike she was unaffected, almost callous.

"Whether we gave them time to think or not, they would be shocked. But before we went to court, we had breakfast with them, and I explained how everything changed between us when he took another wife. I told them I would cut off their balls if any of them ever took more than one wife."

"Ouch. You said that in front of your husband?"

"Yes. My ex-husband. And my eldest son Raed said I was doing the right thing in getting a divorce."

"What a great guy."

"Raed isn't afraid of Mohammed. Actually, Mohammed is afraid of Raed. My son even went to court with us and held my hand in the judge's office. He said he was proud of me for taking a stand for all women. Out loud. In front of the bearded judge."

A FEW HOURS LATER, ZAYNA WAS IN HIS APARTMENT. They sat on the couch facing the television. He turned the television on.

"No, please turn it off. I want to sit with you without any distractions."

Mike took what she said as a cue to being intimate, so he moved closer to her. "I want to kiss you so badly, Z."

"Look, I know the first time you met me I had taken off the hijab to go to the barbecue with you guys. But that was a spur-of-the-moment kind of thing. It was a big mistake, and I regret it. I even felt guilty talking to you while I was married. And I don't want to increase my feelings of guilt. I'm still a traditional woman. Sorry, I'm rambling."

"You once told me you wanted to remove the hijab, remember? Your mom made you wear it."

"Yes, but it's a part of me. I kind of feel naked without it. I mean I wish it hadn't been imposed on me, don't get me wrong, but it's too late."

"I understand, babe."

"I'm sorry I can't kiss you now. I want to, but I won't kiss a man I'm not married to. I'm not asking for marriage, but that's just who I am."

"I totally get it," Mike said, disappointed. He had wanted to make sure they were sexually compatible before committing to anything serious, but he would have to trust their chemistry.

THE NEXT FEW WEEKS, MIKE AND ZAYNA SPENT ALL their free time together. Amy had assured him Zayna would marry him, and he was waiting for the right time to propose. It had to be romantic. It was local tradition to ask the family for permission, but he wanted a private engagement with her first. Mike would broach the subject with her, then find the right location to get down on his knees.

"Zayna, I know this is fast, but I'm serious about you," he said, one night after they had dinner at his apartment. "But would your family ever approve of us?"

"Mike, I'm not young. I have three sons and am a divorced woman. They'd practically throw me on you." Zayna laughed. "They won't like that you're younger than me, but they won't stand in our way. The best part is that you converted before you met me. So they'll know you're serious about the faith. And Raed promised to have my back. He's happy for me."

"He knows about us?"

"Yes. Since my divorce we've gotten closer. Raed's my rock. He wants me to live my life without thinking of society."

"Wow. That's shocking. Your son?"

"He's all about women's empowerment. He's more of a feminist than any woman you'll meet. Raed can't wait to meet you. But I told him to wait."

"I liked the sound of him when he said you were doing the right thing divorcing Mohammed. Cool guy. You raised him well."

"Trust me, he didn't get these ideas from me. I don't know how he turned out like that with a religious father and submissive mother."

"You're not submissive. You left your husband."

"Yeah, but I grew my wings after he married Lina. Trust me, I was a meek wife. You can't even imagine the hell I go through as a woman. It's refreshing to meet a man who lets me be myself. Thank you."

"Don't thank me. I wish we could blend our cultures together. It would be the right mix. Our kids can have the best of both worlds."

"Oh my love. You want kids with me? I'm kind of old."

"Science, my love. Science and technology. Or we can adopt. If you don't want kids, that's fine too. I just want you to be happy, kids or no kids. We don't even have to discuss this. It's not an issue for me. Your decision."

"Why are you so perfect? I can't wait for you to meet my parents."

"I can't wait either. When do you think is a good time?"

"Let's wait until my divorce waiting period is over. I'll tell them I met you at a parent-teacher conference at Isa's school."

She was the right woman. Not the one, but the right one for him. Their relationship was rushed, but Mike was relaxed. He squeezed her hand, and she moved it away abruptly. Mike apologized, but she smiled warmly at him. They met every day, until the weeks became months and an official engagement was approaching.

"HELLO, MIKE."

She said she had gotten a divorce a couple of months before. She explained how she had turned into a typical local during her marriage. She even underwent a procedure to sew her hymen so her husband didn't know she wasn't a virgin. Aisha spoke of her daughter Dania, and how her husband had turned out to be gay. She made him swear he would not tell anyone because her husband's father was one of the richest, most famous men, locally and around the globe. She confessed she had been in touch with an ex of hers right after the divorce, but he broke her heart by taking revenge on her for the way she left him in the past. He was the guy she dated after Mike and before her marriage. She begged Mike not to do the same if he took her back. Aisha added she had stopped drinking after they had broken up but had started again after her divorce. She spoke of a friend named Salma, whom she deceived with her chaste alter ego. Hopefully, you can meet her one day, Aisha told him, but you have to pretend we just met.

"I'm sorry I left," she said. "I know now that money isn't

everything. I don't know what else to say, Mike."

"You don't know what to say? You call me out of the blue after all these years? Oh, hello Mike. Um, well, I wanted to let you know that after I left you, I met a guy, but we broke up, then I married another guy, who turned out to be gay, so I went back to that guy that I met after you again. And guess what? He ditched me and now I realize I want you. Go to hell Aisha. I'm sorry. But I won't let you play me again."

"Mike, I'm here now. Don't let your pride get between us. It was a bumpy ride finding myself back to you, but I know you still love me. I can feel it."

"When did this ex of yours, not your husband, the other one, leave you?"

"D-d-day b-b-before yesterday." She was blubbering. Why was he being cruel when he had been waiting for this moment? But how could Aisha go back to another ex after leaving her husband? Why wasn't he first on her list?

"Man, you're cold. You jump from one guy to another like it's a game. How can you say he's out of your system? Are you insane? You don't get over someone who breaks your heart that fast, especially since he was an ex. It seems you're more affected by your breakup with him than your divorce. And, remember, you wanted him when your marriage fell apart, not me. You're back to me now 'cause he dumped your ass."

"No, Mike. I just needed to see him one more time. Please give me a chance. No man has ever treated me better than you. You're good for me."

"You think you can come running back to me because I was good to you?"

"Let's meet tonight. We were meant to be. After all these years, I still feel for you."

"Yeah, but you felt that for the guy you went back to right after your divorce. Who's after me? Another ex?'

"I could've not mentioned I had gone to another guy first. I'm an idiot to have thought my honesty would be appreciated."

"Oh, you're really good at turning things around, aren't you?"

THE NEXT NIGHT THEY WENT OUT TO DINNER. THEY MET at a Chinese restaurant Mike suggested.

"Sorry. It's not elegant, but you wanted a low-profile place. A teacher I work with suggested it," he said when they sat down at the table.

"I don't care. I'm just glad to see you. It's been way too long."

"Too long." He held her hand across the table, but she looked around nervously and gently moved her hand away. They caught up, ordered food, and Mike couldn't take his eyes off her. He was afraid she'd disappear if he looked away.

"You look different."

"Well, I got my teeth fixed. Veneers. And my acne's under control. Laser."

"You're beautiful the way you are. You don't need to fix anything."

"Whatever."

He blurted out his upcoming engagement to Zayna.

"Seriously? Two women during their divorce waiting periods? What are the chances?" She was smiling.

"Yeah. Synchronicity."

"May I?" she asked gesturing toward his plate. He

nodded. She leaned over toward his plate and poured soy sauce on a prawn dumpling. Aisha used her chopsticks to eat it. Then, she dabbed a napkin on her mouth.

"Aren't you just a little bit jealous. Can't you at least pretend to be?"

"I don't want to get in the way of your future again. If this girl's the right one for you…"

They sat facing each other in silence. He had no appetite. Aisha was slurping her tom yum soup. The restaurant was dim. There were red paper lanterns hanging from the ceiling. The air-conditioning was on full blast. He shivered.

"Are you cold babe?" Aisha asked.

"No."

She was looking at him. She bent down and fumbled in her oversized purse. She took out a pashmina shawl. "Here."

"No thanks," he said, self-consciously.

"Oh come on, Mike. Nobody's here." He took the fuchsia shawl and wrapped it around his shoulders. It smelled of *oud*. "So what're you going to do?"

"There's only you," he said, as he inhaled her fragrance. The waiter brought them a hot plate of sizzling shredded chicken and jasmine rice.

"Are you sure? Don't you need time to think?"

"You were sure about us on the phone yesterday. Do you have cold feet?" He put chicken and rice on Aisha's plate.

"I didn't know you were engaged."

"It's not official yet."

"Yeah, but it's a serious relationship. I don't want to wreck anyone's relationship."

"I've waited for this frickin' moment for ages. I can't be with her now that you're back. But you have to promise me you've thought this through. I don't want my heart broken again."

"Babe, as soon as the *idda* is over we can get married. I wouldn't have come back." She was devouring the food on her plate. The girl could eat. "Aren't you having any chicken?"

"I had a heavy lunch." He was biting his fingers.

"What's wrong?"

"I'm scared. Why do we have to wait?"

"Oh come Mike. We're having dinner together after a bloody long time. Can't we enjoy ourselves?"

"You brought this up yesterday. I'm just carrying on where we left off. We need to discuss this. I'm not doing it the other way round. Look what happened last time. Let's lay all our cards on the table. Then I can relax."

"I promised Hussam I wouldn't tell our families the truth about why we got divorced. If I suddenly introduce you, they'll think you were the reason. It'll look like the marriage fell apart because of me."

"Am I crazy to put all of my trust on you again?"

"There's a woman in between us. I don't want to get involved until I'm sure you're not in a relationship with her. I'm not telling you to leave her. But you need to think carefully about what you want. It's your future. I want what's best for you and so should you."

Aisha asked for the bill. She told the waiter she would pay in cash. Aisha couldn't drop him back to his apartment because she was meeting Salma. He was still wearing the shawl when he got home. But he could no longer smell her traditional perfume. It smelled of garlic.

———

THE NEXT NIGHT MIKE INVITED ZAYNA OUT FOR DINNER. He was afraid to take her to his apartment. At a restaurant, even a secluded one, Zayna couldn't shout.

They ordered dessert, and Mike waited until after his second spoon of tiramisú to say he couldn't be with her anymore. He told her he thought he wanted to get married but he can't. It's too much pressure for him.

"We don't have to get married now, Mike. I can wait for as long as you want."

"I don't ever want to get married," he lied.

"I don't understand. What happened?" Zayna was scratching her eyebrow. She got up, adjusted her abaya, and sat back down.

"I can't do this. Please forgive me. I wasn't thinking straight, Z."

Zayna patted the corner of her eyes with a red-and-white checkered napkin.

"Do you need time away from me to think about it?"

"I'm sorry. This isn't working."

He leaned over across the table to touch her arm, but she pulled it away. She took off her hijab, dangling it before him.

"Is this what you want? I'll take it off. This is who you were interested in when we met, right? Me without the hijab?" She threw it on him.

"Z. This has nothing to do with the hijab. Please, put it back on." He handed her headscarf back and she put it back on, quivering.

"So, it's over? Just like that? Tell me you're not serious. Please. Is this your idea of a sick joke? You asked to marry me. What happened?" She waited, but he said nothing. "Is there someone else?"

He looked at her without saying a word.

"I need to know. It's the least you can do. Tell me."

"No."

"You're lying. Tell me the truth. There's no other explanation. Tell me."

"Yes," he whispered.

"What?"

"I said yes, Z. Yes."

"Oh Mike. No. Do you love her?"

He nodded. He cupped his head in his hands.

When he raised his head, mascara was running down Zayna's face. Her cheeks were red. He cared deeply for her, but nothing mattered to him more than being with Aisha.

She asked for the bill, and though she usually insisted on paying or they'd split the bill, when the waiter came to their table, she gestured toward him and walked away.

Then she walked back toward him.

"If you ever, and I mean ever, try to get in touch with me again, I'll cut it all off," she said as she gestured toward his private parts. "Do you understand, you son of a dog?"

Mike took out his wallet and paid the bill.

He called Aisha as soon as he was in a taxi and told her he was single.

"That was fast."

"It wasn't fast enough for me. I love you."

"Can I come over?"

"Please do, my love."

———

AISHA HAD AN OVERNIGHT SUITCASE WITH HER.

"I'm spending the night at Salma's," she said.

"Oh, Salma knows?"

"Of course not. I told Salma I was spending the night at a feminist lecturer's house. I made up a project we are working on and said we would be up late and I didn't want to drive back home. And I told her to pretend I was at her house. I'm still using the angel alter-ego on Salma."

"You *are* an angel, Aisha. You're my angel. It's who you are inside here that matters." He touched her breastbone. "What you do and who you sleep with has nothing to do with your heart." He pressed his ear to her chest to listen to her heartbeat.

"I lie all the time, Mike. My whole life has been a lie."

"Aisha, I love you for you. I want you to know you can be yourself with me. You don't need to lie to me."

"Thank you. I missed this. I missed you."

Aisha spoke on and on about how she would cover her tracks when she went back home.

"Tomorrow, I'll tell Salma we finished the project. Then I'll go to her house for lunch and ask her to spend the night at my place. That way if we walk in together, it would look even more credible to my parents."

She was caressing his hair now.

———

THOUGH THEY SPOKE ON THE PHONE A LOT, HE DIDN'T know when he would see Aisha and it frustrated him. It's the quality, not the quantity, she reminded him. She also warned him not to call her first because she slept in the room with her daughter at her parents' house. Since the divorce, Dania couldn't sleep by herself.

"I have a trip coming up," she said. "We can be together an entire weekend. It's for a book launch. I'm excited because I paid extra to have a private Q&A session with the author."

"That sounds amazing. A one-on-one?"

"Not exactly. It's a VIP meet and greet package, so who-ever paid for it can attend. I asked the organizer, and seven people have registered so far."

Though Mike had a master's degree and was a teacher, Aisha's knowledge impressed him. She was a voracious reader. And even though she only had a high school diploma, she was intelligent and he learned a lot from her. He was excited to join her on this trip.

Aisha had booked a first-class ticket, and he was flying economy. He would stay at another hotel upon arrival.

"Your hotel is on the other side of town. Stay with me," Aisha said.

"OK, but let's split the room bill. I can pay you back in a couple of weeks."

"Roohi. Don't worry about it. Just cancel your reservation."

The hotel lobby was stunning. But Mike couldn't enjoy the beauty of the gilded walls, black-and-white marble floors, and pink champagne-colored chandeliers because Aisha paid for everything, including tips for their personal butler, the concierge, and the porter. Still, he was willing to trade in his discomfort for a life with her.

"Aisha, how can I afford this when we get married?" he asked her when they were sitting on a plush purple velvet sofa in the hotel lobby waiting for their car. He put his arm around her, but she got up and moved away, facing him on a fluorescent green plexiglass stool.

"Don't touch me in public. Someone could see us."

"We're out of town."

"I lost count of how many times I've bumped into

relatives or people I know here. Everyone flies out here for the weekend."

"Isn't that stool uncomfortable? Come sit here. I won't touch you."

Her phone rang. She walked away, then waved at Mike to get his attention, and he trailed her to the entrance of the hotel. She went through the revolving door, and he followed her. It was humid outside. The driver opened the door for Aisha while Mike walked to the opposite side of the car. The driver came rushing behind him and opened the door for him.

The car was spacious inside. The interior was soft beige leather. And there were footstools, two television screens and bottles of expensive water. He picked up a bottle of water. It was room temperature, so he put it back in its place.

"You want cold water?" Aisha asked. Mike cringed at how Aisha had read his mind. He watched her open a compartment and take out a bottle of water. It was chilled. He opened the water and drank it in three gulps. He was thirsty when he was nervous.

"This is too much for me. This car has a frickin' fridge in it." His eyes widened.

"It's a cooler, not a fridge, dummy."

"Same difference, silly."

He fidgeted in his chair. Aisha told him to adjust the seat if he wasn't comfortable. The seats were reclining, she informed him.

"No thanks. I'm fine. Just excited." He had no idea which button to press. Instead, he reached for a magazine. Aisha turned on a light for him. He flipped through it and put it back in the car-seat magazine holder.

"I'm excited too, Mike. I want to travel all over the world with you."

"With me, you'll be riding on a camel. Or a motorbike, if I get a promotion."

"Camels can be more expensive than motorbikes."

"Yeah, true. God, I love you so much. But I need to know we're going to get through this hurdle."

"What hurdle baby?"

"Can you love a pauper this time around?"

"I don't need your money. Keep it for yourself. I'll take care of us. You know what? I'm tired of depending on my family. I want to start my own business."

"What do you want to do?"

"I'm not sure yet. But I need to stand on my own feet for once. I mean, I can start with all the money I've been getting from my parents and Hussam, but I want to do my own thing."

"I feel bad. Like I'm mooching off of you."

"If it were the other way round, you'd be taking care of me. That's love. And I don't want to be a part of a patriarchal system where the man is financially responsible for everything. That's what's making you feel uncomfortable."

"I don't know. It's more than that. I don't want any part of you to feel I'm a burden."

"I can afford four of you," she laughed. She pressed a switch, and Mike watched a screen go up in front of him. In the movies, that was when a character wanted to avoid the gaze of a driver. Aisha squeezed his hand and kissed it. "Look, I'm here for a book launch of a famous feminist. I don't want to be a hypocrite anymore. I don't need a man to pay for me."

"What did I do to deserve you?"

"No. What did *I* do to deserve *you*?"

"I could sleep on a mattress on the floor in a ghetto with you and feel like a king."

"Well, when we're married, I'll show you what it feels like to be a real king. I was too paranoid to buy you a first-class ticket this time because I didn't want you to sit next to me."

"Are you kidding me? You don't have to justify that. I've never even flown business my entire life. We can travel economy together. I don't care which class we're on as long as we're together."

"Well, I care. Economy? Me?"

They laughed.

"I hate talking about money. It gives me anxiety," Mike said.

"I don't want you to make a fuss each time I spend on you. Hussam is richer than me. He spoiled me. And I let him. Won't you let me spoil you?"

"You were still from a rich family. I'm not."

"Let go of your conditioning. I know you're not with me for money. So relax and enjoy the ride."

Aisha was right. It was the patriarchy that made him uncomfortable. And he loved her for her. Most importantly, Aisha was as desperate to get married as he was. What else mattered?

AFTER THEY RETURNED FROM THE TRIP, AISHA CHOSE an expensive Japanese restaurant and insisted on paying, and Mike was no longer ashamed he wasn't rich. And on their next date, he took her to a coffee shop where they ate sandwiches. He paid.

Now, all he was waiting for was her post-divorce period to end. He couldn't wait to spend the rest of his life with the woman of his dreams.

12

MESHARY

"It's hard to come by people you value a lot."
—Martha Unaida

"Hello, Meshary."

He would recognize her voice if she were calling from the moon.

He listened to her go on and on about her life after their relationship had ended and how she had never stopped thinking about him. Aisha told him she had a daughter and she wished Dania were his.

"Hussam, the son of Abdul-Aziz Salama, is gay?" Meshary asked her.

He had seen photos of Hussam on the night of Aisha's wedding in newspapers but wouldn't have ever suspected it.

"Yes. But please don't mention it to anyone. His father knew before we got married, but he wants to keep a low profile."

Was Aisha telling the truth about Hussam? She was the best liar he had ever known.

"Why are you calling me? I don't get it."

"I got a divorce yesterday. Imagine that, Meshary, yesterday. And all I could think of was being with you. You can't imagine how much I missed you. You're the only man I ever loved."

"Look, I'm over you," he lied. "It took all of me to move on, but you can't call me after all this time and expect things to go back to the way they were. I would've had ten children with you, even if I couldn't afford it, but all you cared about was money."

"You don't know how much pressure women face here. We're expected to marry into the same status or higher. I couldn't bring shame to them by—"

"Shame? Was I shameful to you? You're such an arrogant person. And since when do feminists listen to society and marry within their so-called status? You're a hypocrite." Meshary hung up on her. She called right back.

AISHA CALLED HIM EVERY DAY FOR TWO WEEKS. SHE begged him to take her back.

"Meshary, how long is life? If we're both still in love, this is worth it."

Nobody was more straightforward than Aisha. He liked that about her. She didn't hide her feelings and gave him the courage to express his own. But he couldn't profess his love for her.

"Are you deluded? Who said I'm in love with you?"

"Aren't you?"

"No. I'm not."

"Look. I'm going to ask you one more time. If you say no, I promise you won't hear from me, and I'll move on. So here it goes: Are you in love with me?"

"Yes, dammit." He took a deep breath. "Yes. Now what?"

"Now, it's you and me. Let's not let this go. Ever."

"Why didn't you get in touch with me?"

"I was married. I had a new life. You were a reminder of my old life. Drinking, partying. I left all that behind. And I didn't want to cheat on Hussam."

"Why wouldn't you want to marry a guy who didn't care where you've been or what the heck you do? I didn't give a damn."

"I was selfish, materialistic. Hussam fit the bill."

"If you hadn't found out he was gay, would you have stayed with him?"

"Yes, I would've. I'm not going to lie. But this is why I'm so desperate to be with you. I won't settle again. I want you."

"Come show me how much you want me."

And that was it. He was back with Aisha.

MESHARY HAD FIRST MET AISHA YEARS BEFORE AT THE parking lot of his university.

"Is this your car?" she had asked him.

"Yes."

"I'm sorry. Look, I hit the bumper."

There was no dent, just a tiny scratch. "Oh, come on. I don't see anything. Don't worry about it."

"I left my number on the windscreen. Get in touch and I'll pay for the damages."

"What damages? It's nothing paint can't fix. And why were you waiting here if you left your number?" Meshary asked her.

"I didn't wait that long."

"Really?"

"You love questions, don't you?"

"Isn't that a question?"

"Behave."

Meshary wasn't attracted to Aisha, but he was intrigued by her boldness and asked her out right away, confident she would agree. Women rarely turned him down, and he was certain from the way she was eying him that Aisha wouldn't.

"Let's have coffee," he suggested.

"Only if you don't interrogate me further."

"Can I ask about you?"

"Maybe. Oh and this is a big deal for me. I don't like to be seen in public with guys. But you make me want to make an exception. I like you. Yeah, this is like at first sight for me…"

At the coffee shop, Meshary found out she was on campus to attend a lecture on feminism and tradition.

"You don't want to go to college?" he asked.

"You make it sound like a crime."

"You were at a lecture, so I thought you were interested in education."

"I am interested in education. I don't need a degree to prove that. I can afford not to work."

"Oh, Baba pays your bills," he sneered.

MESHARY WASN'T INTERESTED IN MEETING UP WITH HER again. Her arrogance repelled him. But she called him the following week.

"Are you ghosting me, Meshary?"

"Hi Aisha. Look. I'm sorry. I'm busy with my studies. I'll call you later."

"I can distract you."

Meshary had never dated a girl who wore the hijab. He was afraid to approach veiled girls on campus. There was one, Dana, in his accounting class who was stunning, but he had tried to speak to her once. She turned away from him and said she was there to study not socialize. Most of the guys in his class had tried to approach Dana, and she rejected each of them, one by one.

But Dana was an exception. He was used to girls pursuing him. All of his friends were jealous because they'd faced plenty of rejection, but Meshary never had trouble with the opposite sex. He was a handsome young man, as his mother kept telling him. Girls his age were interested in money, but even the rich girls made an exception for Meshary. A friend called him a ladies' man because Meshary had one woman after another. He was irresistible to them.

"WHERE DO YOU WANT TO GO, AISHA? A PRIVATE PLACE?"

"Yes, please."

"My friend lets me use his family's chalet. Let me check if it's available. When do you want to meet?"

"The sooner, the better."

They spent all their free time together. Aisha was an animal. She even brought a sex toy to bed once and asked him to use it on her.

"Aren't I enough?"

"Yes, you are, my love. But it ain't a crime to spice things up."

ANOTHER TIME, AISHA HAD ASKED HIM TO MEET HER AT a coffee shop in a mall. He waited twenty minutes for her until he received a text from her: I'm the girl wearing the niqab across from you. Meshary looked up from his phone. Aisha was the lady in black sitting in the corner when he had entered the place. She was wearing an abaya, and her whole face was covered except for her eyes. And, I'm naked underneath, she added to the message. She fulfilled a fantasy he never knew he had. How could anyone compete with that?

It was the most memorable night. He was falling in love with her. And not just because of his physical attraction. She mentally stimulated him. Aisha taught him about literary feminism and was constantly buying books for him.

"AISHA, I LOVE YOU." IT WAS THE FIRST TIME HE HAD EVER said that to any woman he had dated. Meshary had called her during a lunch break at university because he couldn't wait until their date that evening to tell her.

"Oh, Meshary."

"Look, I know it's only been a few months, but I'm graduating soon. I'll get a job right away and propose to you. I have to go now. See you later."

"Wait, one more thing."

"Tell me."

"I love you too. Can't wait to see you tonight."

THAT NIGHT, AT HIS COUSIN'S APARTMENT, SHE SPOKE to him about her past. He teased her and said he now knew why she was good in bed. She told him her last serious relationship was with a foreigner. She hadn't been in love with him, but she liked being with him because he was different than locals. When he asked her what she meant by different, she told him he treated her with respect. Meshary insisted that she was stereotyping local men and that he was respectful of her, and Aisha retracted her statement and said that she'd had bad luck with local men, but agreed Meshary had changed her mind.

"Why'd you guys break up if he was good to you?"

"This feeling I have with you is what I've searched for my entire life. He was just a phase and on a string budget."

"Babe, you know I'm on a string budget too. And my dad's on a government salary."

"I could live in a hut with you, baby," she whispered in his ear.

WHEN MESHARY GRADUATED, HE FOUND A JOB AS A graphic designer. He applied to several prestigious firms before he graduated, and two companies were vying for him. He called Aisha to tell her he picked the one with a higher salary so he could support her.

"I can't live up to your standards, Aisha. Are you sure you want to marry me?"

"I couldn't marry anyone but you. My parents give me a monthly salary. It keeps increasing each year. And we can move in with my parents."

"We can get married in a few months, when my probation at work is over. It's for three months. But, I can propose now."

"I don't want to overwhelm you."

"Are you kidding me? I can't wait to meet your parents."

"I consider myself engaged to you. And you can meet my father when you sort out your finances. There's no rush, *habibi*."

"You're right, *habibti*."

"Remember how crazy I am about you. OK? No matter what happens. Even if we break up, for whatever reason, you're the one for me, the love of my life."

"Stop talking like that Aisha. You're scaring me."

"Life's unpredictable. I'm being realistic. Anything can happen."

"I said stop it. Say you love me."

"I know that even if I don't say it, you can feel it." Aisha sighed.

"Yes. I can. And that's why I'm the luckiest man alive." He looked up at the ceiling and silently mouthed thank you. "Gotta go now, my love. I'll call you tonight."

A FEW MONTHS LATER, AISHA BROKE UP WITH HIM BY text message. He had to read the message over and over again. She had written that they could not be together because of his financial status. He tried calling her, but she had blocked him from her email, phone, and social media. Meshary called her from various numbers, but she must have known it was him, because she ignored all his calls. He managed to get through to her, after months of trying, when he called her from overseas.

"Hello?"

"Aisha. I miss you. Please come back."

"Meshary, I'm engaged now. I wouldn't call back if I were you. Please move on with your life." And she hung up on him.

⸻

AND NOW, THEY WERE IN A RELATIONSHIP AGAIN. But could Aisha have changed? Was he making a mistake trusting her? Maybe she was bored. Or lonely. Or shell-shocked by her husband's sexuality. And even if she was serious about him, he was renting a cheap two-bedroom bachelor's apartment and had a secondhand car. She couldn't be with him after Hussam. She would leave again. It was best to dump her.

But he couldn't intentionally break her heart. She was a mother. Still, how could he forgive her? He cringed, recalling how his friends wouldn't even mention her name to him when she had broken up with him. How would they react when they found out he was talking to her again?

Meshary called his best friend Yaser.

"What do you mean you're back with her?"

"She got a divorce, and one thing led to another."

"Are you sure about this? She broke you last time."

"I'm not planning on staying with her. Are you crazy?" He told Yaser his plans to break Aisha's heart.

"Revenge is stupid, man. If you don't want her, what better revenge than telling her you don't? That way your conscience is clear, and she'll regret what she did to you. Simple."

"Thanks, buddy. But I know what I'm doing."

THREE WEEKS LATER, AFTER DAYS AND NIGHTS OF LOVE-making everywhere in his apartment except for the bathroom, Aisha came over with a small wheeled suitcase.

"I'm spending the night, baby. I told Salma to cover for me." She took off her hijab and hugged him, and he breathed in the watermelon fragrance of shampoo on her damp hair.

They walked straight to his bedroom.

"I thought she didn't know about us."

"She doesn't. She thinks I'm at a moderator's house. I'm glad she no longer attends these lectures since she's obsessed with spirituality now."

"What do you mean?" He was trying his best to pretend he was interested in what she was saying, but why couldn't they have sex and save the conversation for later?

"Well, she's into meditation and all that. I think it's a phase or a crisis. Anyway, Salma thinks I'm with a fellow feminist, and my parents think I'm with her. But here I am with you. Isn't this exciting?"

"It's not exciting. It actually scares me that you're still such a good liar. We even met on a lie. Remember? That whole innocent game about denting my car at the parking lot."

"That doesn't count. It was an excuse to meet you." Meshary watched her as she twisted a strand of her hair around her index finger. He had read that women do that when they are sexually frustrated. But how could she be frustrated when they have sex all the time? Why was every gesture of hers so beautiful? Why was he still in love with her?

"Were you stalking me that day? Come on, baby, you can tell me now that I'm yours." He grinned.

"I was at a lecture, right? And I had parked next to you. You caught my attention right away, and I had to talk to you, but I didn't have the courage. When the lecture was over, and I saw that your car was still there, I thought, hmm…I have to talk to this man. So I waited. And that's about it folks."

"And so you hit my car?"

"Lightly."

"Crazy woman."

"A girl's gotta do what a girl's gotta do."

"Come here, stalker."

Meshary kissed every part of Aisha's body. He spooned her as they slept.

IN THE MORNING, AFTER MESHARY BROUGHT HER BREAKfast in bed, they made love, and he took a shower. How could he leave her? Wouldn't he fall into depression again? Meshary had resisted taking medication after they broke up, but after cutting his wrists in the shower one night, there was no other way around it. He stayed on the pills for more than two years, until the psychiatrist weaned him off them.

"Aisha, wake up. Aisha." She had fallen asleep again, so he patted her cheek gently. She lifted her head off the pillow. He had a towel wrapped around his waist and his hair was wet. Aisha was looking at him seductively. Why was she such a nymphomaniac? He frowned at her.

"What happened, roohi? You seem upset."

"Get up and come to the living room." He walked away from her.

Ten minutes later, she came out of his room and sat next to him on the couch. She was wearing his bathrobe. He turned the television off and faced her.

"I can't do this anymore, Aisha. I took you back to get you out of my system. And I have. We're not the same standard. You're a low-class woman, even if you are richer than me and from a good family. Class has nothing to do with money. I deserve better than you."

"Are you kidding me?"

"No, I'm not."

"You can't be serious. I thought you had forgiven me. All this was a lie?"

"Maybe now you'll know what it feels like to be lied to."

"I didn't lie when I said I loved you. This is evil, spiteful."

"It takes an evil person to know one."

"Meshary, please get a grip on yourself."

"No. It's over. We're done. And if you want the number of a therapist, let me know. You're going to need one. Now get out of my face before I call the police and tell them a whore broke into my apartment."

"You're sick. And one day you'll regret this. Your pride is more important than love."

"I guess we have more in common than we think. And I don't love you anymore. You're going to be alone for the rest of your life."

"No, I'm not. I have another man who loved me before Hussam too, even before you. I'll call him now. He'll take me back in an instant."

"Listen to yourself, you messed up woman. What are you, an ex collector? We're not toys you can play with and throw away."

"You're the only one I have ever loved. Hussam was security, and Mike—a security blanket. Nothing more."

"Mike, huh? Is that the name of your victim? A foreigner? Let's see how long that lasts. He's an idiot if he takes you back. I bet you're not going to tell him you chose me first."

"Of course I'll tell him. He was never judgmental."

"What makes you think this guy isn't married or has moved on or still lives here? Have you been in touch with him?"

"No. I haven't. But, I'll try…And if not him, there are plenty of other fish in the sea. I'm a fool to have thought you were the one for me."

Though the idea of her with another man made him sick to his stomach, she must be bluffing. She was trying to make him jealous and it was working. He couldn't breathe. But watching her sob now, the way he had, strengthened his resolve. Now it was her turn to carry shock around with her. He couldn't even be around people for a while after Aisha had left him. Meshary wouldn't ever obsess about her again. He was over her. At last.

Aisha got up and walked to the bedroom. He followed her. She picked up her clothes from the floor, and put them on. She had such a great body. Maybe he could touch her one last time. Aisha was wearing red-soled nude designer heels, black-and-white trousers, and a denim trench-coat.

Her style was unique. And Meshary had developed an appreciation for fashion after meeting her. He watched as she kneeled on the floor and neatly packed her lingerie and toiletry bag. When Aisha stood up, she held the arch of her back and stretched for a few seconds. Then she bent over again, fumbled through her suitcase, found a safety pin and secured her hijab with it. She was now crying uncontrollably. She walked out of his room. Click click click. There was silence. Was she coming back? Then the sound of her heels, once again, and squeaky wheels across his living room floor.

The door slammed shut. Who would marry her again?

He picked up the phone and called his best friend Amy.

13

AMY

"Because when you have an unfulfilled dream,
sometimes your lifestyle changes as a result."
—Hassan Malhib

Amy liked Meshary. She had met him when a female colleague, Tina, invited her to a party at his apartment. At the party Amy and Meshary clicked right away. They spent the whole night talking to each other, but it was purely platonic. She had found a new friend. The day before his next party, Amy wanted to take Mike with her, so she asked Meshary if she could bring a guy with her. He told her if the guy was her boyfriend or husband he didn't mind, but he preferred not to have single men at his parties. She told him he was just a friend, so Meshary said it was better to come alone. He said single men always hit on his female friends and it was uncomfortable. In time, Amy noticed there were many single men at the parties, but they were all Meshary's friends. Maybe he didn't want his friends to have competition hooking up with the single women at his parties, she thought.

AND NOW, A COUPLE OF YEARS INTO THEIR FRIENDSHIP, they were in Meshary's bedroom after a party. She had spent the night many times at his place, but they had never been intimate with each other, nor did they even sleep in the same room. He had never even tried to kiss her, and she respected him for his decency and chivalry. Meshary had a guest room, and Amy left her razors, pajamas, underwear, and toothbrush there. He called it her room.

MESHARY WAS LYING ON HIS BACK WITH HIS ARM COVER-ing his eyes. He was slurring his words and kept spacing out mid-sentence.

"So wait," Amy said, "You loved this girl ages ago, but she dumped you and then got married? Then she came back to you a day after her divorce? And you dumped her less than a month later?" She'd had too much to drink that night and nausea was building up in her throat.

"Yup."

"Why did you keep all this a secret from me while it was happening?"

"I didn't think I had to tell you. And I guess I didn't want to make a big deal about it, because I knew I was going to ditch her." She watched Meshary take his shirt off and throw it on the floor. Then he took off his jeans and got into his bed in his boxer shorts.

"That's brutal, Meshary."

"Yeah. Well, this girl is brutal. We made a good team."

"Wow. You can be callous with women, you know?"

"Go to sleep, Amy. Can you turn my lights off? And don't forget to turn off the lights in the corridor on the way to your room. Good night." Meshary pulled the covers over himself.

THE NEXT DAY, AMY WOKE UP WITH THE WORST HEADache ever. It was four in the afternoon. She walked to the television room.

Meshary was sitting on the couch, draped in a blanket. She could tell he was hung-over too.

"Let's eat, Amy. I'm starving. Do you need to go home?"

"No."

They sat in the living room eating leftover Chinese noodles Meshary had found in his fridge. She asked him who the lucky girl was, but he said he didn't feel like discussing her. Amy had learned during her first year in the country that local men refrained from mentioning girls' names. It was her. Or my wife or my girlfriend. Or the woman. Or the mother of the children. They spent the next hour talking about 'her', but it was challenging for Amy to understand the nature of his ex, because Meshary was guarded.

TO AMY, MESHARY AND MIKE WERE LIVING IN A SOAP opera. Meshary had taken revenge on his mystery woman, but instead of feeling vindicated, he seemed distracted, almost regretful. And Mike had left Zayna for his ex, Aisha. When she pressed them for more information regarding their girlfriends, they both seemed enigmatic, as though they were leaving significant details out. She once asked Meshary about his girl's ex-husband and why she had gotten a divorce, and he said it wasn't important. Of course it was important, she thought. It said a lot about the girl's character. Was it her fault? Had she cheated on her husband? Did he cheat on her? It also spoke volumes about whether she loved Meshary. If her husband had left her or was abusive, then Meshary may just be a backup. Mike was also secretive. He told her he swore to Allah that he would never mention the reason of Aisha's divorce to anyone.

Though Amy had never met Aisha, since she had been living back home the first time Mike had dated her and because he was not ready to introduce them now, she was wary of meeting her. Mike deserved better. Aisha would probably break his heart again.

She had never even seen a photo of Aisha, and she wondered what Meshary's nameless lover looked like. It was strange that her two best friends were both excluding her from their personal lives.

When they spoke of their lovers, they made her nostalgic for love and marriage. Growing up, she had dreamed of a white wedding like many of her friends back home. There was one serious boyfriend in college, Larry, but they broke up because he proposed to her in a restaurant filled with people and she said no. You could've pretended to say yes, he had told her on the way back home. But you broke my heart *and* embarrassed me.

She had been waiting to settle down her whole life. But they had only been dating for a few months. Larry had told her it was an engagement, not a marriage. They could stay engaged for two years, even three, four if she wanted. Amy still said no. Five? Please Larry.

Was she in love with him? Yes. Was she attracted to him? Yes. Could she spend the rest of her life with him? Yes. But that night, after chocolate fondue and three shots of limoncello, she said no. She had regretted it later, but Larry had moved on. Why couldn't they have stayed together as boyfriend and girlfriend for a few more years? If he loved her, he would've waited, right? Maybe he thought if she loved him, she would've said yes.

And now, lost in Mike and Meshary's love stories, Amy fantasized about Larry more than ever.

But even amidst Mike and Meshary's dramas, Amy was mostly concerned for Zayna. It was becoming a challenge to console her. Once she had called Amy in the middle of the night. Amy was awake because she had just come home from a party.

"Who is she? Please tell me," Zayna begged.

"Look, Z. I'm in an uncomfortable position. Mike's a friend. I can't talk about his personal life with you." It was late. Amy was tired.

"Please, Amy. I beg you. I won't tell him you told me. I swear."

"I don't mind you venting about him, and I want to listen to everything you say and be here for you. But I don't want to discuss who he's dating. I would protect your secrets too."

"It's not a secret. You know he admitted it to me. Is she a local?"

"Z, please don't do this. I can't betray him."

Zayna sighed. "I understand. I've never experienced

this feeling before. Mohammed was a husband to me, and I became obsessed with him, but with Mike, it was different."

Tears rolled down Amy's cheeks. "It's called love. I gotta go now, but I'll call you back in the morning. I'm here for you every step of the way. Love you."

"You're such a good friend, Amy. Love you more."

THE NEXT MORNING, AMY CALLED ZAYNA AGAIN TO check on her.

"Why don't we go shopping or watch a movie?" Amy asked.

"Can I come over? I feel like chatting."

"Sure."

Zayna stayed for an hour, talking about Mike and how much she missed him. When Zayna was in the bathroom, her phone, which she had left in the living room, rang.

"Who is it?" Zayna yelled from behind the closed door.

"It says Salma."

"Oh, don't answer. I'll call her in a bit."

Zayna came out of the bathroom. Amy watched her dial a number.

She spoke in Arabic. She picked up a few words she understood: *Inshallah. Habibti.*

When Zayna hung up, she told her Salma asked her for the phone number of her tailor.

"After my divorce from her uncle, she finds random excuses to call me. Such a sweet girl. I think she wants me to feel I'm still a part of the family."

"Oh, that's the girl you told me about once, right? The so-called free one?" Amy asked.

"Yeah. That's her," Zayna said. "Anyway, thanks for inviting me over. I needed this. Where's my bag?" Zayna glanced around the room.

"I don't think you had a bag when you came in."

"Are you sure? God, my memory sucks lately."

"Well, you've got a lot on your mind."

"You can say that again." Zayna hugged Amy.

"You don't have to leave."

"I know. But I'm tired. I want to go home and take a nap."

"Well, come over every day if you want."

"I wish the world had more people like you."

AMY LISTENED TO MESHARY RANT ABOUT HIS EX-WITH-out-a-name again. One minute, he would speak highly of her, and the next moment he was infuriated by her.

"So what're you going to do?"

"I'm going to take her back."

"If you still love her, why did you throw her out?"

"I wanted to take revenge on her. Then I changed my mind. I behaved irrationally."

"Well, good luck, crazy boy."

"Thanks. I'm going to need it. I'll call her after dropping you home."

"Wow. You must really love this woman."

A FEW DAYS LATER, MESHARY'S NAME FLASHED ON THE screen of Amy's mobile phone.

"Well?" Amy asked.

"She never wants to see me again. She went back to

another ex."

"Oh well. It wasn't meant to be."

"You don't know this girl. She loves money. She'll leave him. I'll wait for her."

"She sounds materialistic. And she's already with another guy. Is that the kind of women you want to end up with?"

"She told me she would go back to him when I dumped her, but I didn't take her seriously."

"I'm sorry. I don't know what to say."

Amy had expected Meshary's ex-girlfriend not to take him back, but was surprised she was already in a relationship with another man. She felt sorry for the other ex this girl was dating. She was probably using him as a rebound. And would she go back to Meshary? She was determined to help Meshary out of his predicament, even though the girl sounded unstable, jumping from one ex to another. They must have a strong connection if they were still holding on to each other. And she wanted Meshary to be happy.

Maybe she was judging his ex harshly. Wasn't she acting like a hypocrite since she had broken Larry's heart and had tried to get back together with him? He had been polite when she reached out to him, but he told her he was engaged and it wouldn't be fair to his fiancée if they stayed in touch. She should be blessing Meshary's union with his ex. At least she could live vicariously through them now. Their story was giving her hope, even if it was false hope.

"Say anything. I'm dying here."

"Look, I'm not exactly a fan of your story. The girl sounds unstable. And so do you, when it comes to her, but this time *you* messed it up, not her."

"What do I do, Amy?"

"Fight for her."

"How?"

"Keep calling her. Don't give up. Send her significant songs, messages professing your undying love. Women love that shit. Tell her you guys are even now. Be honest with her. She's hurt, but it's a good sign she hasn't blocked you."

THE NEXT WEEK MESHARY CALLED AMY.

"We're back together."

"What the hell?"

"I fought for her, like you told me to. And I'm going to make her my wife."

"Wow. You're brave. Or stupid. Either way, I'm happy for you."

"Amy, I'm the love of her life. She admits she was materialistic. But she came back to me. We're even now. She's the love of my life too. I don't want to wait."

"Incredible. You guys adore each other."

"Well, she's still technically with her ex, but she's going to leave him."

"Poor ex."

"Well thanks to you, I got her back in time. She was going to get married. But she said she was never in love with the poor bugger."

"How dramatic. But I'm happy for you. And lucky girl, she had her ex-husband, you, and another guy all within a short period. I can't even find one guy to call my own."

Meshary and Amy laughed.

"How can I ever repay you, Amy? You have to meet her soon, but don't tell her you made it happen. I want her to think it was all me."

"It was destiny."

"Yeah, but I don't want her to know we discussed this."

"Your secret's safe with me," Amy promised him.

THE NEXT DAY SHE CALLED MIKE, BUT HIS PHONE WAS switched off. He called her back a week later.

"Sorry I took long to get back to you. I needed a break. I don't get it, Amy. We were getting along well. I even stopped worrying about our financial differences. I thought we made it. I don't get it."

"Oh no. Not Aisha again. Dammit Mike."

Why would Aisha leave Mike so abruptly? According to Mike, their relationship was solid this time around. How could she break Mike's heart again? Was Aisha a cruel woman? Was she cheating on Mike? Or maybe Aisha needed to have been with Mike one more time before ending it for good. She had a friend back home who had done the same thing. She was on and off with this guy until she broke up with him for good. Got him out of my system finally, she told Amy.

Mike was crying. It made her uncomfortable. Her mother had once told her she was extra-sensitive, and a psychic had explained she was an empath. Mike's pain became her pain. She started crying too.

"We were so close to getting married."

"What happened?"

"Out of the blue she said it wasn't working and she couldn't see us together."

"After all that?"

"She's messed up. I'm done with women. I'm such a fool."

"She's the fool. I can't imagine how awful this must be for you. Come over. I'll cook us dinner."

"Amy, the last thing I want to do is eat."

"OK, come by for a chat."

"I can't leave the house."

"I'm coming to you then."

SHE SPENT THE NEXT FEW NIGHTS WATCHING MOVIES with and cooking for Mike. He barely ate anything.

"I don't want to talk about her ever again, Ame." He had never called her Ame before. It was a nickname only Larry and her parents used.

"I never trusted that girl. I'm glad I never met her. I would go to her house and beat the living daylights out of her."

"I thought the first breakup was painful. But this time around is worse. I don't know if I can make it through."

"Time is a healer. I promise you. She'll regret it." Just like I did, she wanted to say.

"This is killing me. I can't even talk about her."

A FEW WEEKS LATER, AMY AND MIKE WERE WATCHING television at his apartment when Mike told her he was going back home.

"I hate it here. I want to leave this country." Mike was fidgeting with a box of tissues.

"You said you wanted to retire here."

"Not anymore."

"Mike, don't let Aisha change your life. This is home for you now. You can't leave because of her. You have a great career." Her ankle was throbbing. She ran on the treadmill earlier without warming up. Should she use an ice pack or warm water?

"This place has too many memories." He scratched his chin.

"All places do, Mike. Good and bad. It's the way things are."

"Well this place has too many memories. It's too much for one place."

"Oh man. I can understand. Do what's best for you. Wait, you signed your contract for the upcoming academic year. You'll have to pay a large fine if you bail on it."

"Well, I'm giving it one more year, then I'm outta here. I'm done with this country."

ANOTHER NIGHT, HANGING OUT AT AMY'S APARTMENT, he asked her how Zayna was doing.

"Mike, why don't you call her?"

"She'll never take me back. She said if I got in touch with her…" He used his hands to gesture scissors aiming at his private parts.

"Yikes."

"Uh-huh."

"Look, I think she'll take you back. I'm breaking a cardinal rule of mine here by revealing this to you, but she asks about you all the time."

"I can't see myself with her again. I can't. I mean she's a good person, but I think I got caught up in the fantasy of her because she reminded me of Aisha."

"I get it."

A WEEK LATER, AMY CALLED MESHARY.

"Hey there. I'm detoxing for a while. I'm grading exams. Then, I'm heading back home for the holidays. I'll call you when I'm back in town."

Amy had a relaxing vacation. It was peaceful being away from Mike and Meshary. Their drama was draining her. Her family was exactly what she needed. It was refreshing to be in nature again. She didn't miss the desert and heat. She hiked, swam in the ocean, played Frisbee in the park with her sister's dog, and spent most of her time outdoors. One day, during a neighbor's barbecue, her father offered her a can of beer. She declined.

"You quit drinking?"

"No, Dad, but that place can make you sick of alcohol. I need a break."

"I thought you said it was illegal there."

"Go figure."

"I don't get it."

"Dad, they have a saying there: What is prohibited is desired. It's illegal, but I've never seen or drank that much alcohol in my life."

WHEN AMY WAS BACK, SHE BOOKED A DAY AT THE SPA. Amy had to stay awake during the day to adjust her sleep cycle, so she opted out of a massage. She got a manicure, a pedicure, and a body scrub. It was careless of her to spend money right after a holiday, but the jet lag wore her out. She spent the next couple of days shopping. She went back to work and a few days later called Meshary.

"Hey, sorry to call you this early in the morning on a weekend. Anything scheduled for tonight? I got back last week, and my jet lag is out of my system."

"Welcome home. How was your holiday?"

"Oh, I missed you but not your drama." Amy laughed.

"I have so much to tell you. Can't wait to see you."

"Oh dear. Here we go. What's the latest episode?"

"OK. So here it goes. I did it. I married Aisha."

It was the first time he had revealed her name. How strange both Meshary and Mike loved a girl with the same name, but it was a common name locally. And it was strange he didn't call her my wife, but voiced her actual name.

"Oh my God. Wow. I can't keep up with you. This is the season finale. When did you guys tie the knot?"

"Last week. She's still asleep in the bedroom. We're going to move in with my in-laws next month."

"I thought it was the bride who moved in with her in-laws."

"Well, that's the norm. But, in our case, it's better for me since she has a daughter, and I can't afford either of them. She's the rich one."

"You didn't tell me she has a daughter. That's so cool. You're a stepdad now, Wow. I'm happy you guys managed to let go of the past. You must really love each other."

"Yeah we do. She used to call me PLG. And now she started calling me that again."

"What does PLG mean?"

"It's an acronym for Parking Lot Guy."

"Huh?"

"That's where we met. At a parking lot."

"I want to hear that story."

"Not now."

"So tonight? Are you guys free?"

"We're busy. But I can host a party next weekend if you want. You can finally meet her."

"Cool. Can I bring a friend? He's a guy. He's single and I'm not dating him. Is that OK?"

"Of course."

"Of course? Who are you? And what have you done with Meshary?"

"I'm in the greatest mood ever. You can invite as many single guys as you want."

MIKE AND AMY WERE IN THE TAXI, ON THE WAY TO A party at their mutual friend Casey's house.

"So you remember that guy Meshary I told you about? The local guy?" she asked him while putting on her new fuchsia lip liner using an inscribed compact mirror Larry had bought her. He had told her to look closely for his reflection staring back at her since they were one. She shoved the mirror back in her handbag after rubbing her lips together to let the color blend with her pale pink lipstick.

"The elusive one who doesn't let you bring single guys to his parties?"

"Yeah, well, he's having a party next weekend. And I can bring you along. He's in a great mood. He just got married."

"Lucky guy," Mike said.

"It's a complicated story. Kind of like yours."

"But with a different ending." He sounded more sad than bitter.

THE WEEKEND HAD ARRIVED. THEY WERE ON THEIR WAY to Meshary's. Mike was staring outside the window. It was obvious to Amy where his thoughts had taken him. Even after all she had done to him, his heart remained open to Aisha. Did Larry love her like that? Was the new woman in his life still his fiancée or were they married? Would they ever get back together again? Why had she said no to Larry?

She squeezed Mike's hand. "You deserve happiness."

"Look, Amy, tonight I want to unwind. Let's celebrate this guy's wedding and have a blast." He kissed her forehead.

"I'm glad you feel better now."

"I wouldn't call it better. Let's call it numb."

"Whatever you call it, I wish you'd get her out of your system. I'm sure there are going to be a lot of hot girls tonight. You ready?" She turned to look at Mike. He was looking out the window again. She wiped the place he had kissed her on her forehead with the back of her hand. Mike had a nasty habit of licking his lips, so his kisses were wet. The worst was when he kissed her cheeks.

"I was born ready."

A part of Amy wished Mike would settle down with Zayna, because they were both kind people who could commit to one another, but she wouldn't broach the subject with him again. It was obvious he was no longer interested in Zayna. No, it was obvious he would never get over Aisha.

"Where'd you go, girl?" Mike asked, smirking at her.

"Oh, far away. OK, enough thinking. We're going to have a great time. That's our mission tonight."

The taxi came to a halt. They thanked Iqbal and both her and Mike paid him separately. Amy told him she would call him half an hour before leaving. Many people found it strange that both Amy and Mike used a taxi all the time, but Amy didn't have a local license and Mike couldn't afford a car.

Mike linked arms with Amy. "Come on. Let's do this."

It was their routine to walk into parties together. Then, once inside, they'd go their separate ways. Amy would usually go to the bar, and Mike would scan the room for a girl.

"Are you going to hook up with someone?" Amy asked.

"Nope. Tonight I'm going to fall in love again."

"Easy, Mike."

They were outside of Meshary's apartment door. Amy rang the doorbell. Music was blasting from inside the apartment and someone shouted: Coming!

It was going to be a good night. Of this she was certain.

EPILOGUE

"With God, everything is at peace even when it may not seem [that way] to others."
—Zoe A. Davis-Almes

I ma watched as Guru Shantiji bowed his head and brought his hands together in prayer pose. During her first week volunteering at the retreat, two years prior, Guru taught his disciples to align the tips of their fingers with the third eye chakra in the middle of the forehead between the eyes when saying Namasté. The word had such a beautiful meaning: The divine in me recognizes the divine in you. Ima even repeated it silently to her reflection while brushing her teeth or washing her face.

Unlike other gurus around the world who traveled and gave sermons, Guru Shantiji stayed at his ashram. He didn't charge anyone for accommodation or for his retreats and relied solely on donations. But the money flowed in, and Guru had told her it was a blessing from God. There were fifty rooms, each with twin beds and an en-suite bathroom. The ashram was full during retreat season, and rooms were given on a first-come basis. Up to three hundred devotees attended each retreat, so the majority of disciples bunked in nearby budget-friendly hotels. One luxury resort, two miles away, offered a seventy percent discount to anyone attending the retreats.

Ima admired Guru Shantiji because he didn't sit on a platform higher than his disciples, even though his own teacher had taught him from a dais. He faced attendees while sitting on a cushion on the floor. And all participants were asked to bring the same cushion provided to them in their rooms so they would be seated on the same level as him.

It was the first day of the new retreat. Guru held many retreats throughout the year, but Ima never tired of attending them or being around him. A year into her first visit, she called her family and informed them she would not be returning home. She would spend the rest of the Guru's life serving him. He was two years older than her. If she died before him, she asked him to perform her burial rites.

After two hours of silent meditation, Ima informed the attendees it was time for a Q&A session with the Guru. A young lady raised her hand.

"How do we deal with heartbreak, Guru?"

It was Salma who asked the first question. Ima had met her the night before. Salma had told Ima her traditional mother wouldn't let her travel alone, but one night she had a severe panic attack after arguing with her and had to visit a doctor. She was prescribed a sedative, but Salma refused to take it. Her mother bought her a ticket to India the next day but had no idea she was coming to an ashram.

"Speak some more," Guru said. He gestured to Salma to come closer to him. Ima watched as Salma made her way through people to sit by his side. "That's better, *bachcha.* Now go on."

Ima was fifty years old and Guru Shantiji still called her child as well. Even if a devotee was older than him, he addressed him or her as *bachcha.* Salma was in her twenties, so she could truly be Guru's child.

"I met a man years ago, and I loved him. And I'm trying to ascend, but it's hard because I can't get him out of my mind. Is he my soul mate?"

"A soul mate does not leave, acha? OK? When two people are spiritually ascended, they find each other and stay. We were designed to love one person, to share our bodies with one person throughout one lifetime."

"Do we know immediately if we have found our true love?"

"The heart knows. The ego will pretend it has found it. It will rush to find a mate to feel validated by society, and to start a family without listening to the inner guidance. Why settle down? Why not settle up? Otherwise, it is abusive to the children we bring to the planet."

"And what if we don't find that one person?"

"You have ascended when it becomes your reality. It could take lifetimes. If we are taught at a young age one is a divine number, we will understand the journey is from the one to oneness. The final stage is evolving from the need for a soul-mate to a yearning for divine union."

"So if we are in a relationship, it means we are not yet enlightened?'

"Not at all. Even people in relationships become enlightened. But sex takes on a new meaning. We are here to rise from the realm of animals. On the final rung of the ladder, celibacy becomes the natural state. It could happen in old age when the body can no longer engage in sexual activity, or in another life. That person was not your soul-mate. Let go. No more pain. No more need for Hollywood Bollywood romance drama mama."

Ima and the devotees laughed. Even Salma was giggling. Then silence.

"WHAT HAPPENS WHEN WE CURB SEXUAL DESIRES?" IMA recognized the voice of the person asking the question. It was Blythe, a celebrity singer who attended the retreat every year. Though she was famous, the retreat members neither bothered nor fawned over her. Blythe once told Ima it made her feel more at home, among peers and fellow human beings on a collective journey. Ima told her most people who came to Guru's ashram weren't too concerned with pop culture.

Two years prior, a paparazzo followed Blythe all the way to the retreat and took pictures of her inside the ashram, which is forbidden. The police were called. She filed a lawsuit against the photographer, but the case was settled out of court, because Guru emphasized forgiveness. Then the following year, the paparazzi waited for her outside the ashram, but they didn't manage to take a photograph of her. Unbeknownst to them, Blythe sent her car out first. The photographers followed it, hoping to take pictures of her at the airport. Instead, Ima hid her in the bus. When they reached the airport, Blythe was wearing a white cloth covering her face. Ima led her to the check-in area where her security team was waiting for her. She boarded the plane without incident, and not one picture appeared in any tabloid.

"Curbing sexual desire does not necessarily mean celibacy. For some, it leads to our twin flame, the person who will guide us toward higher realms. With this mate, sex is evolutionary," Guru responded.

"Is it possible for everyone on this planet to give up promiscuity?" Ima craned her neck. It was Isaac. She had ushered him to his room the night before. Like Salma, he was a newcomer. She learned Isaac was a thirty-five-year-old recovered drug addict who was now taking courses to be certified as a yogi. He had come to the retreat to learn how to silence his mind.

"Each person is at his or her level. But since you are here, you must be ready even though you don't realize it. The spiritual path will destroy all you thought you were. You will see how promiscuity keeps you away from awakening."

"Can being with one person monogamously curb excessive sexual desire?"

"No, child. Some people are animalistic even while married or with one person. It does not necessarily mean we have transcended our desires."

"Why do people make such a big deal about marriage? If we have sex with one partner, without a piece of paper, isn't that just as holy?"

"Marriage is indeed a product of a man-made system, but can reflect divinity when our hearts are open. In most cases, only our minds and bodies are open to it. We have turned marriage into a prison and are easily distracted by temptation. We get bored of our spouse, because the relationship was based on lust, carrying the bloodline or convenience. Cheating begins. You could even sleep with your spouse's best friend if you were sure you would not get caught. But lust is never satisfied. It has a big mouth with fangs of guilt that will eat you alive." Guru growled.

Ima cherished the sound of laughter in the room.

"AND WHAT ABOUT HOMOSEXUALITY? WHY IS IT SUCH an issue on the spiritual path?" Isaac spoke loudly.

"*Bachcha*, we have made it into an issue by defining a person by his or her sexual inclinations. We are not physical bodies. We are souls. The sexual energy in us is here to manifest as creativity and self-realization. When in doubt about anything, ask the divine if any action or union is aligned to love. I can guarantee if you ask God and are a sincere devotee, circumstances will pull you away from any action or individual that will thwart your ascension whether you are gay, straight, or whatever. Let us collectively stop defining people according to labels in the meantime."

"I think most people are afraid of homosexuality because of scripture."

"Love doesn't punish. It is unconditional, welcoming, all-inclusive. Invite people to love. We are here to rise above the collective."

Nejoud Al-Yagout

Blythe asked Guru how she could help others align themselves. Ima was certain she was talking about others in the music industry. Blythe had often complained to Ima about how her managers pressured her constantly to reach the top of the charts. She was tired of seeing her photographs every day in tabloids or online gossip sites. Blythe said even going out for a cup of coffee was a challenge, because paparazzi stalked her every move. She had to seek therapy because she was becoming paranoid from all the attention. Meditation relaxed her, she had said. When Ima told Guru what Blythe had told her, he said Blythe would one day leave the music scene and use her divine gift to only sing songs of ascension and awakening. Ima asked him how long he predicted it would take for Blythe. He said: When the suffering becomes unbearable. He told Ima the artists who come to the retreat are the ones who are evolving in consciousness. Where they chased after fame, lovers, and money, they were now searching for God and ways to transform the world. He said if all artists honored their calling, their art would no longer be for wealth, a lavish lifestyle, or to attract groupies or followers, but to invite others to a higher way. He insisted when the shift of consciousness was full blown, there would be a focus on sacred love and spirituality. Then, he closed his eyes, pursed his lips, and meditated.

The room was silent. They were waiting for him to answer Blythe's question.

"Be concerned with your own alignment. And look within yourself to see what is asking to be surrendered or what needs to change in your life. Simply focus on yourself as a spiritual seeker. When your heart takes over, all these mental questions about alignment, misalignment, right, and wrong will disappear. You will have risen above duality."

"Guru, we are advised to love everyone while on the spiritual path. That's not easy. Any tips?" It was Paul, a regular devotee. In the past, she would've referred to him as a hippie. Long hair? Check. Floral shirt? Check. Bell-bottoms? Check. A guitar and a necklace with a peace sign pendant? Check. Check. She once told Guru hippies thought they were spiritual by the way they dressed. Look at the soul of others and not the clothing, he told her. Let them be hippies. They are all here for the same reason as you, and that is what matters.

"At the beginning of your path, if you do not like certain people, let it be because of their personality, not their race, gender, sexual inclination, religion. Let it be because you cannot handle toxicity. Let it be because you need silence and space and cannot handle low frequencies. Eventually, even these feelings and judgments will pass, and you will have compassion for all."

"It's hard to make important decisions in our lives. How can we use discernment?" It was Salma again.

"Let your discernment use you. Get out of the way."

"Is there a way to practice celibacy in the mind?" Ima couldn't identify the person with a high-pitched voice asking the question.

"Rise from the thoughts. Observe and do not feed them

by delving into fantasies."

"Is the purpose of rituals to rise from our thoughts?"

"Yes, in the beginning. This is why most religions encourage chanting, praying, meditating; these help to quiet the mind. Instead, we smoke, take drugs, drink alcohol, listen to music that invites us to indulge in our base instincts, or watch movies or look at pictures that fire up our lust, because we think life is boring without all these distractions. A free society is not one where we have the right to do all these things. True freedom comes by being liberated from the shackles of desire, *acha bachcha*?"

"Some people say sex can help us. But why is it so shameful in our society then?"

The guru closed his eyes. He closed his left nostril with his right finger and inhaled and exhaled loudly from his right nostril. He then let go and did the same with his right nostril and left finger. After a few minutes of going back and forth from one nostril to another, he placed his palms on his lap and opened his eyes.

"It is shameful only because of how we use it. Sex has become a pawn to encourage people to buy things. You want to sell cars? Put a video of a scantily clothed woman bending over and washing it. You want to sell magazines? Show breasts. But it's not only about nudity. The force that objectifies naked women is the same as the one that covers women up because the patriarchy views women sexually."

"How can we change that?"

"One must not impose rules on anyone. The most conservative societies in the world sometimes have the most perversions. We must allow people to be who they are until they realize it is actually not who they are."

"Isn't that a lengthy process?"

"Everyone will return to God in his or her own time. With proper education, we can speed up the process. By education, we are not talking about schools or books, memorizing or turning pupils into robots, but about meditation, prayer, and universal love."

"Can we also ascend faster by being of service to the community?" the same voice asked.

"Most people say we have to ascend first, but I say to you helping others is a sign of ascension, even if the ego does it for selfish reasons at first. At least it is choosing glory through service. Eventually, you will have to rein in the ego and let the source work through you when giving to others."

"How do we do that?"

"Ask to become a vessel. Ask to surrender your ego. When your desire to transform becomes stronger than your desire for being recognized, the miracle comes forth. It all depends on divine grace, but asking for it means we are on the path."

"DOES READING SCRIPTURE TRANSFORM US?" SALMA asked.

"In scripture, the divine message, a diamond in a mine, is hidden beneath the illusory verses of the ego. Scripture is a rung on the ladder of consciousness. But reading can become a trap of the ego on the spiritual journey if we do not grasp the message. When we are awakened, we understand the text was a portal. And then we no longer want to read anything. No novels. No poetry. Nothing."

"We will forego reading?"

"All we will look forward to is being with God and taking

care of God's manifestations: man, woman, and all living beings." Guru breathed in and exhaled loudly. His eyes remained closed for a couple of minutes.

"Does religion help or hinder the process?"

"If religion is mental, then it hinders the process. If it touches the heart, then religion helps. Most people embrace religion mentally. They do things for rewards or to avoid punishment. Or, they choose desire in this world over connecting with the divine. This is why there are even religious people who engage in sex, drinking, smoking. Do not judge them by calling them hypocrites. They are merely asleep. The message has not touched the Anahata, the heart chakra."

"I don't understand why some religious people can be extremists while others are peaceful."

"Anyone who suppresses their darkness, be it lust or anger, for a ticket to paradise will explode. The denial manifests as intolerance toward others, especially those who do not adhere to their ideology. And they will quote verses to justify their contempt."

"Some scriptures are violent though."

"The way you interpret scripture is a measuring stick for the distance of your ego to God. If you are rigid, you are far away. The closer you are, the more loving and tolerant and all-inclusive you become. You will recognize the text that has been filtered by the ego."

"Guru, how can we recognize the religious soul who loves God?"

"These devotees no longer focus on appeasing a deity but bask in awe of the All-Pervading. They are at peace, and God dwells in them. They don't try to convert anyone. But people rush toward them and follow them without being prodded, because they emit divinity. Rituals and service, if and when performed, become celebrations of the divine."

"Guru, how do we know when we have transcended dogma?" It was Isaac asking.

"When you recognize beauty in all the paths to God. When you grasp all are God's chosen ones. All land is holy. Borders are man-made, *bachcha*. We erect temples. God's land is not just on our planet. The universe is filled with consciousness and design. When you transcend dogma, you can no longer judge or separate believers and unbelievers. You will also drop the human ego and respect the life source in animals, nature, even insects. The divine spark is everywhere."

"Guru. What about atheism?"

"If you cannot fathom God, then search for yourself. Engage in self-inquiry. You will surely know God." Guru closed his eyes again.

As soon as Guru opened his eyes, he looked in Ima's direction. This was his cue to end the session. Guru didn't like to speak much. During his one-week retreats, he spoke to his followers only on the first and last days. All days in between were designated for meditation and silence. He responded to questions because he told Ima it was his service to others and in one's early stages of awakening, words were important for disciples. People from around the world came to learn about spirituality, and he had to respect his guests by sating their curiosity before retreating to his room.

"We thank you for your time, Guru Shantiji. Namasté to everyone in the room. Dinner is now served in the cafeteria. But first, Guru will leave you with one more nugget of wisdom before this session ends," Ima said. She turned toward the guru, waiting for him to sum up the dialogue as he did at each retreat. His final statement was brief but left a lasting impression on her and the devotees who understood his enigmatic messages. Only a few people in the room would grasp what he said, and her instinct told her one of them would be Salma. Ima couldn't figure out why, but she recognized in Salma a soul on the verge of awakening.

***

"Say: I ask to know the one. And if not that beloved, then the beloved," Guru said.

"Huh? Two beloveds?" A man in the front row asked. He was facing Guru.

"The first beloved is with a capital b." Then, he stood up and walked toward Ima and the rest of the volunteers, and they left the room.

ACKNOWLEDGMENTS

This book began crawling in February of 2018. And if a book could say thank you for teaching it to walk, then *Motorbikes and Camels* would express its gratitude to Patricia Marshall, Kim Harper-Kennedy, Jamie Passaro, and Melissa Lund of Luminare Press. And to Jade, Ashley, Meredith, Missy, and Nadia for editorial and cover design feedback.